£2.4G

ALSO BY KAREL VAN LOON

A Father's Affair

KAREL VAN LOON

The Invisible Ones

Translated by David Colmer

Published in 2006 by
The Maia Press Limited
82 Forest Road
London E8 3BH
www.maiapress.com

First published as *De Onzichtbaren* by Karel Glastra van Loon,
Uitgeverij L. J. Veen Amsterdam/Antwerpen in 2003
Copyright © 2003, 2004 Karel Glastra van Loon
English-language translation © 2006 David Colmer

ISBN 10: 1 904559 18 2
ISBN 13: 978 1 904559 18 4

A CIP catalogue record for this book is available from the
British Library

Printed and bound in Great Britain by Thanet Press

The Maia Press is indebted to Arts Council England and the
Foundation for the Production and Translation of Dutch
Literature for their financial support

All characters in this book are fictional except General Ne Win, Daw Khine May Tan, General Aung San, his widow Daw Khin Kyi, their daughter Daw Aung San Suu Kyi, U Thant, Prime Minister U Nu, Brigadier Aung Gyi, Captain Sein Lwin and Saw Ba U Gyi.

The place names Min Won and Pan Thar are also fictional.

In Burma, people's names are often preceded by a title: in Burmese this is Daw for women and U for men; in Karen it is Naw for women and Saw for men.

U Saw Min Thein was born of a hundred stories.
The Invisible Ones
is dedicated to the people who told me those stories.

Love Poem

This mountain ridge
Teems with fierce tigers
Come with me, my love
Let's go pick bamboo shoots

Kyi Aung

PART I

Fish Crazy

Come, take me by the arm and lead me away from here, out of the darkness in my hut and into the pale light of morning, where I will show you a world I have never seen with my own eyes yet know as well as the town I grew up in. We will tread carefully on the steep track that leads down to the bottom of the hill, where it splits and splits again, forming a delta of paths and side-paths until the bank of the river. In the cool morning air the smells are still diffuse – hints rather than statements – but the sounds are sharp and clear. From all sides we will hear cocks crowing and children shouting as they get ready for school. They dawdle and fool around as if they've stopped the clock.

I will show you the way between the houses to the river and you will help me climb five worn wooden steps on to the bridge. Then I will free myself from your grip and walk ahead until the middle of the bridge. There, above the clear water, we will pause in the first tentative sunlight, filling our lungs with the metallic air of the mountains. You will look at the clouds of mist rising up the wooded slopes and see an eagle tracing circles in the white sky. 'Look! There!' And only then will you realise that I cannot see the bird.

Downstream, the river winds off in a north-westerly direction, a twisting ribbon of placid water in a bed of pebbles. On the right bank are the vegetable gardens tended by the children from the orphanage. They fill big plastic watering cans from the river and empty them over the fertile clay in which they grow corn and yellow beans and banana trees. The orphans wear T-shirts printed with the names of their benefactors: Christian missionary organisations from distant, northern lands. They do their work in silence and with great dedication. The watering cans are brightly coloured: red and yellow and blue.

I know what you see, even though I do not see it, I have heard it described a hundred times. What's more: I hear, I smell, I feel. I have learnt to see in the darkness.

13

Two women are washing in the water at the foot of the bridge. They exchange the latest news: about a feverish child and about the arrival of a distant relative who was presumed dead.

'Things have been happening,' I hear one of the women say, 'things he's better off not knowing.'

'Is he planning on staying?' the other asks.

'Yes, I think so.'

'Then he'll find out. Nothing stays secret here.'

Then they fall silent, perhaps because their own words have frightened them, perhaps because they have seen us standing on the bridge, within earshot.

We will walk on and climb the opposite bank. There, the path leads to a teak plantation: trees in orderly rows, the soil stamped down and swept clean, a hard floor for a cathedral of trees in which you occasionally hear the rustling of a withered leaf floating down like ominous tidings from another, higher world. The plantation is the responsibility of the students from the nearby Bible school. Every morning and every evening they sweep the leaves into a pile and burn them to stop them from building up into a crackling brown blanket that could easily catch fire later, during the hot dry months. We will hear them softly singing, their voices scarcely audible above the rhythmic brushing of their brooms. We will stop briefly to listen and their song will reassure us. For a moment you will be convinced that this is the most beautiful place in the world.

I will ask you to take me by the arm so that I can lead you to the street where the Muslims ply their trade and it's as noisy as a carnival or a village fair. Under an awning of bamboo and palm leaves we will drink sweet milky tea and eat martabak *with coconut and chocolate, while listening to two different soundtracks: one Hollywood, the other Bollywood. The movies are being shown in cramped rooms where teenage couples who should be at school hold hands in the dark. Jarring chords suggest tension, a chase perhaps, while at the same time the sweet tones of a sitar evoke images of a long-awaited embrace.*

There was a time when you could find me here every day of the week – I never had to pay admission. Sometimes I tried to imagine what was on the screen, more often I relaxed into the sound, letting it wash over me like the warm water of a lowland river. Sometimes I took advantage of the darkness to weep.

In the afternoon we will retreat to the shade of the trees near my house, where we will doze until the worst heat of the day is over. My sister-in-law, Tamla Paw, will wake us with a meal of rice and yellow beans. Afterwards we will play a game of chess.

'Pawn e2-e4.'

'Knight g8-f6.'

You move the pieces on the board, I move the pieces in my head. I find it hard to concentrate and feel like you're deliberately holding back and could win easily. When the sun disappears behind the ridge, a chilly evening mist will roll into the valley and you will suggest we call it a draw, an offer I will accept joylessly. Like every other evening and every morning, the Thai national anthem will play over the speakers of the camp's public address system. To remind us that we are only guests.

My house is not large: two rooms and a verandah. It is made of bamboo and, like all the houses here in the camp, it is raised up on teak stilts. That helps to keep out vermin, but the main reason is the flooding during the rainy season. In those three, wet months I am totally housebound. The paths get so slippery that only children can walk them without constantly losing their footing. My world shrinks so much that I am sometimes afraid that there is no room left in it for me at all, that I'll be washed away with the mud and the dead branches and the dead leaves. On days like that, I don't dare to get out of my hammock.

There are holes in the palm-leaf roof; that's why there are pieces of canvas strung up over the sleeping places. I have a hammock, two sleeping mats, two chairs, a blanket chest and a small table. I own some clothes, some photos, some cutlery and a few plates and glasses. That's *about it. People who flee can't take much with them. On the walls are a few colourful pictures Tamla Paw has hung up for visitors and for herself: a mountain lake reflecting snow-capped peaks; the Shwedagon Pagoda, our holiest Buddhist temple, shining in the late-afternoon sun; Jesus of Nazareth sitting on a stone and surrounded by blond children; a Karen National Union calendar with photos of our leaders. Hanging above the door is a small sign with the word WELCOME.*

If you wanted to, you could use the spare room, Tommy's room. For years Tommy was my guide, y'meh klee po – my little eyes. But Tommy isn't here now and there are times when I am convinced that he won't be coming back.

You can sleep on the mat in his room. The toilet is outside, between my house and the neighbours', a small bamboo and leaf construction. Inside it's not much more than a hole in the ground above a septic tank, but the neighbours keep it clean. The washroom is next to the toilet. At this time of year there is no shortage of running water so you can wash as often as you like. The food is plain, but there is plenty of it, and Tamla Paw, who looks after me, is a good cook.

If you will be my eyes in the darkness now and then, I will tell you what you see and where we are. I will tell you how we live here in the camp, how we love and hate, how we die here. I will tell you about the Burmese people they call the Karen, who imagine themselves one of the lost tribes of Israel, and about their struggle with the mighty Burmans, the largest ethnic group in Burma, who say of the Karen: 'Don't trust them, they do what they say!'

I will tell you about the comforting wisdom of Gautama Buddha.

Together we can climb the Mountain of Salvation and Prayer and imagine, for a moment, that we are closer to God. We can visit the Cave of Oblivion, home of a hermit who talks to birds. And in the evening we will sit on the verandah and I will tell you about the events that made me who I am: a blind refugee from Burma in a camp in the Thai jungle. Through these stories I will show you my country just as you can see a garden in a dewdrop.

And if I find the courage, I will tell you Tommy's story.

One

My mother's eyes were closed. She smiled. Her face was close to mine. She had covered her forehead and cheeks with the paste she made from the finely ground bark of the thanakha tree. As the paste dried, fine cracks appeared. Carefully I picked at the flakes with my nails. The skin of my mother's face was wonderfully soft and light, much lighter than my own. She opened her eyes and I smiled at her. From this close I could see the strange patterns in her irises: dark brown and ochre radiating from the black of her pupils. In her left eye, there were three black dots that formed a perfect triangle. I liked to pretend that I was the only person who had ever noticed them.

My mother was getting ready to go somewhere, a party or a ceremony. A carefully ironed pink silk blouse on a hanger was dangling from the wardrobe door. She poured herself a glass of water and sat down for a moment at the long teak table in the middle of our front room, fanning herself to cool off a little. It was the hottest hour of the day and very muggy, even in this room, which was generally cool.

I knelt on the table and stared at her.

My mother looked at me, I saw her pupils dilate. My mother was able to smile with her eyes, making them gleam and sparkle until flakes fell from her cheeks. Soon she would put flowers in her hair and rub herself with coconut oil. Long after she had left, I would be able to smell her perfumes. That made it easier to bear her absence.

Behind me the front door opened, letting the noise of the street drift in. My mother's pupils constricted. She looked past

17

me at the doorway. Then something strange happened: her pupils got very big, then as small as the dots in the triangle, then big again. Her eyes turned black. Dozens of pieces of dry thanakha paste flaked off and drifted down to the table. My mother opened her mouth, closed it, and opened it again.

I turned around.

My father was standing in the doorway. He was wearing his uniform, but not his cap. His hair was sticking up from his head in strange tufts. He was standing with his legs wide apart and holding something big and heavy in his arms. Drops of water fell to the floor, glittering in the sunlight. My father took two steps forward, then slowly crumpled, as if the burden he was carrying was dragging him down. Behind him a truck drove past, very slowly. I saw the eyes of cows between unpainted planks. I smelt diesel exhaust. I didn't dare to lower my gaze.

My mother screamed, loud and high. I closed my eyes and covered my ears with my hands.

If I think of my brother, I think of fish. And vice versa: if I walk through the market and smell the fish stall, I think of my brother, even now, after all these years.

We had rolled up our longyis and were standing up to our knees in muddy water. Thrashing around us were gouramis and torpedoes, mango fish and butter fish – enormous, terrifying catfish with cold heartless eyes. We grabbed the fish eagerly, lifting them up into the air and holding them over our heads like trophies. Sometimes one managed to escape, slapping back into the water; sometimes one slid down through our arms, leaving a trail of slime and scales on our bare skin. At the end of the day my brother and I were fish among fish, and for days afterwards our mother would pinch her nose shut every time we came too close. When he was born, my parents named my brother Hla Than, but as long as I could remember we had called him Ngar Yoo, 'Fish Crazy'.

My brother lay on the cement floor, wet and lifeless, and it seemed as if my mother would never stop screaming. My father stared at her with dull, black eyes. He didn't say a word, he didn't do anything, he sat on the ground beside the body of his eldest son and waited. I looked at my brother. Little puddles were forming around his head and feet. There were bits of grass and water plants in his wet hair.

My mother screamed.

My father waited.

I watched.

On the street behind my father a small crowd formed. I saw faces I knew and faces I had never seen before. I saw the girl from up the street with a silver tray on her head with pieces of watermelon that were starting to sweat in the sun. I saw a surly-looking man with a cropped moustache peer shamelessly into the house. And I saw Maung Maung Aye, the neighbours' little boy, who let out a peal of laughter. Then my mother finally stopped screaming.

I took a deep breath. Inquisitive children thronged around the door. My mother stood up and walked around the table. She knelt down next to my brother. My father followed her with his eyes. She put her hand out to my brother's head and carefully picked the rubbish out from his hair, then laid her fingers on his eyes and closed them.

'He's . . .' my father said. 'They . . .' Only now did I see that he was trembling. His whole body was trembling, as if a mysterious force of nature was gently shaking it. My mother ignored him. She stood up and walked to the door, the children moved back.

'Ngar Yoo is dead,' I heard a strange female voice say. Only later did I realise with a shock that the strange voice was my mother's.

It's a trick as old as the universe: first comes beauty, to seduce and reassure, and then evil arrives, striking when you least expect it.

What killed Siddhartha Gautama, the Buddha? Diarrhoea! He, the Peerless One, who had associated in the heavens with gods and devas and known himself to be their superior; He, the Enlightened One, who had perceived the unutterable and indivisible Truth; He, the Perfected One; died of a trivial infection of the gastrointestinal tract. A smith called Chunda from the land of the Mallas gave the Enlightened One truffles to eat, the truffles had gone off, and the next morning the Buddha was dead. Of course, the believers say that the Great Recluse chose the moment of his death, that he knew that there was something wrong with the truffles and ate them anyway. After all, three months earlier the Blessed One himself had predicted his imminent demise!

The strength of religion lies in the way it makes unbearable events bearable by weaving them into a web of stories. But those who witnessed the death of the Buddha, his most faithful followers, did not have those stories at their disposal – the stories came later. His most dedicated pupils had to make do with harsh, unadorned reality: a man they loved like no other had died from eating spoilt truffles. The most sublime beauty had been destroyed by a petty ailment. And the disciples behaved the way that people in situations like that can be expected to behave: they became unreasonable, undignified and vengeful. They went in search of a scapegoat and found one in the Buddha's closest confidant, his cousin Ananda, who they accused of not trying hard enough to convince the Master to live longer, and of course in Chunda, the smith who served the spoilt truffles.

According to the holy books of Buddhism, the Master spoke to his followers from his deathbed, saying, 'If one of you still has the slightest doubt, speak now and ask frankly.' But they were all silent. And Ananda said, 'Strange as it seems, Oh Lord, none of the monks here present has the slightest doubt.' Whereupon the

Buddha answered, 'You have spoken from faith, Ananda, but I speak from knowledge. I know that none of the monks here has any doubt.'

It is by virtue of this statement by the Buddha that the faithful revere his first followers to this day as saints, just as the first disciples of Jesus of Nazareth are holy in the eyes of Christians. The pettiness that their master's death brought out in them does not detract from their saintliness, on the contrary, it is this proof of their humanity that makes them saints. That is the mystery of religion: rather than undermining it, contradictions only strengthen it.

There are people who claim that, of all religions, Buddhism is the only one that is in harmony with science, but by doing so they show that they understand the true nature neither of science nor of religion. Religion is not a science and science is not a religion. Both involve searching for truth, but the truths they seek are very different. Those who measure religion with the tools of science find only emptiness; those who practise science with religious means invite catastrophe down on their heads.

The founders of modern Burma believed that they could guarantee prosperity and happiness by correctly choosing the moment for the rebirth of our country. They consulted astrologists and fortune-tellers, men of impeccable behaviour and uncontested wisdom, who were devout Buddhists to boot. Acting on the advice of these holy arithmeticians, they declared independence on the fourth of January in the year 1948, at twenty past four in the morning. Every year since then, we have commemorated that happy occasion on that day at that same impossible hour – in the full awareness that independence has caused more misfortune than all of the oppression and exploitation of the entire colonial period put together. What was supposed to be the most beautiful moment of our history became the first black page of yet another chapter full of horrors and darkness. You could say that we Burmese have made that universal trick with beauty and evil part of our national character. Because there are two things that come easier to us than to any other nation on earth: smiling and waging war.

The Buddhist temples of my motherland are decorated with murals depicting the life of the Buddha. They always show the same scenes: the young Siddhartha experiencing his first ecstasy, seated under an apple tree; Prince Siddhartha Gautama, who wants for nothing, leaving his palace, cutting off his long princely hair and going in search of Truth; the Seeker of Truth almost starving to death in the forests of Uruvela in the vain hope of finding Enlightenment through chastising the body – until he remembers the moment under the apple tree and tells himself, 'Of course! Happiness can only be achieved through Happiness!' They show him being visited by Mara, the Evil One, who cunningly tries to lead him away from the Middle Way by instructing his daughters to seduce him, by besieging him with the help of the Sins, by letting the fiercest monsters from the deepest depths of the earth loose on him – all to no avail. Whereupon Gautama becomes the Enlightened One, the Buddha.

Those few stories, those few moments in the life of the Wise One, made him who he was, they defined him, and they define the faithful to this day.

Our own, insignificant lives are like that too. Between our birth and our death, a few events take place that determine our whole lives, who we are, how we define ourselves, and how others will remember us.

We are, each of us, a small collection of stories.

Two

'I know something no one knows,' my brother said. 'I've seen something no one has ever seen.'

We were sitting in our back yard in the shade of the acacia. Ngar Yoo had the hard-back scrapbook in which he recorded the things he discovered about the world. He didn't usually share his discoveries with me, so I awaited his announcement nervously.

'Look,' he said, holding the opened scrapbook out to me. 'Who is this?' He pointed at a photo he had torn out of a magazine. It was a slightly fuzzy picture of a doll or a statue, with a shiny face and a peculiar, swollen body. I had no idea what it was supposed to represent.

'That is the Mahamuni Buddha in Mandalay,' my brother said. 'They say the statue was made in the days when Buddha himself was still alive. That it's a faithful representation of what he looked like in real life.'

I bent over the picture once again. The Mahamuni Buddha had a remarkably large nose and a broad flat face that shone as if it was behind glass. It had a strange hat that made the face look even broader, and shoulder pieces that looked like wings. It was the least human statue of Buddha I had ever seen. And this was supposed to be what the Great Sage had looked like in person?

'Look here, next to it?' my brother ordered. He took his hand off the page and I saw another somewhat blurred photo, this time from the newspaper. 'That is Yuri Gagarin,' he said, with the self-evident authority of an older brother initiating a younger sibling into the secrets of life. 'The first man in space. A

23

Russian cosmonaut! Now compare him to the Buddha of Mandalay.'

I looked from one photo to the other and back again, and it was true. There were a few remarkable similarities: the flat, unnaturally broad impression that both faces gave, the swollen, ribbed arms . . . 'Gautama Buddha,' my brother declared, 'was a cosmonaut! A space traveller!' And with a triumphant bang, he closed the scrapbook.

My father was a Burman and a Buddhist, at least, until he lost his faith and up to the day, just before his sixty-seventh birthday, when he suffered a fatal stroke. My mother is a Karen and a Christian. Our neighbours were Muslims from Bengal. My brother and I grew up with the traditions and values of two religions and the self-evident presence of a third – until my brother drowned in the canal behind the Bengali mosque and stopped growing forever.

'Allah must have willed it so,' said the imam, one of the many potential witnesses questioned personally by my father. The imam hadn't seen a thing. Neither had my brother's school friends. Or the one-legged beggar who always hung around on the Nat Sein Street bridge. Or the dealer in bags and suitcases who first saw my brother's dead body floating in the water and raised the alarm. Whereupon Kyaw Win, the son of the shoemaker who resoled my father's boots, jumped into the canal and dragged the body to the side. What happened afterwards can be reconstructed in detail, but no one was able to say anything about the events that preceded the gruesome discovery. As a result my father, who was possibly the most respected police officer in the town, was obliged to conclude the investigation into his own son's death without having discovered the answer to a single relevant question.

Why did my brother die?

Because Allah had willed it so?

Because God had different plans for him?

Because it was predestined by his karma?

No, no, no! My brother, Hla Than, died because he was *ngar yoo* – fish crazy. He must have believed that he was a fish, just as he believed that Gautama Buddha was a cosmonaut.

Years later I saw the Mahamuni Buddha with my own eyes when I was in Mandalay for a meeting of the Burma Bar Council. In reality the gigantic statue is much less peculiar than it looks in photos – in photos the reflections on its golden face make it look flat and unnatural. The strange bumpiness of the body of the Perfectly Enlightened One is caused by the immense amount of gold leaf that the faithful have applied over the years. It is definitely an unusual and impressive statue and the thought that it was made in the likeness of the living Revealer of Truth fills the faithful who visit the temple with deep awe and great joy. But I don't think a single one of them has ever thought of the Buddha as a cosmonaut.

Three

The car jerked and jolted, a boat at sea in a heavy storm. My father sat straight-backed at the wheel, concentrated, as if leading a military operation. His willpower was greater than the forces shaking the car. This was how wars were won. Next to him sat my mother, gripping the door with one hand while trying hard to keep her hair out of her face with the other. She had wound down the window to let the warm breeze blow into the car. My brother and I bounced on the back seat. We were on our way to my grandfather's farm.

We lived in Burma in the provincial town of Min Won, but my mother's family came from the country. Karen trust clay more than brick, they prefer bamboo to concrete – and that was definitely true of my grandfather. He owned land that was bordered by two rivers. In the rainy season a lot of his fields were under water, which meant that every year they were naturally fertilised with the country's finest, richest clay. My grandfather grew six kinds of rice and more than ten different vegetables. There were big mango trees on his land. He had a banana plantation and fields where he grew pineapples and papayas. He kept chickens and pigs, a few water buffalo for the heavy work in the paddy fields, and an ox to pull the cart. In a few strategic places my grandfather had dug ponds that disappeared when the river water washed over them in the rainy season. When the river shrank again, the ponds reappeared, now filled with enormous quantities of fish.

Burmese farmers are magicians with water. People who grow wet rice in a country where it rains heavily for four months and stays dry for the rest of the year must know how to impose their will on water. My grandfather was a master at it – or perhaps, I should say, my grandfather's overseer was a master at it. His name was Tender: a tall skinny man whose facial features suggested Indian blood, even though he considered himself a Karen, like my grandfather and my mother. It was Tender who decided where to dig ditches to flood and drain the land, and where to build the dams and sluices. Tender was also the one who mapped the constantly changing pattern of streams and pools after each rainy season and worked out when and where to position the barriers and fish traps to catch the spawning river fish. When it was time to scoop out a pond to harvest the fish, it was Tender who chose the best spot for the *kha-nwe*: far enough from the bank to be able to scoop deeply, but not so far that the water would run back into the pond. On my grandfather's farm, Tender's word was law – that was as true for the farm workers as it was for my brother and me, and I believe it even applied to my grandfather.

When it was time for the fish harvest, my grandfather would call my mother and we would leave for the country on the next free day we had, with my brother and I excited on the back seat of our old Morris Minor, but forced to stay calm by stern glances from my father.

Our country's roads were in a terrible state and those drives took forever. Often my father would have to negotiate the bumps and potholes at walking pace to avoid wrecking the car, hurting us, or making us all carsick. And then my mother still insisted on stopping somewhere along the way at a stall or a teashop to eat watermelon or *mohinga* or have something to drink. As if we couldn't get all the *mohinga* in the world at my grandfather's, and *nga-peat-ye*, and as many papayas as we could eat, and big glasses of fresh pineapple juice, and of course the most delicious fish soups.

And the length of time my mother could spend over a single glass of tea!

The sun would already be setting when we finally reached my grandfather's farm. But once there we didn't need to waste another minute. Because while my parents and my grandfather enquired about each other's health and the latest gossip, Ngar Yoo and I had already headed off with Tender and a group of workers to the first pond. Tender knew that nothing he could do would make us happier than involving us as much as possible with the work. And so he let us help carry the tools, position the *kha-nwe* and put the fish baskets out in preparation. Once all that had been done, we sat down on the grass beside the pond and watched the water go down.

With every inch that the water level sank, our excitement grew. And once we saw the backs of the first fish tracing nervous lines over the surface, there was no stopping us. We rolled up our longyis and stepped into the water, which still came up over our knees. We wiggled our toes in the warm slippery mud and grabbed wildly at the fish, which got away easily, but would soon become an easy prey once the water was so low that their fat white bellies were rubbing over the bottom of the pond. And we weren't the only ones screaming with delight, the workmen too were soon caught up in the feverish excitement, yelling at each other in languages and dialects we didn't speak, but seemed to understand at moments like these. The men grabbed the fish without hesitating and threw them into the baskets from a great distance without ever letting a single fish get away. My brother and I tried as hard as we could to do the same.

It was Ngar Yoo who taught me to grab the fish just behind the gills, so that the pectoral fins would help me to keep my grip; he'd seen the workmen do it that way. He also taught me how to recognise a swamp eel and how to grab a dwarf catfish, a *ngazin yaing*, without pricking myself on the poisonous spikes of the dorsal fin. He would have been furious with me if he had known that I would later let a no-account fish like that prick me, and in my eye of all places! At first the wound didn't seem anything to worry about, though it was itchy and it stung! And, of course, it got infected and, of course, I pretended that it was nothing, lying to my mother that I could still see perfectly. It was treated in the hospital, by a real specialist, and for a while it even improved a little, but in the end I still went completely blind in that eye.

Would all that have happened if my brother had still been there? Who can say?

The only thing that's certain is that after his death I never swam again.

What do we have left after the loss of a loved one? Nothing except words and memories.

After the death of Gautama the Buddha, his disciples gathered to decide how to continue the *dharma*, the teachings of the Completely Enlightened One, and the *sangha*, the brotherhood of monks. And after they had taken their frustration and sorrow at the death of their beloved master out on his cousin, Ananda, their thoughts returned to the Buddha's words as they remembered them and, softly singing in unison, they repeated the Transcendent Wisdom and the Indivisible Truth and they sang continuously for seven months until they had repeated all of his words.

For the first three centuries after Buddha's death, no one wrote down his words, which were passed down orally by the monks of the *sangha*. And despite this, the faithful believe that not a word was lost and not a syllable was changed! It was only when Prince Mahendra travelled to Ceylon to spread Buddhism there that his followers took on the task of recording the *dharma* in writing. Every good Buddhist believes with absolute certainty that the holy books that were then written do not deviate by even a letter from the words that were spoken in his lifetime by the Great Sage, the Finder of Truth, the Perfect One, the Blessed

One, the Buddha!

If only I could have so little doubt about my memories of Ngar Yoo.

We were standing next to a small pond, no more than a shallow pool of clear rainwater. I saw tadpoles and water insects that shot forward every few seconds as if they'd just got a kick up the bum. A squirming worm here, a slithering snail there. Dangling upside-down from the surface were the semi-transparent larvae of the tiger mosquito. But I didn't see any fish.

'Where are they then?' I asked my brother.

'Look properly!' he shouted.

I looked up at him. He was climbing a tree near the pond.

Slowly I walked around the pond, peering, searching. Was that one? No, a decomposing leaf. A root, a water plant.

'What kind of fish were they?' I asked.

'Climbing perch,' Ngar Yoo replied.

'Climbing perch?'

'Yep.' He turned to look at me and grinned. 'So you're looking in the wrong place.'

He was making fun of me. He'd reached the tree's lower branches, or rather, the place where the trunk split: first in two, then in four, and so on. He squatted inside the fork of living wood and leant forward. Holding on to the tree with one hand, he slid the other down into a hollow under his feet. I watched and waited. He looked back at me and grinned again. He was playing tricks on me.

'Go on, keep looking,' he said, but I knew there was no point. I waited. He waited. And then suddenly his shoulder jerked and his arm shot up: in his hand he was holding a wet, wriggling fish.

'Catch!' he shouted and the fish was already flying through the air. I stretched out my arms, took one step forward, then another and, just as my hands were about to close around the fish, I lost my balance and tumbled forward into the pond. Even with my ears full of water I could hear the shrill shrieks of my brother's laughter.

Later I climbed the tree myself because I didn't believe him when he insisted that the trough of water in the tree fork was full of climbing perch. He was right.

'What are they doing here?' I cried in astonishment. 'And how did they know there was water up here?'

'The fish owl told them,' Ngar Yoo answered. 'He landed on the bank of the pond in the twilight. The climbing perch were hiding in the mud. 'Your days are numbered,' the fish owl whispered. 'The rainy season is over. The sun keeps on creeping out from behind the clouds. Soon it will dry up the pond, and then you'll all die!'' Ngar Yoo had put on a strange, nasal voice. He was speaking to the empty pond, as if the climbing perch were still there, as if they could hear him and understood his words. 'Your only chance,' said my brother the fish owl, 'is that tree there. In the fork of the boughs, there is a deep hole that's full of water, and the most important thing is, that water's always in the shade! The sun can't get to it! You'll be safe there!' A treacherous frown appeared on my brother's face. 'But what good's that,' he squawked, 'how's a fish supposed to get up a tree?'

Ngar Yoo stood up straight. In his normal voice he said, 'That night the fish owl sat in the top of the tree looking down. It saw the climbing perch creep out of the pond one by one, and watched them hop over to the tree like deformed frogs. They climbed up into the tree and jumped down into the hole. That's where they are now. And every night the fish owl comes to eat one up. Look!' my brother walked around to the other side of the tree. I followed him. He pointed down. At the base of the trunk, on the grey clay, between the herbs and the lush green grass, lay the white bones, scales and heads of four, five, at least seven climbing perch.

I stared at my brother in disbelief.

'Yes, Min Thein,' he said in the voice of the fish owl, 'it's a strange world.'

Four

For four days and four nights Ngar Yoo's body was laid out on the long table in our front room and all that time I didn't dare to leave my bedroom. Family members and neighbours, friends and acquaintances came by to mourn with us. I heard their voices, sobs and laughter. I smelt the food my mother and aunts prepared for them, I smelt the incense and the candles and the sickly smell of flowers that opened at night. Now and then someone came upstairs with something for me to eat or drink: caramel cake and coconut bars, sweet popcorn or jackfruit and lime cordial. Sometimes my mother sat silently on the edge of my bed, sometimes I cried in her arms, sometimes I slept on her lap.

One night I dreamt that I was being swept along by a swirling current. I tried with all my strength to keep my head above water but it kept dragging me under until finally I gave in and saw that it wasn't water that had engulfed me but an enormous fish. Deep inside the fish, where everything was lit with a dim green light, I discovered my brother's body. He was lying in a puddle of water with his eyes closed, just as I had last seen him on the floor of our front room. I walked up to him, shouting out his name as loud as I could, but instead of sound, air came bubbling out of my mouth. My brother didn't move and, just when I was bending over him and stretching my hands out to bring him back to the land of the living, just in that instant, the door of my room opened and I woke with a start.

It was Tender.

'Were you asleep?'

'Yes, I was asleep.'

'Were you dreaming?'

'Yes, I was dreaming.'

He stood in the doorway and looked at me. The candlelight threw strange shadows on his face. I sat up and rubbed the sleep out of my eyes. It was quiet in the house. Tender stepped into my room and closed the door behind him. He was wearing a colourful shirt I had never seen before with red and yellow flowers on it. Seeing him standing there, in my room, by the light of a single candle, the man I only knew as the boss of my grandfather's farm, was comforting and worrying at once – and the same applied to what he said.

'When you dream,' said Tender, 'your *k'la* wanders, the spirit that makes you a living creature. That's why you always need to be careful waking up from a dream: you have to give the *k'la* time to return to your body, otherwise . . .'

'I saw Ngar Yoo,' I blurted.

'That doesn't surprise me at all.' Tender stared into space for a moment, then looked at me again and sighed.

'Ngar Yoo's *k'la* misses your company,' he said. 'It will try to lure your *k'la* away to where he is now.'

'He was inside the belly of a fish.'

Tender smiled. 'Take my advice, keep your distance from him.'

I nodded, even though I had no idea how to do that: how to keep my distance from him.

Tender said, 'I often watched you and Ngar Yoo catching the fish in the ponds on our land. One day I started noticing that your brother threw all the fish neatly into the basket except the climbing perch. If he caught a climbing perch, he'd always let it go again. First I thought it was because he couldn't get a grip on them, that he was hurting himself on the spiny fins. But after watching him longer, I saw that he did it on purpose. He let them escape. One afternoon I bumped into him when he was wandering around by himself. I asked him, "Ngar Yoo, why do you let the climbing perch get away? Don't you know that they make a delicious curry, even better than chicken?" He felt caught out, I could see that. He turned away and shrugged. But I insisted, "Come on, Ngar Yoo, it's nothing to be ashamed of, you can tell me, can't you?" And do you know what he said? He said, "Tender, the climbing perch and me, we go back a long way."'

There are some people who attach great significance to the synchronicity of events – I am not one of them. But I make an exception in one case: on the night that Tender came to my bed and told me about Ngar Yoo and the climbing perch, a military coup took place in our capital, Rangoon. The democratically elected civilian government of the first prime minister of independent Burma, U Nu, was overthrown by troops led by the commander-in-chief of the Burmese army, General Ne Win. Since then I have never been able to completely escape the idea that the course of my life, my fate, is linked in some dark way to the fate of my country. It is totally irrational and no doubt the product of a seriously exaggerated sense of my own importance, I know that as well as anyone, but that doesn't make it any less real.

Buddha said, 'Those who think the unreal is real, and see the real as unreal, are in the realm of false thinking. But those who know the real is real, and see the unreal as unreal, are in the realm of sound thought.'

The question is, are we capable of determining for ourselves in which of the two realms we live?

Five

I was standing in the room where my brother's body was laid out on the table and studying the family photos on the wall – anything to keep my eyes off the coffin. Between the old black-and-white portraits there was one colour photo, taken less than a month before in the photographic studio of the Chinese, U Kyi Nyo. I studied my brother's face carefully. Unlike me, he looked a lot like my father: the same small eyes, the same broad chin. There was also a photo with my father as a child around the same age as my brother. The similarity was almost frightening, as if, during his own lifetime, my father had been reincarnated in the body of his elder son, who, as I now knew, would never become the determined, handsome young man that my father was, as displayed in a third photo, taken on the day he married my mother.

I was startled out of my reveries by a loud bang. Despite myself, I immediately looked at the coffin, as if the noise could only have come from my dead brother. The coffin didn't look any different. I looked to the side, where Tender was now sitting. Tender was asleep with his head on the table. That must have made the noise: Tender's head falling forwards in his sleep and pulling his neck and shoulders along behind it, just as my brother's dead body had made my father go down on his knees.

With Tender asleep, I was even more terrified of looking at the coffin. And so I went back to concentrating on the photos.

The most prominent, in a gilded frame with lots of curlicues and flowers, was a posed portrait of my father's family. It showed five people: three big, two small; two standing, three seated – the photographer knew what he was doing. My grandfather, a man with an inscrutable face and eyes that seemed to bore right through the camera, was sitting on a chair with a high, straight back. The back of the chair – turned and carved wood – stuck up quite a bit above his head, making my grandfather look dignified and majestic as well as, paradoxically enough, small and insignificant.

My grandmother was sitting next to him on a chair that was just as straight but not as tall. In the photo she was a young woman, but there was already something elderly about her. Her hair was draped over her right shoulder in a luxuriant ponytail, but the flowers she wore in it did not dispel the sombre and unhappy impression she gave. Standing between the parents was the elder son, Than Tun, my father, who must have been about ten. He was wearing a glistening silk longyi and a leather belt with an ivory dagger hung from it. The sheath was delicately carved and the young Than Tun had his hand on the hilt, as if he might bare the blade at any moment. His chin was raised and he was staring at the camera provocatively. A mocking smile was playing on his lips.

The contrast with his younger brother, my Uncle Thet Tin, could hardly have been greater. Thet Tin was sitting on a leather pouffe at his father's feet. He too was wearing a longyi of glistening silk, but without any show of arms or boyish bravura – on the contrary. His shirt was made of silk as well and that, together with the fact that his head was turned slightly downward, so that he was looking up shyly at the camera, made him seem somehow vulnerable, almost girlish.

The fifth person in the photo was a maid, a squat young Kachin with a face like a full moon, standing off to one side behind my grandmother and the only one not looking at the camera, but beside and below it.

The photo told the story of an unhappy family.

My grandfather had been a middle-level administrative

officer, a not altogether insignificant cog in the mighty bureau-
cratic machinery that ran Burma in the British era. His wife was
a doctor's daughter and an actress who, in her day, in her part of
the country, had brought down the houses with her renditions of
wicked women in the traditional *pwe*. My grandmother had too
much talent and ambition to be happy in the remote provincial
town where her husband was posted for most of their marriage.
She took out her embitterment on the servants and took solace
in her youngest son, the sensitive, artistic Thet Tin, who
reminded her strongly of her younger self.

And the elder son, Than Tun, my father?

Ah, my father, a little sergeant major even then! A proud
fighter for an independent Burma! And still blissfully unaware of
the tricks life would play on him . . .

How often I stood before that photo: that night as a small,
frightened little brother, ignorant and taken by surprise; later as a
young adult, armed with knowledge but still unable to defend
myself against the crushing message that photo conveyed. The
message that, more than anything else, what and who we are is
determined by all the things we *could have been*, but never
became. And doesn't that same thing apply to our country?

When the first European merchants and adventurers came to
Burma in the mid-sixteenth century, they were stunned by the
wealth they encountered. They visited the capital of the most
important kingdom, Pegu, and gazed at its beauty. The city,
located on a plain, was built in the form of a gigantic square and
surrounded by walls and a wide moat that was home to innumerable crocodiles. There were twenty gates, five in each of the
four walls, and a bridge for each gate. In the palace gardens there
was a courtyard where they kept dozens of elephants, including
several pure white ones – white elephants are lucky.

And the goods you could get, there in Pegu! Gold and silver,
rubies and sapphires, pepper, lead, rice, wine and sugar – even

though they could have exported much more sugar if the foolish natives would only stop giving it to the elephants to eat, and using it so extravagantly in their own meals and delicacies. Our forefathers were just as wasteful, in the eyes of the European traders, with that most coveted of all precious metals, gold. The country's holiest temple, the Shwedagon Pagoda, was entirely covered with gold even then. Travellers praised it in their journals as the most beautiful building ever made by human hands, but at the same time they lamented the native custom of squandering gold on such vanities and noted that otherwise there would be much more available at much lower prices.

The stories of opulence the merchants took back home with them and the books they wrote about it, which were read avidly in all the major European ports, led to an endless supply of new adventurers willing to risk the long and hazardous journey east to present themselves on our shore in the hope of making a quick fortune.

But even then, Burma was a land of beauty and of war.

At the end of the sixteenth century, the Arakanese in the west and the Siamese in the east marched on the kingdom of Pegu. When the invaders withdrew, the once mighty kingdom was completely destroyed. The impoverishment and famine were so terrible that parents ate their children, and children their parents. The strong lay in wait for the weak, like wild animals, killing people who were reduced to skin and bones so they could fill their stomachs with their organs. They even slurped the brains up out of the skulls, they were so desperate.

Soon the jungle swallowed up the plantations, and the palaces and temples became ruins. And the traders avoided that accursed land, because the fields and roads were full of the bones and skulls of the poor Peguans, murdered or starved to death, or thrown into the river in such numbers that their carcasses blocked it and made it unnavigable.

Which evil spirits reside in our people, what kind of bad karma keeps us imprisoned, making us drown every new hope of a better future in blood?

In the 1930s and '40s General Aung San led the Burmese to freedom. He defeated the British with the help of the Japanese, then defeated the Japanese with the help of the British. At the end of World War II he travelled to London and successfully argued for a complete British withdrawal from Burma. An Executive Council, chaired by Aung San, was charged with the preparations for a new constitution for an independent Union of Burma. On 19 July 1947 armed men stormed the building where the council was meeting. Together with six others, General Aung San, the people's hero, the father of the nation, was murdered.

That night, in that gloomy room, with Tender sleeping with his head on the table and my brother lying in his coffin, I looked at the family photos and gradually realised that I was no longer scared, I wasn't even sad; instead a feeling I can best describe as lightness had taken hold of me − briefly it was as though I was being lifted up, as if gravity no longer had me in its grip. I felt the way that someone who has been carrying a heavy load and is finally able to put it down must feel. This feeling confused me so much, that it took a long time before I was able to give in to sleep, and all that time I quietly sang a song that Ngar Yoo had once taught me:

> *The rivers here don't flow to the sea*
> *The rivers here flow to the north*

Army trucks drove through the streets of Rangoon without their lights on.

'Have you heard the news? Turn on the radio, quick! Turn on the radio!'

'What's happened?'

'What's happened? There's been a coup, that's what's happened! General Ne Win has seized power!'

'When?'

'Last night!'

'Last night?'

'Turn the radio on, now! He's about to make a speech!'

We were going to bury Ngar Yoo that morning. I was sitting in the corner of the living room on my mother's lap. The house smelt of incense and flowers, cigarette smoke and women's perfumes. My mother had put her hair up and was wearing a dress of dark-red silk. My head was resting on her breast. I could hardly keep my eyes open, I was that tired. But as soon as a neighbour rushed into our house shouting something about a coup and U Ne Win, I was wide-awake. General Ne Win was one of my father's heroes, his portrait hung over the bedroom door. During the war, U Ne Win had worked side-by-side with Aung San. Later he had led the country for a while, when Burma's first democratically elected government was in danger of collapsing from internal conflicts. Many times I had heard my father announce, 'The General is a real patriot. In difficult years he saved our country from chaos.' And although I didn't know what that was, a patriot, and couldn't imagine what chaos in our country would be like, I understood that the former was something admirable and the latter, dangerous.

Our neighbour's arriving with this great news about the General on this sad morning seemed to me to be a reason for joy. It would surely cheer up my father! Someone immediately ran upstairs to call him. Meanwhile, no less than five people began searching for the radio, which Tender found first. By the time my father joined us, a cheerful march was already blaring through the room. I wasn't surprised that everyone had stopped talking. In a moment the great patriot, my father's hero, Aung San's former comrade, would speak to the people! We would take in his words and then, fortified and determined, we would complete the task ahead of us, Ngar Yoo's funeral.

'Here it comes!' said the neighbour.

'Quiet!'

'Turn it up a bit!'

'Shhh!'

The radio hissed and crackled but the voice of the General reached us loud and clear. Did I listen to what he said? Probably not. Would I have understood his words? Definitely not. I was six years old, my world was small and contained, it wasn't big enough for words like 'national unity', 'conspirators' and 'civil war'. I just watched my father's face, which looked gloomy and stayed gloomy, and that was something I couldn't understand because this was his hero speaking. And in such a difficult hour!

When the General had finished, another march started up and my father turned off the radio.

'Come on,' he said, 'we have to bury my son.'

Years later I realised that on that particular morning the General gave the following explanation for the military putsch he had ordered: various leaders of ethnic minorities had plans to leave the union. The unity of the state was at risk. And, according to General Ne Win, it was the patriotic duty of every Burmese to defend that unity and thwart the separatists.

He also gave another reason for the military takeover: it had been General Aung San's wish that Burma become a socialist state. And that goal had come no closer in the years of independence to date. General Ne Win was going to make sure that the wish of his former comrade-in-arms would be fulfilled. On 4 July 1962 the formation of a new political party was announced: the Burmese Socialist Programme Party. Three days later, on the campus of Rangoon University, the General's troops emptied their guns on students protesting against the coup. According to the authorities there were fifteen dead. But people who were there say that several hundred unarmed students were shot dead. One of the young casualties was my mother's cousin, Day Law, the son of her uncle Saw Eh k'Kyaw, who had a leading role in the Karen independence movement.

Six

If I'm honest – and you tend to be honest if you're blind and a refugee, with your life behind you instead of in front of you – if I'm honest, I have to admit that I wasn't sad about the loss of Ngar Yoo for nearly as long as I should have been. The very first night, when I was lying in bed with my eyes wide open, straining my ears to catch scraps of the conversations being held downstairs – a word, a sentence, a burst of wailing – even then it occurred to me that the death of my brother could have positive consequences for me. Of course, I immediately tried to banish the thought – how could I, how dare I! – but it kept fluttering around the back of my mind, like a brightly coloured butterfly in a darkened house. After all: suddenly everyone would be worrying about me! I would be the oldest and the youngest child at the same time! My mother would spoil me even more! And my father – my father would finally notice me.

That's what I thought.

But I didn't know my father.

What could I actually say about him? That he had served in the army in the 1940s. That he had been decorated several times (he had pinned the ribbons and medals on to a piece of black velvet and framed them; they hung on the wall in my parents' bedroom). That he had been promoted after the war (next to the ribbons hung a photo of the promotion ceremony, showing my father and the commander-in-chief of the Burmese army, General Ne Win). I knew that my father was still proud of what he had achieved in the army. I had often stood by those photos with Ngar Yoo while my father told stories about surprise attacks and night manoeuvres, about ambushes and hostile movements. And time and again my brother helped the story along by mentioning things he remembered from earlier stories, knowing they were about to come up but unable to wait, or not wanting to wait, because he wanted to show that he had paid attention last time. And time and again I was too late with my own little contributions to the story – and if I ever did manage to get in before my brother, my father would simply ignore me, while my brother would lay a quasi-paternal hand on my shoulder and say, 'That's coming, Min Thein, we're not up to that yet.'

I still couldn't get enough of those stories, I still drank greedily from my father's verbal fountain, as if I had a premonition of the terrible event that would come – the event that would dry up the source forever. When my father told us about the war he was like the proud, energetic boy in the family portrait: the kind of person who doesn't let anyone or anything get in his way. And I know that back then I often thought, if Ngar Yoo wasn't here, my father would . . .

I remember an afternoon not long after Ngar Yoo's death. My mother was out visiting relatives, I was at home alone with my father. We were sitting in the front room. My father was reading the newspaper, I was drawing wavy lines on a piece of paper with a pencil. I kept going until the sheet was full and then took another one. My father turned the page and started a new article. I looked at the newspaper hiding his face. On the front page there was a photo of two men in uniform holding up a shiny cup.

'What are those soldiers doing?' I asked my father.

'That's good,' he said absently.

'What are they doing?!' I repeated.

'Who?'

'Those soldiers. On the front page of the paper.'

'Oh, them. They've won something.'

'What have they won?'

My father sighed, closed the paper, and glanced vaguely at the picture. Then he said, 'I don't know,' opened the newspaper again and went back to reading.

'I'm going to join the army later too,' I said.

My father ignored me.

'I'll get to be a general at least,' I said. 'I'll tell everyone that they have to stop fighting. And then the army will make sure that it's always peace.'

My father read on imperturbably. Now and then he nodded his approval, at other times he frowned, puckering up his forehead and making a deep vertical line appear on his face from just under his hairline to the tip of his chin, with two short interruptions for nose and mouth. My father has two faces, I thought to myself, the left stands to attention, the right droops a little. I wondered whether Ngar Yoo would have ended up like that as well, but I didn't want to think about him, so I quickly changed the subject.

I asked, 'Why didn't you ever become a general?'

But my father didn't answer, and when I repeated the question he folded up the newspaper and went upstairs. I felt like shouting something out after him, but I didn't know what, so I walked despondently out into the garden and flopped down with a sigh on the chair next to the door, where my mother liked to sit at sunset so that she could see the neighbours coming home from the mosque and exchange the day's small talk with them.

I swung my feet back and forth. I used a splinter of wood to pick some dirt out from under my toenails. I waited for something to happen. For a very long time nothing happened. Then I saw the kid from next door, Maung Maung Aye, come around the corner. He was holding a piece of rope in his hand and there was a piglet walking along on the end of the rope. Maung Maung Aye was wearing his *jobba* and his *topi* – he must have just been to his Koran lesson. I knew immediately: this is going to be trouble, a Muslim kid with a pig.

'What are you doing with that?' I called out to him.

'Nothing,' said Maung Maung Aye.

'What do you mean, nothing?'

'Just nothing.'

'Where'd you get it? I mean, you don't just find a pig on the side of the road. Did you buy it or steal it?'

'No.'

'No, what? No, you didn't buy it, or no, you didn't steal it?'

'Neither.'

'Neither?'

'No, neither.'

I'd had conversations like this with him before. If there was something Maung Maung Aye didn't want to tell you, you wouldn't get it out of him. He must have been about six at the time, but he was as stubborn as an old ox.

'Pigs are unclean. At least, according to you Muslims, they are.'

Maung Maung didn't say anything. He looked back at the piglet, which had settled down on the warm sand.

'It's called the General,' he said.

'The General! That little pig?' I burst out laughing. 'Did you make that up?'

'No, that's just what it's called.'

'That's what it was called when you got it?'

'Yes.'

'Who told you that? Who'd you get it off?'

Maung Maung Aye kept quiet again. 'Come,' he said after a while, tugging on the rope. The General grunted, stood up and scampered up to him obediently. He patted the animal on the head and started walking.

'Your mother's going to be pleased . . .with the General!' I called out to his back. He shrugged and walked on. At his front door, he grabbed the rope close to the General's head, kicked the door open with one foot, and disappeared pig and all into the house.

I waited. First, in front of our own house, then halfway between our house and the neighbours'. Finally I leant against an electricity pole, just to one side of the door that Maung Maung Aye and the pig had disappeared through. My patience was amply rewarded.

It started as banging and rattling, apparently caused by a box or tin being knocked over and causing other, noisier and more fragile objects to fall over in turn. Someone ran downstairs. I heard screaming. A woman's voice, Maung Maung's mother. Then swearing. Then Maung Maung himself whimpering. And finally the horrible shrieks of the piglet itself. The animal came flying out through the air with all four legs stretched out straight ahead, squealing loudly, its little eyes bulging and its ears flapping in the wind. The landing was far from gentle. It came down on its hams and scraped over the rough, cracked asphalt for at least three feet, which silenced it completely for a moment, until it burst into something midway between the cry of a newborn babe and the shrill of a steam whistle.

I never saw the pig again.

My uncle Thet Tin told me what went wrong with my father's military career: he married my mother. The marriage of a Burmese officer and a Karen woman was problematic enough, but that woman's also being a close relative of one of the main leaders of the struggle for an independent Karen state was more than army command could tolerate. Soon after the wedding my father was given a job at a large but meaningless desk, far away from the battlefields that gave birth to national heroes – and high-ranking officers.

'But your father didn't break,' said my uncle. 'He kept his back straight and his chin up, he didn't utter a word in anger. He suffered in silence. One day he found a job with the police and handed in his resignation. On his departure he gave a glowing speech about loyalty and obedience, self-sacrifice and discipline. His superiors were deeply moved, his men clapped their hands raw and burst into a nationalistic song. Your father left the army the way he joined it: determined and filled with a passionate love for his motherland.'

Still, something deep inside him must have been ruined even then, I realise that now. Buddha said, 'Do not underestimate evil, thinking it will not affect you. Just as dripping water can fill a jug drop by drop, so evil fills mankind, little by little.'

When my brother drowned, my father was probably no more than a shadow of the man he had once been, even though he still did his best to resemble him. The death of his elder son suddenly brought that change to the surface, making it visible even to me, as young as I was.

The morning after my brother's funeral, I saw my father leave the house in his perfectly ironed uniform, his shiny boots, cap on head, pistol in holster: impeccable and determined. I sat at the long table in the front room eating the mohinga that my mother had made that morning, just like any other morning, and which she had put down in front of me with a smile that had so much sorrow in it that I had the greatest difficulty in getting a single mouthful down my throat afterwards. And I don't know whether it's pure imagination or whether my memories are coloured by the person my father became later, but thinking back on that morning and the way he came out of the bedroom: hair combed, cap in hand; the way he sat on the bench next to the door to pull on his boots; the way he said a distracted goodbye to my mother and put on his cap, pulled down the visor, opened the door and stepped out into the bright light of morning, I see a man desperately trying to hide something that everyone else could see at a single glance – that fate had succeeded where his superiors in the army had failed: my father was a broken man. And no matter how hard I tried to take my brother's place, in an attempt to make the unbearable loss a little more bearable, I would never succeed.

'Your father and you,' Uncle Thet Tin said, 'are like a cat and a dog living in the same house. You use the same rooms, eat the same food and breathe the same air, but you'll always be strangers to each other.'

Seven

I have never met a woman in my whole life who loved fish unless it was nicely cooked on a plate. It's men who go fishing and men who make a hobby of putting fish in aquariums. It's easy to understand women not liking fish – the scales, the slime, the cold eyes . . . But the fascination that so many men, and especially boys, feel for fish is considerably more difficult to explain.

After Ngar Yoo died, Maung Maung Aye, the boy from next door, became my new fishing buddy. The big advantage was that I was better at fishing than he was. Maung Maung Aye was six months younger than me and not altogether right in the head. Older boys would often tease him, but because my father was in the police, they always left him alone when we were together. Maung Maung Aye liked going fishing with me and we did it often.

The town of Min Won lies at the end of a bay in a place where three rivers flow out to sea. There is an inexhaustible supply of fishing spots and the number of different kinds of fish you can catch is overwhelming. Thanks to the knowledge I acquired at my grandfather's farm and thanks to Ngar Yoo, it wasn't difficult to impress Maung Maung Aye. I taught him how to catch razor fish with just a line, a hook and a piece of martabak. I taught him the difference between a tilapia and a gourami (the shape of the pelvic fin and the position of the jaw; tilapias are more fun to catch as well, they put up more of a fight). And of course I told him about the climbing perch in the tree on my grandfather's land. Once I found a similar tree beside a stream on the edge of town. I climbed up with pounding heart, but in the fork I only found a tiny bit of water that was crawling with wrigglers. It was not the only time that my status was challenged. The day I got spiked in the eye by a dwarf catfish was also the day that Maung Maung Aye caught more fish than me for the first time.

We were standing waist deep in the warm water of a pool that was almost completely overgrown with water hyacinth. We had made bamboo rods and lowered our floats in the rare openings between the hyacinth. Whenever we got a bite we had to pull the rod up quickly to make sure the fish didn't shoot in between the plants and tangle the line. Maung Maung Aye turned out to be better at it than I was – to my considerable frustration. It was high time I caught something as well.

My float disappeared underwater with a tug.

I jerked up the rod – fast, hard, too hard.

The fish (it was tiny, not more than four or five inches long) flew through the air at great speed. 'Watch it!' I shouted to Maung Maung Aye, who was standing close to me and had just got a bite as well. But he wasn't the one who was in danger. I had hardly spoken my warning when the vicious, poisonous spike on the dorsal fin of the dwarf catfish speared into my left eye. It took me a moment to realise, it all went so fast, and the hole it had pricked in my eyeball was so minuscule. The fish fell into the water in front of me and immediately dived down between the plants. My line got so tangled that I had to break it. My eye was watering. And it stung – not intensely, but unpleasantly.

'What was that?' asked Maung Maung Aye, who was removing his hook from the mouth of a greenback mullet.

'A catfish.'

'A *kitten*fish, more like it.'

'Whatever, a *kitten*fish. Just throw your line back in.'

We stayed until late. I pretended there wasn't a problem. I almost caught up. There was no question of me admitting to Maung Maung Aye that I had done something stupid, that something serious had happened.

It will go away by tomorrow, I told myself.

Don't think about it.

Don't touch it. Do not touch it!

It didn't go away.

Two months later the specialist at the hospital ascertained that I had been permanently blinded in the left eye.

First there was the tension of climbing up. My hands clamped around the slippery bamboo, my feet seeking a grip, the rapid, purposeful movements, briefly giving me the illusion that, if I wanted to, I could master even the greatest of obstacles. If only I'd been a little more careful that time in the water hyacinth . . .

With one eye it's difficult to judge distances. With one eye you'll never become a soldier, or even a humble police officer. With one eye it's more difficult to climb scaffolding. The only advantage is that you're not as likely to be afraid of heights.

Fearlessly I climbed up to my uncle, Thet Tin, who was sitting on his platform painting at least twenty feet above the temple floor. I sat down next to him and casually dangled my feet. There was a nice smell of paint up here. My uncle was putting the finishing touches to a depiction of the Buddha's First Sermon, the third in a series of murals that had to be painted just below the ceiling of Payagyi temple. When the job was finished, a band of paintings would run around all four walls, starting in the east with the birth of Prince Siddhartha and ending in the north with the death of the Great Sage after eating the spoilt truffles of Chunda, the smith from the land of the Mallas.

During a previous visit, my uncle had told me about Queen Maya's miraculous dream announcing the birth of the Buddha. In her dream, according to my uncle, four kings took her to a holy lake high in the Himalayas. There she was washed by four queens who sprinkled her with the most exquisite perfumes and dressed her in the most beautiful robes. They took her to a golden palace where she rested on a verandah with a view of a mountain that was bathed in light. While she was lying there, a white elephant came rushing down from the mountaintop, an animal that was bigger and stronger than any she had ever seen before, with six tusks and limbs as hard as diamond, an animal of preternatural beauty. In its silver trunk the elephant was carrying a white lotus flower. On reaching the queen, it ran around her bed three times, then stopped abruptly. Gently it tickled her right side with its trunk, then disappeared immediately. In her dream Queen Maya knew where the elephant had gone: it had entered her womb.

'That was how the arrival of the Buddha was revealed to his mother,' my uncle said.

I looked at the mural he was working on. I saw the newborn Siddhartha awash with golden light and his mother, Queen Maya, joining her hands in devotion before him. I saw the gold mountain in the background and I saw the white elephant and the lotus. I saw trees whose boughs were bending under the weight of flowers and birds, and I saw brightly coloured butter-flies – yellow, pink and light blue.

My uncle said, 'It is written that when Prince Siddhartha was born, a gigantic lotus flower rose up out of the earth. They say that the gods appeared in the heavens to look down on the babe in curiosity and that a stream of warm and cold water descended from heaven to wash him. There are stories that the little prince was able to stand immediately and that he took seven steps to the north, while the gods protected him with a white parasol, and that he roared like a lion and shouted that the whole world belonged to him. But I don't believe that bit, because in all of his miraculous life the Buddha never showed any interest in worldly power.'

Every time I visited him, my uncle would tell me the stories that went with the painted scenes – and yes, I paid attention, and no, I haven't forgotten anything!

A monk came into the temple to check the progress of the work. He joked with my uncle and warned me to be careful and stop dangling my feet over the edge of the scaffolding. Reluctantly I pulled up my legs.

My Uncle Thet Tin was a kind man, who, especially after Ngar Yoo's death, smothered me with care and attention and a love that was so selfless that I sometimes caught myself gaping open-mouthed at him for minutes at a time, as if, by studying him in minute detail and absorbing each movement of his hands, every nod of his head, and all of his expressions, I might somehow discover the secret of that selflessness. Through my Uncle Thet Tin I began to understand something of the awe-inspiring wisdom of the teachings of Gautama the Buddha. And I believe that it was by virtue of those teachings that I finally reconciled myself to both my father's indifference and the far too premature death of my brother.

My uncle taught me these words of the Buddha's: 'Those who hurt living creatures are not noble; only those who do not form a danger to any living creature are noble.' Through my Uncle Thet Tin, I finally gave up fishing.

Eight

My mother said, 'Take your questions to Uncle Thet Tin, he can
tell you anything you want to know.'

'I already do that, that's not the point.'

'What is the point then?'

'I just want to know what it's like.'

'You should have thought of that two years ago. You're too
old now.'

'So two years ago you would have let me?'

She hesitated. And I knew, I'd got her! 'Well?' I insisted.

'Yes . . . Yes, I think I would have.'

'And now I'm not allowed because I'm too old?'

'All the other boys in your class went ages ago, didn't they?'

I knew it. I had her. I had her! 'Not all of them,' I said. 'Do
you know Kyi Lwin? He hasn't been either. He's going next
month. After the Water Festival. Can I go with him?'

My mother sighed. My mother always sighed before giving
in. 'All right,' she said.

I ran up to her, wrapped my arms around her waist and
pressed my head against her chest. 'Thank you,' I said. 'You're
the nicest mother in the whole world.' I knew how much my
mother loved to hear things like that. I knew she liked it when I
pretended that I was still her little boy. Lately my mother was
always saying, 'You're growing so fast!' and 'You don't need to
be in such a rush to grow up!' She smiled when she said it, but it
wasn't a happy smile. I looked up at her. Her eyes were gleaming.
'Thank you,' I said quietly. She looked me straight in the eye.
How old she suddenly looked! And her eyes were so sad!

'I'll still believe in Jesus as well,' I said quickly. 'I promise.' But my mother broke free, saying, 'Stop it, don't talk nonsense.' Then she sighed again, very deeply.

I went outside. Maung Maung Aye was in the middle of the street. He was on his knees, looking up at the cloudless sky. Then he bent over and pressed his nose against the asphalt.

'Maung Maung Aye, what are you doing?'

He looked up, but didn't reply.'

'I'm going into the monastery,' I said. 'With the Buddhists.'

'Then I'll come with you,' Maung Maung Aye said.

'You can't, you're a Muslim.'

'So? You're a Christian, aren't you?'

'I'm not a Christian. My mother's a Christian.' I said it as quietly as I could, hoping my mother wouldn't hear me.

'You go to church with your mother, don't you?' Maung Maung Aye said.

I couldn't deny it.

'Then you're a Christian.'

'I'm still going into the monastery. After the Water Festival.'

'And I'm coming with you.'

'No, Maung Maung Aye, you're not.'

Maung Maung Aye bent over again to press his nose against the ground.

'You're praying with your bum to Mecca,' I told him. 'You're insulting the Prophet, peace be upon him.'

He acted like he hadn't heard. I picked up a pebble and took aim at the circle of his backside. But at the last moment I changed my mind. *Only those who do not form a danger to any living creature . . .* I dropped the stone.

It is an old custom for all Burmese boys to join a Buddhist monastery for a few weeks around their tenth birthday, so that they can be initiated into the teachings of the Great Sage. At least, it's an old custom for Burmese boys with Buddhist parents. My having to win my mother over to the idea of me going into the monastery at the age of twelve had everything to do with her faith in Jesus, the carpenter's son from Nazareth – and with my father's unbelief.

We were sitting in the garden and drinking tea by the light of two kerosene lamps. My uncle was visiting. My father said, 'Have you been putting ideas into the boy's head?'

'What do you mean?' asked my uncle.

'Him suddenly wanting to go into the monastery.'

'Oh, that,' laughed Uncle Thet Tin. 'Tell us, Min Thein, is that because of me? Am I responsible for that folly?'

I didn't know how to reply. Of course, it was because of him, but would I get him into trouble by saying so? And wouldn't wanting to go into the monastery on my own account be more of a sign of character? And anyway, what was my father complaining about? I was only going for two weeks! And everyone did it, all the boys in my class except the Muslims. Kyi Lwin was going too, wasn't he?

'I don't know,' I said hesitantly. 'Maybe a little. But I want to . . .'

My father interrupted me. He said, 'Why is Burma still a backward country? Because we are the prisoners of a backward religion.'

It was like having a bucket of ice water thrown in my face: I had never heard anyone say anything like that before! What had got into my father? What kind of demons had taken charge of him?

'Not so fast,' said my uncle. He seemed neither shocked nor surprised by my father's blasphemy. 'Are we ruled by Buddhist monks,' he said, 'or by a military dictatorship? Who's the boss in this country?'

'Of course,' my father replied, 'the General is the boss. But what can he do, faced with a population that . . .'

' . . . asks him to act like a good ruler?' Uncle Thet Tin interrupted my father. 'A good ruler according to the precepts of

Buddha! What's so unreasonable about that?'

'It's not that,' my father grumbled, 'it's all that superstitious fatalism. About living a thousand lives and if you don't find the Truth in this life, you can try again in the next . . .'

But his brother wasn't going to be put off that easily. 'If anyone is superstitious,' he said, 'it's the General: he'd rather listen to fortune tellers and stargazers than the people he rules. What did Buddha say about good rulers? Which qualities do they need to have, what standards do they have to live up to? The Buddha says that kings have Ten Duties, Ten Duties that apply to all leaders through all ages and in all corners of the globe.'

'I knew you'd been putting ideas into the boy's head!' my father said. 'You and your constant preaching.'

'A good ruler is generous,' said my uncle, who had now turned towards me and was completely ignoring my father. 'And he keeps to the five moral precepts: do not kill, steal, commit adultery or lie, and do not indulge in intoxicants.'

My father had got up out of his chair to stride furiously back and forth on the lawn behind my uncle.

'The true leader,' said Uncle Thet Tin, 'is prepared to sacrifice himself to save his people.'

'If there's anyone who's sacrificed himself for this country . . .' my father said, but he didn't finish his sentence. Instead he gouged a hole in the lawn with the heel of his right boot.

My uncle said, 'In all he does, the honourable ruler is guided by Truth and Truth only.'

My father had pulled a cheroot out of the breast pocket of his shirt. With a firm bite from his incisors he removed the end of the cigar, spat it out on the ground and used the nose of his boot to nudge it into the hole he had just made.

'The wise king is a shield for the weak,' my uncle continued. 'He is filled with pity.'

My father stamped the grass down over the end of his cheroot and pulled a silver lighter out of his trouser pocket.

'He is austere.' *Clink-ssshk* went the lighter. 'He has banished anger from his life.'

'Ha!' my father mocked, drawing back furiously on his cigar.

'He renounces violence . . .'

'Ha!'

' . . . and he is tolerant.'

'Of course he is.'

'Lastly,' said my uncle, 'the good monarch has a duty not to resist the will of the people. Is it really so strange,' he asked, turning to face my father, who was still pacing the grass behind his back and smoking furiously, 'that the people ask their ruler to adhere to these principles? Wouldn't our country be better off if the General kept to the teachings of Buddha?'

'How could anyone govern this country,' my father replied, 'without using violence? The country would fall apart immediately! And what use is tolerance when others preach intolerance? Don't the Arakan Muslims wage holy war against the infidels? And haven't the Karen, misled by their own leaders, who should know better, maintained an armed struggle for a state of their own for years? And what about the blood-thirsty Wa warriors and the cunning, battle-hardened Kachin troops, are you really going to resist them with pity and gentleness? Buddhism might be beautiful inside the monastery walls, as far as that goes, I don't mind him there' – he gestured in my direction with his left thumb – 'spending a couple of weeks in the monastery. Some people just aren't up to much more than meditation and prayer, and learning holy books off by heart. Maybe that's true for him too' – again that thumb – 'but don't come telling me that those holy books have any meaning and significance in affairs of state.'

'The important thing,' my uncle said, 'is that our people's morals, the ideas we have about what really matters and what doesn't, what's right and what's wrong, those ideas are rooted in Buddhism and we are groaning under a government that has turned its back on them because of its craving for power and its fear of the people. This government tries desperately to prove its moral legitimacy by building a new pagoda here and renovating a monastery there. And, of course, there are monks who let themselves be appeased! Of course some of them toady up to the regime! But the people see through it! The people know our leader's deeds. How could they forget those who have fallen in the struggle for freedom? How could they forget the prisoners who are in jail for no other reason than speaking up for their beliefs? How can you keep on justifying all those crimes, Than Tun? How can you?'

It was quiet in the garden. I imagined that I could still see my uncle's words hanging in the air and I hoped in vain for a breeze to blow them away. I had never heard him talk like this before. He was putting us all in danger.

My father's face was sweaty and the crease that divided it in two, the borderline between his determined self and his defeated self, was sharper and deeper than ever. And my uncle? My uncle's face was almost unrecognisable, it had changed that much. There was nothing left of the gentle features I loved so much, there was no sign of the relaxed concentration that was on his face when he was painting. He looked like he was gritting his teeth in pain, his jaw was that tense, he was staring that fiercely out into the dusk.

Were my uncle's words true: was my father justifying the crimes of the General and his henchmen?

Could that be why my mother had been angry with my father for so long?

Was my mother really angry with my father?

Or was she just sad?

And my father? Wasn't my father right that our country would immediately fall apart if its leaders renounced all forms of violence?

Didn't my mother have an uncle who was fighting in the

jungle against the Burmese army, the army of General Ne Win, the army that had liberated our country from the British and the Japanese – the heroic army that my father had been a part of?

Was that why my father was angry with my mother?

Was my father really angry with my mother?

Or was he just sad as well? Saddened by the death of his son? And angry with me, perhaps, because I wasn't my brother and never would be?

All these thoughts beset me that evening in our garden, by the light of the kerosene lamps. I caught snatches of children's voices from neighbouring gardens. I heard my mother in the kitchen. The acrid smell of fish paste drifted out through the open window. A stray cat stuck its nose up in the air.

I stood up and walked around the house to the street. Suddenly I no longer felt like going to the monastery. I picked up a stone and threw it as hard as I could at a mangy dog that was sitting in the middle of the road scratching itself behind the ear. The animal ran off yelping.

I have two very clear memories of my days in the monastery. In the first I am skulking behind a fence. I peer anxiously down the street that runs past the monastery. I'm waiting for Maung Maung Aye. It must be about three o'clock in the afternoon. Even in the shade, the air is so hot that you feel it burning in your lungs. And I'm hungry. I'm terribly hungry! Very early in the morning I had done a circuit of the neighbourhood with the monks and the other novices to collect alms. Slowly our begging bowls filled up with rice, vegetables and fish. Later we had breakfast. In a monastery you are not allowed to eat anything after midday, that's something that the Buddha, in all his wisdom, once decided. But my boy's body can't go that long without nourishment! Every afternoon my stomach screams out for food! Yesterday evening Maung Maung Aye came by. I asked him to help me. And now I'm sitting behind the fence, out of view of the monks, peering down the street in search of a figure with Maung Maung Aye's characteristic gait: bent slightly forwards, rocking a little, as if he's not altogether steady on his legs.

Is that him? Yes! No! Yes, it is!

A little later I'm stuffing my mouth with martabak.

The other memory is about a monkey. The monkey lived in a tree in the garden of the monastery. On one of its legs it wore a steel anklet with a thin iron chain attached to it. The other end of the chain was fixed to a branch. A fat monk with an impressively large, bald head looked after the monkey. He was the only one who could approach it without being attacked. The monk had bought the monkey years earlier from a travelling performer who was trying to teach it tricks by beating it with a stick. The monkey was eternally grateful to the monk.

One morning the monkey was hanging dead in the tree. The sun hadn't come up yet, the sky was a bluish purple, the monkey's free leg was sticking up in the air at a strange angle, its hands were pressed tightly over its face. The fat monk released his dead friend from its chain. There he stood, in the half-light of early dawn, with the dead animal in his arms. No one said a word. The monk turned the stiff body over and over, his fingers searching through the fur, pushing hair aside, trying to move its arms. Suddenly he stiffened. His eyes were fixed on something between his fingers.

'They murdered him,' he said.

We thronged around, all speaking at once.

'What?'

'Where?'

'Who?'

There was a small round hole in the monkey's coat, in a fold of its neck. Around the hole the hair was black and stuck together. The monkey had died from a fatal bullet wound.

There is a saying in Burma that goes: for a married man, the happiest day of his life is his wedding day; for a prisoner, it's the day of his release; and for a novice, it's the day he gets out of the monastery. I have my own ideas about the first, and I don't have any experience of the second, but I can vouch for the last of the three: more than anything else, my two weeks in the monastery taught me that monastic life was not for me.

'Thank goodness,' said my mother.

'Not that either then,' sighed my father.

'What was so bad about it?' asked my uncle.

'Everything,' I said. 'Getting up early. Going around the neighbourhood with a bowl for food. I felt like a beggar.'

'Humility, my boy, humility!'

'And the passages we had to learn! They were so . . .'

'Incomprehensible?'

'Exactly. And not being allowed to eat anything after midday!'

'Ha-ha, yes, I couldn't stand that either! But wasn't there anything you liked about it?'

'There was,' I said. 'The robes were beautiful. And the paintings in the temple, of course!'

I never told him the story of the monkey.

PART II

Karma is the Mother,
Karma is the Father

Come, take me by the arm, then we'll climb the hill in the middle of the camp and visit the Pagoda of the Silent Wind. The paths are narrow and steep, even if we choose the easiest route. My first impression is that it's not difficult for you to walk uphill, but gradually I notice your strength ebbing. I feel your clothes grow clammy with sweat. I hear the rasping of your breath. Twice you lose your balance and let go to avoid dragging me down on top of you. You curse in your own language – it makes us both laugh. When we finally reach the monastery, just below the top of the hill, I hear you brush the dirt off your trousers and I suspect that you are using a handkerchief to wipe the sweat from your face, the way white people do when they're hot.

We are invited into the great hall, where the monks are sitting on the bamboo floor in their yellow and red robes. They are watching a video of a Burmese boxing match.

'Who is fighting?' you ask, after the others have made room for us to sit between them. A novice who speaks a little English tells you the names of the boxers: Saw Nga Mai and Thu Ra Aung Dai. You taste the names on your tongue, mouthing them to practise the pronunciation. 'Thu Ra means brave man,' says the novice. 'The brave man is a Burman, the other one is a Karen, like us.'

The men are equally matched. The monks cheer and barrack, making a loud show of their dislike for the Burman boxer. To no avail: his Karen opponent loses on points.

'Do you get Burmese television here?' you ask.

'No,' says the novice, 'this is a video cassette. Most of us have seen it at least ten times.'

We are light-hearted as we climb the last part of the hill. By the pagoda that marks the top, I kneel down to show my respect for the Enlightened One, Gautama the Buddha, who has shown us the Middle Way, and I hope that you do the same, out of politeness or genuine piety, I don't care which. Then I ask you to look out over the valley, over the thatched palm-leaf roofs of the houses, over the schools and churches, the mosque and the temples, the office of the Thai Authority. I see nothing, but I hear everything, and I know where everything is and what it is.

I tell you where to look to see my house on the opposite hill. I point out the clinic where they treat the Aids patients and educate people about this strange and treacherous disease – there, on the shaded side of the football pitch. I ask you to look at the bush on the mountain's eastern slopes and see whether you can make out the road that connects the camp to the rest of the world, and I point out Pastor Marcus's Bible school. Not far behind that is the cliff where the valley ends and the river disappears into the mountain. I tell you about the rainy season of a few years ago when the cave got blocked by branches and mud that had been washed there by the river. The valley filled up like a bathtub. I say: 'On the second floor of the Bible school a line has been carved into one of the hardwood trunks that support the roof: that's how high the water rose in those anxious, wet, September days. A child and an old woman drowned, their bodies were never found.'

On our way downhill, a young woman speaks to us. Her name is Ta Eh Shee, which means 'clear love'. She asks about my health, and I ask her about her children. She answers in short, measured sentences, a few of which I translate for you.

She doesn't say a word about Tommy.

When we walk on, I ask you whether you noticed that she is missing her lower left leg. You hadn't noticed, you say, you were looking at the daughter she was carrying on her back.

I say, 'Six months ago Ta Eh Shee was walking along a path in the forest, not far from her home in a village in East Burma. She stood on a mine planted by one of our own fighters. It took three days to reach the nearest clinic. They refused to help her unless she paid for each treatment and all the medicine. Her brother and two of his friends then carried her over the border. That took another four days. The wounds on her leg had *got infected and the hellish pain had exhausted her so much that the doctors at the Thai hospital didn't think she was going to make it. Her left leg had to be amputated below the knee. Now she lives in the camp with her two small children. Her youngest daughter has never seen her father. He disappeared two years ago.'*

When we walk on, your steps are heavier. You lean on my shoulder as if I am leading you.

One

I first saw her in dappled light under old trees. She had a book pressed against her chest and her steps were hesitant, as if she was lost in thought. Maybe it was how slowly she was moving, as if time had a different rhythm for her. Maybe it was the softness of the light on her face. I sat on the grass and watched her until she dissolved into the green from which she had emerged.

How can one human being move another so much when they haven't exchanged as much as a glance, when they haven't spoken a word to each other?

I sat on the grass, the English grass, in the English park at Rangoon University, a boy from the provinces, uncomfortable in the big city, but at ease here, between the old trees, surrounded by old buildings. Here, love grabbed its chance.

When I stood up my legs were heavy and stiff, but inside my head everything was light and supple. That night I didn't fall asleep until the new day was already visible in the east, but when I woke up again a little later I felt fresh and rested.

When Prince Siddhartha was sixteen, he went out to the fields on a spring day to attend the ceremony of the cutting of the soil. His father, King Suddhona, used a gold plough to dig the first furrow in the black earth. He was followed by a thousand noblemen with silver ploughs and tens of thousands of workers with wooden ploughs that were decorated with ribbons and flowers. The air filled with the smell of ploughed soil and the festive whoops of the villagers. Siddhartha's thoughts, however, were with the birds that had been chased from the land and had seen their nests crushed under the cloven hooves of the oxen. The young prince thought of the creeping animals of the field: the timid mice, the startled grasshoppers, the worms killed by the ploughshares . . . If life is holy, thought Siddhartha, doesn't that mean that all life is holy, that of the unsightliest insect as much as that of the comeliest maiden? And the father saw that his son remained aloof from the festivities and was deeply worried.

The next day the king called his counsellors together and told them what had happened. The counsellors were soon agreed: what the prince needed was marital bliss. And so the king sent messengers through the land to all of the nobles with marriage-able daughters, ordering them to send their daughters to the palace so that Siddhartha could choose a bride. This was done. For a whole day the country's most beautiful young women passed by the young prince. As each came by, Siddhartha reached into a large bowl full of silver and gold bracelets and necklaces that had been made and decorated with gems of many colours especially for the occasion. The king's counsellors watched closely from behind the curtains as the prince handed the young women a piece of jewellery, looking for that one gesture or expression which would betray a preference for one maiden over the others. But it seemed as if he really had no interest in any of them and had only submitted to the whole thing to please his father. When the prince handed the last piece of jewellery to the last maiden with the perfect indifference that he had shown to all of his visitors, the counsellors almost despaired. In that same moment a young woman named Yasodhara entered the chamber. She saw the empty dish and the confusion on the face of the prince, who did not know what to do, and said in a teasing voice, 'What have I done wrong, Your Highness, that you abhor me so?'

Siddhartha looked at this young woman, who had spoken to him so freely, and in that moment he recognised her from a thousand previous lives. He removed a chain of the purest gold, decorated with the most precious of gems, from his own neck, put it around her waist and said, 'All this is yours.'

Not much later, Yasodhara and Siddhartha married. So great, according to the faithful, is the power of our karma.

Days passed, days of expectation and longing, days in which I thought I saw her everywhere, but she was always someone else, until finally I began to doubt my ability to even recognise her if our paths should cross again. More than that, I began to question her very existence and whether she had really walked through the park with a book pressed to her chest, her eyes fixed on the reality behind reality that is hidden within ourselves and has to do with truth and purity.

(Yes, that was how I thought back then, that everything about her was pure, and I already wished that I had never seen her, because after her, anyone else could only seem impure. Love is blind in both eyes.)

And then I saw her again! In a long corridor where Burmese had been spoken for years, but the echoes were still English. And later, on that same happy day, again! On a staircase, with me going up and her going down. Now my eyes caught hers and held her gaze, for less than half a second, but that moment seemed to stretch out endlessly in time, in *her* time, that slow time. And again she was carrying a book pressed against her chest. Ah, if only I had paid more attention – looking more closely, tearing my eyes away from hers, not to look at her hands but at the book – then I might have been able to make out a title, the name of a writer! What did she read? Whose ideas did she embrace?

Once, according to the faithful, Siddhartha and Yasodhara were two tigers wandering side by side through the jungle. The question was: would I ever be capable of such faith?

Two

Her name was Yi Yi Win and she was studying French and English. Like me, she came from somewhere else. Like me, she didn't live on the campus, but was staying with relatives in town. She had two brothers and a sister, and a father in a high position in the government of the province in which she had been born. I found all this out by striking up a conversation with a student I saw her greet in passing. It wasn't that I was planning on talking to him, or that I had any idea of how to bring the conversation around to her if I had the courage to start it up, or that I had the least hope of ever being capable of such decisive action – and yet: it happened, I did it, I astonished myself, I let myself be swept along by something stronger than my natural shyness and the deep-rooted conviction that my life wasn't about me but about others, or actually, about one other, my dead brother, who had drowned at the age of ten in the canal behind the mosque.

For the first time since his death, Ngar Yoo took second place; I think he even encouraged me, whispering, *Go on! Do it! Come on!* I went and I did, and then, when I knew what her name was and what she was studying and where she came from and that she had two brothers and a sister and what her father did, and even what her mother was called (her mother had a Karen name, just like mine!) and saw her again, on a languid afternoon, walking once more in the dappled light under the old trees with her book, I spoke to her, saying, 'Yi Yi Win, I'd like to know what you're reading.'

Her face lit up with a cheerful, surprised smile.

'Why do you ask that?'

'Because I . . . because . . . I saw you . . . Would you like to sit down?'

She hesitated, looked around. Looked at me. I smiled. I smiled what was probably the stupidest smile I have ever smiled in my whole life. More a cramp than a smile, a nervous tick, a spasm.

Yi Yi Win sat down.

'I was just curious,' I said, trying to be flippant, but unable to restrain the deep sigh that immediately followed.

'D. H. Lawrence,' said Yi Yi Win. Again she looked around. Then she said, '*Lady Chatterley's Lover.*'

'Oh,' I said. And then I didn't say another word for a long time. I didn't want to admit to not having read the book, but at the same time I didn't want to pretend that I had, I'm not the kind of person who gets away with things like that.

In the end I asked hesitantly, 'Wasn't that um . . . a very . . . controversial book?'

'Yes,' she said. 'Yes, it was controversial, because it's about . . . well, about a married upper-class woman who falls in love with a gardener. And that love is um . . . described fairly explicitly. It's a very beautiful book.'

That last bit came out with surprising ferocity and then she smiled again. This time her smile was more triumphant than nervous, as if to say, 'What's it to anyone else?' Her confidence was so contagious that I suddenly heard myself saying, 'When you've finished it, can I borrow it?'

'Do you read English?' she asked.

This time I didn't need to choose between bashful silence and bluffing. 'Yes!' I replied truthfully. Suddenly I was eternally grateful to my mother for sending me three times a week after school to Sister Agnes, a pale, nagging British nun who had lived in our town since her childhood and taught for years at the convent school, until General Ne Win nationalised education and forbade foreigners from teaching at Burmese schools. How often I had cursed my mother during those interminable English lessons! The mere thought of the unbelievably boring pre-war children's books that Sister Agnes had made us read from, books about English rural life in the days when the doctor and the vet were the only people with a car, books in which nothing, and I mean absolutely nothing, happened that made any kind of impression on us at all. But now I was prepared to forgive my mother for all of that, I was even willing to forgive Sister Agnes. Thank you, you ugly, pasty-faced nun!

Yi Yi Win said, 'Then I can lend you something else in the meantime, a book I've just finished, *Dubliners*, by James Joyce. Have you read it?'

I hadn't, but I couldn't wait.

She wanted to know where I had learnt English and what kind of things I had read, and I told her about Sister Agnes and the British countryside, and that when I was a kid I couldn't get enough of Shwe U Daung's books about the wily detective U San Shar and his assistant Dr. U Dain Daung, until I found out that the stories were copies of the adventures of Sherlock Holmes, and that since then I had managed to get my hands on a few books by Sir Arthur Conan Doyle and had read them with great pleasure, especially *The Hound of the Baskervilles* – 'Have you read it?'

She had and, more than that, she thought it was fantastic – frightening, hair-raising! Although she was disappointed by the ending.

'Me too, me too!' my heart rejoiced, and I found it extremely difficult to stay calm and avoid making myself completely ridiculous by terrifying her with hysterical laughter or even more hysterical cheering.

'Shall I bring *Dubliners* for you tomorrow?' asked Yi Yi Win.

'That would be great,' I said. And I thought: Where shall we meet? And what time? You sure it's not too much hassle? I'll look after it, the book, I will, really! And when I've read it, shall

I tell you what I think of it? And will you tell me what you thought and why? Yi Yi Win, you are so beautiful!

She said, 'I'll see you tomorrow at three. Same place.'

After she had turned away and was walking over the grass, I realised that she hadn't asked my name.

'I'm Min Thein,' I shouted out after her.

I'd seen them riding high on their floats during the Water Festival: the guys who knew how to go about it. I had never been one of them.

A truck drove down the street. Old and small, it blew greasy clouds of diesel smoke into the air. Big boards were attached to the sides with colourful pictures of Elvis Presley and a fire-belching volcano, two parrots and a palm-lined beach, a big pink flower. Music was coming out of the cab, the teenage idol Than Naing singing *Pepito, Pepito*: 'If she is white, I will be black, if she is gold, I am silver.'

Sitting on the truck and hanging off the sides were the guys from Anyant Ban, the 'Bloom of the Working Class'. All four-teen of them were singing along and they were enviably good-looking in their dark-blue longyis and white shirts, with their dark-blue headbands.

Every year in March, the city's youths form groups of ten to twenty. They make up a beautiful, poetic name for themselves: the Radiant Stars, the Courageous Tigers or the Bloom of the Working Class. They go in search of an appropriate vehicle and decide how to decorate it. Is one of the members – someone daring who commands the respect of the others – crazy about Marilyn Monroe? Then they ask a painter to depict her on the boards, billowing skirt and all. And is there someone else who dreams of taking the girl he loves to a palm-lined beach? Then the float gets a palm-lined beach! The preparations often take weeks, because the Water Festival is the most important festival of the whole year. It is the only time when everyone seems to manage to forget their everyday sorrows, the pressure of living under a dictatorship and the grief about all that has been lost. And for young Burmese, it's *the* chance to meet the love of their life.

The Water Festival lasts a week, but the first days are for children. It's only on the third day that the floats start driving, for four consecutive days. They do the same circuit over and over, through the same streets, where people throw water over each other: young and old, respectable and scruffy, educated and illiterate. And above all, past the same stalls where the local girls are selling sticky rice.

I had seen them standing there, the guys from Anyant Ban, on top of their truck, laughing and singing, I had seen them stretch out their long muscular arms to hand over money and take the rice. I had heard the lines they used on the girls, the quotes from love poems and popular songs: 'If you are black, I will be white. If you are gold, I am silver.'

I heard the girls laugh and I felt the excitement and the longing. I looked and I listened, I took it all in – but I never had the courage to join in.

Oh, yes, I had been asked, by classmates and neighbours. Come with us, Min Thein, this year we're the Passionate Hearts! But I shook my head and turned away. My mother teased me about it. My uncle gave me good advice. ('You have to let yourself go sometimes, Min Thein, just let yourself be happy, it will do you good, it does everyone good.') My father ignored me – and I didn't go, I didn't do it, I refused outright. After all, what kind of girl would be interested in me? None, surely? Girls like adventurous boys. Exciting boys. Boys who have something to say. Who know what to say, and how to say it. Ngar Yoo would have been up to it, I was sure of that, but me? No. I was too boring. I never said anything to girls. I was scared that they would start laughing the moment they disappeared out of my half field of vision.

During the Water Festival I was a spectator, not a participant – and the same could be said of life in general.

Yi Yi Win changed all that.

Three

'There was no hope for him this time: it was the third stroke.
Night after night I had passed the house (it was vacation time)
and studied the lighted square of the window: and night after
night I had found it lighted in the same way, faintly and evenly.
If he was dead, I thought, I would see the reflection of candles
on the darkened blind for I knew that two candles must be set at
the head of a corpse.'

That was the start of 'The Sisters', the first story in *Dubliners*.
Less than a dozen pages long, it was about the death of an elderly
priest and the grief this caused a boy, who had apparently learnt
a lot from him. But despite its pared-back simplicity, I didn't find
it an easy story. It was full of obscure words like 'simony' and
'venial', 'truculent' and 'chalice' – that last word was important
because, according to one of the sisters, that was where it all
began: he started to go downhill the day he broke the 'chalice'.

I took the book to the library and looked up the words I
hadn't found in my own, very limited dictionary. It turned out
that 'venial' meant forgivable. And a 'chalice' was a drinking cup
or a goblet. That didn't clarify things. Still, now that I'd read it
several times, the story started to come to life, more and more,
inasmuch as you could say that about a story that was so clearly
about death. There was one sentence that made me laugh every
time I read it, although I wasn't sure that Joyce had meant it that
way. The sentence went, 'No one would think he'd make such a
beautiful corpse.' It reminded me of the monkey in the
monastery garden.

There was another sentence that make me think of my brother and how I had felt the first weeks after the accident: 'I found it strange that neither I nor the day seemed in a mourning mood and I felt even annoyed at discovering in myself a sensation of freedom as if I had been freed from something by his death.'

'It is an oppressive story and very suggestive,' said Yi Yi Win, when I spoke to her about it the next day. 'What was the relationship between the boy and the priest based on? And what is the meaning of the chalice?'

I waited, hoping that she would answer the question for me, but she remained silent. Finally I admitted, somewhat sheepishly, 'I don't know either.'

She looked at me in surprise, then burst out laughing. 'That was a rhetorical question, there isn't any answer. Or else there are thousands. What matters is thinking about it.'

'Oh,' I said. And I was scared that this would be our last serious conversation. Why would a sharp-witted girl like her waste her time on a numbskull like me? I could learn laws off by heart, I was actually quite good at that. With an ease that astonished even me, I could cut through the wordiness of legal documents and go straight to the core. But the very first goblet or cup in the first James Joyce story I read remained an impenetrable mystery.

I felt – and suddenly I was painfully aware of this – the same as I had felt all those times when I was standing beside my brother listening to one of my father's stories, waiting for my brother to come up with all kinds of details I'd never heard before.

Would I feel like a weight had been lifted if I discovered in the coming days that Yi Yi Win was avoiding me? Would I realise with relief that I rued neither the day nor my part in the loss? No! No! It wouldn't be like that! I wouldn't let that happen!

I said, 'Books like this are new to me, Yi Yi Win. I have never read like this before.'

In the days that followed, she didn't avoid me.

'Look,' said Yi Yi Win, 'this book has been all over the country.'

We were sitting in a teashop, not far from the campus. Yi Yi Win had a book by Jean-Paul Sartre, *Existentialism and Humanism*, translated by someone who called himself U Thet Tin, but was using a pseudonym, according to Yi Yi Win. 'It's an illegal translation and an illegal publication.'

'I have an uncle called U Thet Tin,' I said.

'You have to be careful with uncles,' Yi Yi Win replied. She smiled and I was just about to ask her what she meant when a girl walked up to our table. Yi Yi Win slid the Sartre back under her English grammar textbook.

The girl ignored me and said, 'I wanted to ask whether you were coming to our meeting tonight.'

'Oh, that's right!' said Yi Yi Win. I could tell from her voice that she was pretending to be surprised. I wondered whether the girl could hear it too. 'I'd completely forgotten. And now I'm doing something else tonight, aren't I, Min Thein?' I didn't know anything about any plans for that night, but said, 'That's right,' and smiled apologetically in the direction of the girl, who was still acting as if I didn't exist.

'If you can hardly ever come,' the girl told Yi Yi Win, 'maybe you should ask yourself whether you really want to.' She turned purposefully and strode out of the teashop.

Yi Yi Win watched her go with a mixture of surprise and relief on her face.

'I'll do that,' she shouted, but the girl was already out of earshot.

'What was that about?' I asked.

'Oh, nothing. She has a club that studies the culture of the

Karen. Completely apolitical. Her father's something high up in the Ministry of Justice.'

'My mother is Karen,' I said.

'So's mine,' she said.

'And your father?'

'Burman.'

'Just like mine.'

'Do you speak Karen?'

'Yes, but not as well as Burmese.'

'Me neither. Not very well at all. Even my French is better.'

'You wanted to show me something, from that book,' I said. I didn't feel at ease. Not many people knew that I was half Karen, and I actually liked it that way. It was nice having the same kind of background as Yi Yi Win, but I wasn't really sure what that meant: had there been a Tender somewhere in her life, someone who had told her the ancient stories of the Karen? Did she know the history of her mother's people except from the school textbooks that constantly twisted the truth because the truth didn't fit the image that the military rulers wanted to give of themselves? ('The Karen's leaders have misled their own people, they are motivated solely by self-interest. Only under the just wings of the Burmese Socialist Programme Party can the Karen come to fruition.')

Yi Yi Win looked around, pulled out the book about existentialism and opened it at the last page. She held it out to me. Penned close together in small letters were brief comments and words of praise for the author: '*Sartre est formidable!*' and 'A truly great mind!' each followed by initials, a date and a location.

'It's a floating book,' said Yi Yi Win.

'A floating book?'

'A book that gets passed from hand to hand. Whoever's read it, passes it on to a friend or an acquaintance, or a distant relative who might be interested. After reading it, they pass it on to a third person and so on. Until the book finally comes back to the rightful owner. By then hundreds of people might have read it, all over the country. This book has already been right up to the north, in Myitkyina, and in Sittwe in the west. When I've finished it, I'm going to give it to a cousin of mine in Bassein.'

'I didn't know that things like that existed,' I said.

'Now you know,' she said. 'We have to educate ourselves, Min Thein. The government won't do it.'

That was the beautiful thing about the teashops in Rangoon: people dared to say things that you wouldn't hear anywhere else. There were moments when I felt intimidated by so much frankness. There were moments when I looked at Yi Yi Win and thought, you're like my brother . . . At moments like that I had to force myself to think of something else.

'Yi Yi Win,' I asked, 'have you ever loved someone so much that you were relieved when they died?'

'You're talking nonsense,' said Yi Yi Win.

Four

In Rangoon Yi Yi Win was living with an uncle and aunt who, to their sorrow, had remained childless. Her uncle had a top-level position at the Ministry of Home and Religious Affairs: he was the chairman of the Press Scrutiny Board. He was, in other words, the supreme censor of Burma's socialist government.

Yi Yi Win's uncle was a small, stocky man with a round head. He kept his greying hair cropped short in the style of American film stars of the 1950s. His pale face was dominated by heavy horn-rimmed glasses with thick lenses, behind which his eyes seemed to swim like fish in a bowl. He was a very difficult man to figure out. Yi Yi Win's aunt was a quiet, anxious woman who tried to make herself invisible.

My being received in the home of Yi Yi Win's uncle and aunt without being questioned about my intentions regarding their niece was very unusual. Contact between teenage boys and girls in Burma is a very delicate matter. As soon as that contact becomes in any way regular, it is assumed that they are a married couple, or that they at least plan to spend the rest of their lives together. On the last day of the Water Festival, the day of the Burmese New Year, many Burmese girls decide to stay the night with the young man of their choice. The next morning, mohinga restaurants all over the country are packed with newly weds. A single night is enough to confirm the nuptials. Formal ceremonies are not required and they are only rarely held, especially among the poorer sections of the population.

But what did Yi Yi Win's uncle and aunt expect of me? What did she expect of me herself?

'My uncle and aunt,' Yi Yi Win once told me on the bus from the campus to her home, 'are well-read people. They know that there is a whole world outside Burma, a world with different norms and customs, and different beliefs about love and friendship between men and women.'

I wasn't sure how to interpret that remark. Did it mean that she only saw me as a friend? Should I abandon any illusions I . . .

She didn't give me time to pursue my chain of thought.

She said, 'Did you know my uncle was in prison?'

I looked around. Yi Yi Win didn't have a loud voice, but was it wise to talk about such a sensitive subject in a crowded bus? She read my mind.

'Why should we be secretive about a prison sentence? It's not as if being in prison is something to be ashamed of. It can happen to the best of us. More to the point, in this country it mainly happens to the best of us!'

'Yi Yi Win!' I said. The words shot out of my mouth, harsher than I intended, but still, how could she be so reckless? Talking like that didn't just endanger her uncle, she was putting herself at risk as well. There were spies and informers everywhere, everyone knew that. Here in Rangoon you felt their presence much more strongly than at home in our sleepy provincial towns. And even there you were careful not to make provocative statements in public. What had got into her? What was she hiding behind her smile? But wasn't that the very thing that had attracted me most about her? The fact that behind her girlishness and innocence there was a hidden strength that made her independent and free? A strength I was secretly jealous of?

Yi Yi Win stared at me for a few seconds. Then her face relaxed and she laughed. 'I just suddenly had such an urge to say that,' she said. 'Don't you ever feel like that?'

'Me . . . No, I don't think so . . . Although . . .'

The bus came to a stop. We had to make room for someone

to get past. A little later it was time for us to get off as well.

'Would you like to know what my uncle was sent to prison for?' asked Yi Yi Win. We left the busy road behind us and turned down a lane that led to the tree-lined street where her uncle and aunt lived.

'Of course,' I said.

'So would he.'

'Did you know I photographed Saw Ba U Gyi,' said Yi Yi Win's uncle, 'after his death?'

We were sitting in an imposing, high-ceilinged room with an immense chandelier. It was getting dark outside and inside two candles were the only source of light. The city was suffering yet another of its many blackouts. Yi Yi Win's uncle was sitting in an old armchair in front of a big bookcase with sagging shelves. Yi Yi Win and I were sitting on the floor in what I felt to be a strange, subordinate position. But her uncle didn't seem to notice and Yi Yi Win was as relaxed and self-assured as ever.

Saw Ba U Gyi is a hero to the Karen. He was a minister during the last years of British rule and later negotiated on behalf of the Karen with the first democratically elected government of an independent Burma. When the negotiations failed to achieve the desired level of autonomy – with the Burmese violence against the Karen flaring up at the same time – Saw Ba U Gyi founded the Karen National Union and shortly afterwards the Karen National Defence Organisation. It was in a clash between members of that organisation and the Burmese army that Saw Ba U Gyi was killed in August 1950.

Since then he has been the Karen's most important martyr.

'I was a young reporter at the time,' Yi Yi Win's uncle said. 'With an old Speed Graphic to take photos to go with the articles I wrote. There wasn't usually enough money to send a real photographer out with me.' He had a peculiarly expressionless voice, as if nothing he said really touched him, let alone could have been intended to touch anyone else. At the same time, he never said anything trivial.

'In August 1950,' he continued, 'a few other journalists and I flew to Moulmein in a light aircraft on the invitation of the Ministry of Information. They were going to show us the body of Saw Ba U Gyi. We were told that Saw Ba U Gyi had been found dead after a firefight near a small village outside Moulmein. But even before landing, it was obvious that wasn't true. When pressed, the soldiers who were accompanying us told us that Ba U Gyi had been captured alive by the Burmese troops and shot later while trying to escape. What I suspected at the time, and now know, after experiencing dozens of similar cases since, was that "shot while trying to escape" is a euphemism for summary execution. With Saw Ba U Gyi, that was impossible to ascertain because they had dragged his body through the mud for miles before laying it on a stretcher. Then there were two hot, humid days before we even got there, so what they showed us was hardly recognisable as a human corpse. I remember taking some photos, but I think they came out fuzzy. And, of course, we were only allowed to give the official version: that Saw Ba U Gyi was already dead when he fell into the hands of the government troops.

'The man who got the credit for eliminating Saw Ba U Gyi,' he continued in that same flat tone, 'was Captain Sein Lwin, the very Sein Lwin who is now Minister of Home and Religious Affairs, and therefore my boss.'

Yi Yi Win said, 'You should tell him how you got your job at the ministry. In the bus on the way here, I told Min Thein that you were in prison. He was shocked by my saying that in a crowded bus. Weren't you, Min Thein? But I said that spending time in prison was nothing to be ashamed of in this country.'

'I found it rather . . . um . . . reckless,' I said.

'You're right, Min Thein,' her uncle said. 'There's no need to draw attention to yourself unnecessarily, Yi Yi Win. There's no point in that.' Yi Yi Win spluttered a little, but her uncle ignored her. I was suddenly painfully aware that I had ended up in the wrong camp on this issue. I tried to nudge the conversation in a different direction.

'Of course, I am very curious,' I said, uncomfortably subservient, but undoubtedly influenced by my humble position on the floor, 'about the story of your imprisonment.'

'That's soon told,' her uncle replied. 'After the coup of 1962, a new, much stricter press law was introduced. They set up a Press Scrutiny Board as well to make sure that everything that was published contributed to the General's goal of transforming Burma into a socialist utopia.' The corner of his mouth curled up for a moment in a hint of a smile. 'Criticism of the government of any kind was forbidden. Reports on the independence struggles of the minorities were heavily censored. And because no one could be sure of their own position, not even within the government, a web of fear developed. Anyone who was in any way involved in the press, publishing or the arts got caught up in it. The slightest slip, no matter how insignificant, sent an immediate shockwave through the whole web. I slipped up. I don't know how. It might have been an article I wrote about the cultural richness of our country, in which I got carried away with singing the praises of the Shan craftsmen. Maybe it was a piece about a prominent officer who had fallen from grace and been given a dishonourable discharge. Things like that were always sensitive, still are actually, even if you stick strictly to the official version. I know all about that, given my present position.'

A mocking smile was now definitely playing over his lips. He had tilted his head back slightly and behind the thick lenses of his glasses his eyes looked as if they could come popping out of their sockets any minute.

I glanced sideways at Yi Yi Win. She didn't look back.

'I was in jail for three years, without trial,' her uncle said. 'At Insein Prison, I fell ill. There wasn't any decent medical care. I thought I was going to die. Then I signed up as a member of the party. That was possible, even for prisoners. And I wrote a letter to the General requesting a pardon. In the envelope I enclosed an essay that I had spent a long time on. It was an exceptionally thorough and, above all, an exceptionally boring work on the technicalities and logistics of running a newspaper. At that time, there were still a number of newspapers published by independent publishers. And the readership of those papers far exceeded the readership of the official government newspapers. I thought, if I can convince the General that I can be of use to him, he might be willing to release me. A month later they let me go. Naturally, on condition that I signed a declaration promising that I wouldn't get involved with opposition media.'

Again, that arrogant smile.

'I knew the General from the days when he was just a general and not the leader of the country,' he continued. 'You could even say that we had been friends at that time. Still, I was surprised when I was informed a day after being released that I was summoned to an audience with him.'

He was quiet for a moment, but then he started to laugh. He laughed louder than I have ever heard anyone laugh, before or since. He threw his head back and roared with laughter. His belly, no, his whole body shook with waves of laughter.

I looked at Yi Yi Win, but externally she remained unmoved. She was not looking at her uncle any differently than she had been a few minutes early. She looked like she was studying a cow that was calving, or a dog that was mounting a bitch. Her uncle's laughter petered out. I watched him: he had taken off his glasses and was rubbing his eyes with one hand, while holding the glasses by one arm in the other and letting them swing gently back and forth. Now Yi Yi Win looked at me, I saw it out of the corner of my eye. Her face was completely expressionless. I was shocked.

'Min Thein,' her uncle said, putting the glasses back on his nose and going back to his usual inscrutability, 'you should have seen yourself.' The laughter was still snickering in his voice, but beyond that he seemed to have completely regained his composure. 'What were you studying again?'

'Me?' My confusion was complete. Was he laughing at me? And why? 'I'm doing law,' I said. It sounded like a confession.

'Law. Excellent.' He rubbed the palms of his hands dry on his thighs. Excellent, I thought. It was excellent that I should be studying law. But what did that have to do with his outburst of laughter?

'Fear is a strange phenomenon, my dear Min Thein.'

Fear was a strange phenomenon – yes? so?! I was starting to find him tremendously annoying. And why wasn't Yi Yi Win coming to my rescue? I couldn't get a smile out of her, not even a sympathetic glance.

'I don't believe,' I said, and again my voice sounded thin and small. 'I don't believe,' I repeated, louder this time, 'that I entirely follow you.'

'What I saw on your face just now,' Yi Yi Win's uncle said, 'when I told you that the General had invited me to an audience, was pure terror, elemental fear. And don't tell me that it's not true, because I see that kind of terror every day. It's not something you can control. You're probably not even aware of it. It's the fear a deer feels when it hears a branch crack in a glade. An impulse. A flash. And it's over again before you realise it.'

I looked at the wooden floor. There was dust and dirt in the chinks between the boards. I heard the voice of Yi Yi Win's uncle, but I blocked out the meaning of the rest of his words. Roars of laughter echoed through my mind. Why was he doing this? He was humiliating me in the presence of Yi Yi Win. Was this his way of driving us apart, or was it his normal behaviour? It occurred to me that this was probably how he treated the writers and publishers he received in his room at the Ministry of Home and Religious Affairs. 'You realise that Chapter 3 is entirely unacceptable. It undermines national morale.' 'The word "freedom" on page 4 implies the existence of nonfreedom – surely you don't want to maintain that implication? You know how sensitive the General can be . . .' And then that roar of laughter.

I don't think I will ever be able to recall that evening without feeling ashamed.

Five

There was a story doing the rounds in Rangoon about the day the General showed up to disturb a party. The party was being held in an expensive lakeside hotel, directly opposite the General's home on the opposite shore. A lot of foreigners had been invited, including quite a few diplomats. A band was playing evergreens and the guests danced a quickstep, a bolero and maybe a cha-cha-cha. The party was lively and sometimes noisy but, above all, eminently respectable.

No one knew what was going on in the General's mind that evening, but eventually he stormed out of his house, jumped into his jeep and drove to the hotel at top speed. His bodyguards had the greatest difficulty in keeping up with him. After arriving at the hotel, the General started kicking the dancing couples. When the last pair had fled, the General turned his attention to the band's instruments. His heavy boots splintered a double bass and staved in the side of a piano. Everyone was flabbergasted and too scared to lift a finger to stop him – everyone except one man. This man didn't recognise the General and flew at him. The bodyguards immediately leapt into action: they didn't drag off the General, the fool who kicked the partygoers, the lunatic who destroyed expensive instruments, no, they grabbed the only person in the hotel who resisted the madness. A little later the General left the way he had come: in his jeep, with squealing tyres, leaving the smell of diesel exhaust and burnt rubber behind him.

The story was like an echo of the events of 1962, when Ne Win carried out his coup.

That night, when my brother was laid out in our front room and Tender warned me against the call of the *k'la*, the General went to a ballet by a Chinese dance company, a light-hearted appetizer for the gruesome main course he was preparing.

What powers did the ballerina's dance steps release within him? During the break after the first act he must have shut his eyes and then, awkwardly, almost shyly, looked around. And no one there could have suspected that this unexceptional man would be inspired by the beauty of that evening to commit the greatest evil an officer can commit: overthrowing the civil authority that has invested him with the power of the sword, that pays his salary and provides his uniform, his weapons and his home.

It is one of the hardest lessons I have had to learn in my life: that the beauty that brings out goodness, gentleness, humility, pity and cautious behaviour in one person can, in another, trigger a fury that seems to be aimed at everything that is vulnerable and worthwhile, a rage that ultimately targets not just the beauty that set it off, but also, and especially, other people and humanity itself, including the humanity of the perpetrator. In the years since my flight, my years in darkness, I have realised that many look on unchained evil with horror, but that others see it as a new, superior form of beauty – and thus evil multiplies. To their own horror, or secret excitement, some of those who were cautious and gentle find themselves in the camp of the violent.

After the ballet, the General must have sought his way to the exit, the noise of the street and the starry night. He would have smelt the sweet perfume of the women, and the sweat of the men, whose attendance at a Chinese ballet must have been an ordeal they submitted to only for social status (or to placate their wives). He must have been aware of the looks of recognition, the faces turned towards him or deliberately looking the other way, like monkeys that avert their faces when the hunter shoulders his rifle to take aim for the fatal shot.

The General himself was not a stupid man, but he preferred to surround himself with people who were unburdened by intellectual baggage. He then used the ignorance of his men as an excuse for the excesses they committed, excesses for which he, as president, was responsible. In the better circles of Rangoon, the circles in which Yi Yi Win's uncle moved, they often referred to the General's way of exonerating himself, the way he said, 'You have no idea how hard it is for me to keep my lads under control. I can want it to be like this or that, but those lads of mine . . .'

The General had said something similar to Yi Yi Win's uncle, when he appeared before him after his release. The General said, 'Of course, I would have liked to let you out sooner, but well, you know what my lads are like . . .'

'Then,' Yi Yi Win's uncle related, 'he pulled five hundred-kyat notes out of his pocket. That would get me through the first few days, he said. And then I had to report to the Ministry of Home and Religious Affairs. He had arranged a job that would keep me out of prison.'

And that was how Yi Yi Win's uncle, an enemy of the regime, a journalist who had been a friend of the General's in his younger years and had still ended up in prison for writing something that endangered national security and the construction of the socialist utopia, became the most important official in the state censorship department.

Perhaps that was why he needed to roar with laughter a couple of times every day.

What no one was allowed to write about was that the General was jealous.

He throws a party at his residence.

People are drinking.

The atmosphere is cheerful.

Dozens of intellectuals from Rangoon University are present.

Someone, a guest, makes advances to the General's wife.

Other people joke about it.

They gossip.

The General overhears the gossip.

He orders the doors locked. No one is allowed to leave the house. The conversations hush. The laughter dies. The General walks around between his guests. He looks at this one. He stares at that one. Suddenly he stops. He turns, agonisingly slowly. He raises a fist. He plants that fist with all his strength in the face of the man who dared to make advances to his wife. He beats the man to a pulp.

What no one was allowed to write was that the General was scared – scared and superstitious.

The General stands in front of the mirror and draws his pistol. He is convinced that someone wants to murder him. He shatters the mirror by shooting his reflection because he believes that this will protect him.

The General is scared that others are conspiring against him. He consults his advisers: the stargazers and soothsayers. They say, 'The danger comes from the right.'

The danger comes from the right?

What can he do, what can the General do to avert the danger?

The danger comes from the right . . . from the right . . . from the right . . . He knows what to do!

'From now on our country will no longer drive on the left,' the General says, 'but on the right! That will neutralise the evil forces! Write a law, a decree! Announce it in the state-owned newspapers, on our public radio, through the national public address system and the government journalists: as of today, traffic in Burma no longer drives on the left, that backward custom from the colonial era, no, from now on the traffic drives on the right, RIGHT, RIGHT!'

And that was what happened. From one day to the next. In 1970.

Until this very day, most cars in Burma have the steering wheel on the wrong side.

The General is a genius. Write that down.

The General is the saviour of the motherland and of the fatherland. He is past, present and future, top and bottom, left and right.

The General is no longer a general, but a civil president.

And Burma is a democracy.

Write it down!

Write it down!

Hahahahahaaaaaaa!

Six

And then came the day when Burma's greatest son returned to the motherland, the fatherland. He arrived on a special United Nations aeroplane, he arrived in a coffin. U Thant, the man who for nine years had held the world's highest office, that of secretary-general of the United Nations, wise old U Thant, who on countless occasions had given subtle but unmistakable proof of his abhorrence of the General's dictatorship, he, the most respected of all Burmese, good-natured, astute, tolerant U Thant had departed his weary body. And now, the time had come for the people to say goodbye to that body.

It was 5 December, 1974 and Yi Yi Win asked, 'You going?'

'Of course I'm going,' I said, not because I had thought for a second of actually going there, but because I thought she was testing me.

'Shall we go together?' I asked.

'Of course we'll go together.'

I had avoided her for a while after that terrible evening at her uncle's, because I thought that would be doing her a favour. It turned out that I was actually hurting her. One afternoon she waited for me near the door of the law building.

'Why don't you want to see me any more?' she asked.

' I want to see you very much, Yi Yi Win. But what do you want with a failure like me?'

'You're talking nonsense,' she said. 'Have you finally got round to starting *Lady Chatterley's Lover*?'

I started it that same evening. And in the days that followed we discussed D. H. Lawrence's criticism of the modern age and the parallels and differences between early twentieth-century England and the Burma of sixty or seventy years later – all things that I knew next to nothing about, but not once did Yi Yi Win say, 'You're talking nonsense.' And of course we also talked about the love of an aristocratic woman for a gamekeeper, Victorian morals and the searing heat of desire. But those conversations were between us, between Yi Yi Win and me, and they will stay that way forever.

The stadium was a mountain of steel and concrete, a stone monster that gobbled up people. Anyone who dared to approach was irretrievably sucked in through the black holes of the entrances, up stairs that smelt of sweat and dust and stagnant water, down gloomy corridors and out again, back into the outside air, but no longer outside, inside now, in the middle of the building, under an open sky. It comes as no surprise that sooner or later in the history of virtually all dictatorships, there is a role for the local stadiums. Opponents and agitators driven together like cows to the slaughter, easy prey for the armed guards up on the stands, and everything, thanks to those same stands, hidden from the view of the outside world.

But on this December day the opponents and agitators came to Kyeikasan Stadium of their own accord. This time there weren't any soldiers watching from above, ready to open fire at the first sign of misbehaviour. The regime had obviously lacked the imagination to realise that the special qualities of the stadium, of any stadium, can also have a completely different effect on the masses. Besides overawing and belittling, the size and grandeur of the surrounding concrete can also give people the strength and courage to stand up as one against their oppressors. The sensation of being cut off from the outside world can lead to a self-confidence which the people involved had never dreamed of possessing.

Yi Yi Win and I stood in the burning sun on one of the stands and looked at the black coffin with the bright blue flag of the United Nations draped over it and listened to the speakers, whose words echoed off the concrete and were carried away on the breeze blowing over the city from the delta. Thousands of people had come together to pay their last respects, lay wreaths, and speak their eulogies, full of praise for the deceased, full of scarcely veiled criticism of the General, who considered an ordinary burial at an ordinary cemetery more than enough honour for a man he couldn't hold a candle to.

Could we have known what was going to happen? Were there omens, hints in what was said and not said or in the flight of birds high in the blue sky? And if there had been, would we have acted any differently?

'Do you see that guy there near the coffin?' asked Yi Yi Win, pointing at the small stage on which U Thant's bodily remains were laid out in state. 'The one with the red shirt? That's Soe Nyunt, who goes by the name of Joe. Do you know him?'

Of course I knew him. He was the one who had told me so much about her. The fellow student she had discussed Sartre with, continually confronting him with internal contradictions in his arguments until, driven to distraction, he had conceded all her points, even things he was absolutely certain she was wrong about. When he told me that story, he sounded so annoyed that I burst out laughing, which annoyed him even more. But I didn't tell her any of that. I said, 'We've met, but I'm not sure when and where.' As an answer that seemed safe enough.

'He's horribly pigheaded,' said Yi Yi Win without a trace of irony. 'But beyond that he's a nice guy.'

And suddenly I thought, I love you! Because I too was caught up in the strange magic of the stadium, I too had drawn strength from the concrete and the steel and the energy of the crowd, even if that strength didn't manifest itself in me as rebelliousness, but as the courage to let love take hold of me.

And then there was the flag. And then came the tears. Then there was the monk. And then it all went so fast that afterwards none of us could properly reconstruct all the things that happened, or especially, *how* they could have happened.

The flag was white bunting with a picture of a fighting peacock. It was the flag of the Students' Union of which U Thant had once been a leading member. The General had long since outlawed the flag, but there were still three people who dared to lay it, together with a wreath, by the coffin. A shiver went through the crowd. People were seized by an excitement which let the big emotions that had been churning and seething under the surface for hours escape, just as steam escapes from a cauldron when you raise the lid. Grown men and women burst into tears and soon we too, the young ones, had tears in our eyes. Yi Yi Win laid her hand on mine for a moment. And then the sorrow was immediately followed by anger. Someone shouted, 'General Ne Win is shaming the nation!' Another screamed, 'U Thant! U Thant! Deliver us from these dogs!' Whereupon a monk, wrapped in the mustard-coloured robes of a recluse, took the microphone and declared in a calm self-assured voice, 'The great U Thant, this wise man who has been an example to us all, and should be an example to all those rulers who believe that they and they alone have a monopoly on wisdom, and that they and they alone can decide what is good for the nation, for us, the little people of this country, whose leaders demand such great sacrifice – this proud son of Burma deserves a better fate than to be buried in the cemetery where Daw Khine May Tan lies!'

And new waves of emotion surged through the crowd: indignation, horror and disgust, because everyone knew that Khine May Tan was the General's first wife, a woman who had been the subject of the most terrible rumours and gossip even during her lifetime. And although nobody could say for sure how much of it was true, no one believed she was entirely innocent, let alone that she could in any way approach the dignity and humanity of the great U Thant. Ne Win's decision not to give U Thant a state funeral and the fact that he hadn't even bothered to come to pay his last respects to this great man were disgraceful, but reflected badly on him more than anything else. But his wanting to entrust U Thant's body to the soil in which his first wife was buried, subjecting it to the same creeping vermin that had consumed the flesh of the despised Khine May Tan – that didn't bear thinking about! And now that that unbearable thought had been spoken out loud, now that it had been put it into words by a deeply religious man, a monk who measured himself by the most rigorous of standards and had sought the seclusion in which human beings can best approach the blessed state called nirvana, now that everyone had heard it, the crowd could no longer put that idea aside, it could no longer submit to the course of events.

Something had to happen – and something did happen.

Something incredible happened.

Seven students, including Soe Nyunt who goes by the name of Joe, picked up the black coffin with the blue flag and the body of U Thant in it and carried it out of the stadium! And no one stopped them.

'And now?'

'Where are they going?'

'What are they doing?'

'What's going to happen?'

'We have to help them!'

'The students of Rangoon forever!'

'The Students' Union forever!'

'U Thant forever!'

'Down with Ne Win's dogs!'

'Shh, shh, shh!!!'

'Come on! Come with us!'

'U Thant deserves to be buried in consecrated ground!'

'The students will protect him!'

'We will protect the students!'

'No one can touch us!'

'Who dares to take on the people?'

'We are angry!'

'They won't scare us any more!'

'We'll drive them out!'

'We'll prosecute them!'

'We'll make them pay for their crimes against the innocent people of Burma!'

'The proud people of Burma!'

'The people that gave birth to U Thant!'

'U Thant forever!'

'The people forever!'

'Where are we going?'

'What are we going to do?'

'Let's go outside!'

'We have to see where they're taking the coffin!'

'They're going to bury him in hallowed ground!'

'Where the Students' Union building used to be!'

'The building Ne Win blew up!'

'Death to Ne Win!'

'Shh! Shh!'

'Come on!'

She took my hand. She took my hand! Yi Yi Win took my hand and pulled me towards the exit and she didn't let go again until we were outside in the middle of a crowd that had suddenly fallen weirdly silent. I looked at her and although she didn't look back, I thought, you and me, here and now, in this place, at this historic moment in which the history of our country is taking a dramatic turn, our lives are coming together here, and nothing and no one will ever separate them again! That was what I thought, no, I knew it, I knew it with a certainty I hadn't felt since the day I looked my mother in the eye and knew that there could never be a greater love than the love between her and me – the moment that was so cruelly destroyed by my father's entrance.

We joined the silent flow of people and there was only *one* thing I wanted: I wanted to know what was going to happen.

Later we heard from Joe that they put the coffin in a Datsun minibus. That someone suggested not putting him inside, but on top of the minibus, where everyone could see him. That they had driven off, at walking pace. That they had followed the route the coffin would have taken if it was being driven to the cemetery as planned. That everywhere along the side of the road people burst into tears at the sight of the coffin. That the students who were sitting on the minibus and holding the coffin and the flag hadn't dared to look at each other because they had no idea what they were doing and even less what it would lead to. And that they felt the support of the nation lifting them up, as if they were being swept along by the forces released by the death of this great man, whose body was now their responsibility. That they were scared to death.

'The route to the cemetery passed close by the university,' said Joe. 'That's where we turned off. Someone shouted, 'To Convocation Hall!' And that's where we went. The administrator was there, we chased her away. The rector wasn't around. We occupied the offices. We formed an action committee. That was something at least. Then we put the coffin in the middle of the auditorium.'

Yi Yi Win and I had walked the route the Datsun minibus had driven, we had seen the people lining the roads. It was as if they had just been woken from a long, deep sleep. We found a spot on one side of the auditorium and watched the stream of visitors. We saw professors and gardeners, equally affected, equally moved. We saw writers we recognised from photos in newspapers, and film stars and popular singers, and bus drivers and street vendors and flower girls and families in their Sunday best. We heard people whisper when Daw Khin Kyi, the widow of Aung San, the father of the nation, laid flowers by the coffin. We heard the silence descend.

At the end of the afternoon we took the bus into town where we ate in a small restaurant on 32nd Street without saying very much or paying much attention to the food. Then we said goodbye and I told Yi Yi Win to be careful.

'You too,' she said. She didn't look at me.

Yi Yi Win, I see you approaching down broad avenues, beneath old trees that have seen everything. I see your slim, delicate form, your neck so proud, so vulnerable, the confidence of your smile, which contains everything I lack. Language that needs no words.

Oh, yes, I am careful! In our country love is not something you take lightly. There is no room for free-thinking, let along free love. We know the songs from that other world, far from our own, songs like *Love Me Do* and *Love Me Tender* – but we prefer to listen to them in versions by our own artists, we prefer to listen to Sein Lwin, the idol of all Burmese girls, who sings:

> *Never change your heart, my love*
> *Never change*
> *If you agree with me*
> *Let us go to your parents*
> *Let me ask for your hand*

Love is delicate in our country, like the flowers. It is no coincidence that Karen girls are called Hser Hser Paw and Tamla Paw and Paw Pak Say – 'diamond flower', 'sweet flower' and 'flower that blossoms silver'.

We met in the auditorium again the next day, just as we did the day that followed and day after that and the day after that. People came from the furthest corners of the land to say goodbye to U Thant, to place a donation in one of seven suitcases that were being guarded and watched over by seven monks, money that was being collected to build a mausoleum in which U Thant's bodily remains could be interred with dignity. In the evening there were public meetings in which one speaker after the other turned on the regime, attacking the inefficiency and the corruption, the inequity and the terror. One speaker in particular drew attention to herself, a girl who couldn't have been more than seventeen years old. Fiercely, she attacked the decline of education under the dictatorship. The way that most students were forced to take completely uninspired courses that could only lead to long-term unemployment. While the sons and daughters of the mighty were admitted automatically to the few prestigious institutions that were left so that *they* would be assured of getting the best jobs afterwards, even if they had never given any indication of above-average intelligence.

She ended all of her speeches with the same sentence. 'A government that creates an education system like this,' she said, 'deserves to be overthrown!' These words were so unprecedented that Yi Yi Win and I looked at each other for a moment every time we heard them, as if seeking reassurance that we weren't dreaming, that these things really were being said here, at our university, in this immense city, which had been a tamed monster but now seemed to be on the verge of rising and turning on its masters. 'That girl has the courage of a man,' said Joe one evening.

'She has the courage,' said Yi Yi Win with a ferocity I had never seen in her before, 'that so many men lack!'

I decided to keep quiet for a while.

'But how do we overthrow the regime?'

'What do we do with U Thant's body?'

'Take the coffin to the town hall, that will mobilise a crowd that's big enough to conquer the city.'

'Bury him next to the monument for Aung San, the father of the nation.'

'First Rangoon, then Mandalay, then the whole country!'

Someone had to take charge, but who could you trust and

who was working in secret for the regime? And what was the regime planning? It still hadn't intervened and that wasn't like the General.

On the morning of the fifth day of the people's vigil for U Thant, the small group of students that had taken the initiative by stealing the coffin withdrew into the Institute of Technology for a closed meeting – by this stage they only trusted each other. Yi Yi Win and I waited at a prearranged spot for Joe, who was going to report on what had been said, but when he came running up around midday, he shouted out from afar, 'They've buried him! They've buried U Thant!' We ran along with him to Convocation Hall and from there to where the Students' Union building had once stood.

'Who did it?'

'On whose orders?'

'Who are these people?'

'What will the General think?'

'He will come and crush us!'

'We will resist!'

'We would rather die than bow before him again!'

'Who said that? Who are you? What are you doing here? Why haven't I seen you here before? Who are you working for? Who's giving you orders?'

Ah, Yi Yi Win, I see you asleep on the floor of Convocation Hall, my eye follows the curved line from your throat to your shoulder, the delicate shadow of your collarbone brings tears to my eyes, even now! Even now, after all the years and all that has happened! How gladly I would return to that night, to that place, to those hours when we still didn't know about the soldiers who had prepared themselves, pulling on their boots and picking up their guns, jumping into the back of trucks and heading for us. Your finding the peace of mind to surrender to sleep that night, was that because of trust – trust in us, trust in me? How I would love to answer that question in the affirmative. But if I did, what difference would it make? It wouldn't undo any of the things that happened afterwards. And what's more, I find it difficult to still say the word 'trust' in the same breath as your name.

Someone shouted something I didn't understand. Had I fallen asleep after all in the quietest hour of the night? Our hands must have sought each other, I felt your warmth glowing on my skin.

Cries sounded outside. Voices echoed in the hall. Suddenly everyone was up on their feet, trying to get out. Where are you? There you are! Close behind me.

What's happening? There is the drone of diesel engines, the acrid smell of exhaust fumes, steel tracks rattling over asphalt.

Tanks!

In the semidarkness people are running in all directions, orders and insults are being screamed out. We hurry off towards the grave.

'Where are the soldiers?'

'They'll arrest us!'

'They're arresting every student they can grab!'

'There they are! Quick, this way!'

'Wait! Here! Look!'

'What are they doing?'

'Surely they're not . . .'

'They are!'

'Stop them! Please stop them!'

Shovels are stabbed into the ground. The earth is turned. People scream. Blows fall. Weapons are cocked. People are driven back.

'Get out of here! Go!'

'Us? You! Dogs that you are! Grave-robbers! Ghouls! Traitors! Scum!'

Blood-chilling screams resound as the coffin is lifted up out of the ground. The furious crowd refuses to give in to anyone or anything. Anyone or anything? The first bullets come from the roof of Mandalay Hall. Then they fly from all directions. Who is that holding tight to the coffin? Isn't that her, the girl who couldn't have been more than seventeen years old? The girl who spoke so courageously about the children of the generals who get the best educations while we . . .

Oh, my God! Yi Yi Win! Yi Yi Win, come here, to me, don't watch, don't watch!

I see your pale face in the pale light of morning, as smooth and hard as a pebble in fast flowing water.

Yi Yi Win, look at me!

You avert your eyes, turn your face away, and I know it, even then, I know that it's over, that we are over, that everything I thought we were or could have become has been lost.

Young men's arms carrying a bleeding girl.

Bare feet in red mud.

Red stains on a white blouse.

The last, animal cry of a young girl's voice.

The silence that follows.

The General ordered the university closed. Parents fetched their children back home, away from the campus, away from the soldiers, away from the General's 'lads', whose educational level, according to the students' jokes, went no further than the seventh grade, if you added them up together.

Yi Yi Win's uncle was no doubt working overtime at the ministry. Censorship became stricter, the mistrust greater, the fear that everyone felt became more tangible to everyone. You only had to look at the faces on the buses, in the teashops or at the markets to see what had happened to people.

On 13th May of the New Year the universities re-opened. I took classes on the new constitution that had been approved by referendum the previous year, with 90.19 per cent in favour.

Ninety-point-one-nine per cent. Not one hundredth more, not one hundredth less. Who decided something like that?

I learnt that according to Article 153 'every citizen shall have the right to freely work with creativity and initiative to develop the arts, literature and other branches of culture' – with the proviso that 'acts which undermine unity, national security or the national socialist social order are prohibited'. I also learnt that Article 157 guaranteed freedom of speech, expression and publication for all citizens. Although it was only natural that here too the limitation applied that the exercise of this right must not be 'contrary to the interests of the working people and of socialism'. In a few days I knew the new constitution off by heart. There was no one to distract me.

She was standing in the doorway of her uncle's house. She said, 'What are you doing here?'

What am I doing here?!

'Yi Yi Win . . .' I said.

'Don't you understand?'

Don't I understand what? I don't understand anything! 'What do you mean?'

She had crossed her arms over her chest. 'You're naive, Min Thein, hopelessly naive. You should read more good books.'

I didn't know what to do, what to say, where to look . . . I looked down at the ground, at the crumbling asphalt.

'You didn't really believe we could change the world?'

I didn't answer.

'Yes, of course you did.' She sighed deeply.

The world? I thought. Leave the world out of this! I'm not here for the world, I'm here for you!

But Yi Yi Win said, 'It was a game, Min Thein, and we lost. Because we didn't know the rules. Or because we thought we could rewrite them. Ha!'

Her uncle! That was her uncle's laugh! I looked up at her. I looked her in the eyes.

She said, 'Go away, Min Thein. Go away!'

PART III

Lady C and the
Lieutenant General

Come with me to the house of Saw Ner Tha. With God's help his wife, named Snowflake by her parents because she was born on the coldest night of the year, will bear a child today; her waters broke last night.

We will keep Saw Ner Tha company on the verandah. I have a bottle of Karen whiskey for him.

The month of December is called plü in Karen, the month of the lunar eclipse, the dying moon. December is for burial rites more than births. Saw Ner Tha will need that whiskey.

The whiskey was distilled from rice and herbs by Saw Per Kaw, an old man who lives half an hour's walk from the camp, well out of range of the rigid views the camp authorities hold about the consumption of alcoholic beverages. Saw Per Kaw was the headman of a village that was completely razed during the Burmese army's last great offensive against the Karen independence fighters. Less than a dozen villagers survived the attack, and Saw Per Kaw reached the camp with them a couple of years ago. It was at the time that hundreds of new refugees were arriving every day. Day in day out, we heard nothing but horror stories about the war. There were tremendous tensions within the camp. Between Buddhists and Christians. Between Christians and Muslims. Between the Thai Authority and the refugees.

Saw Per Kaw only lasted three weeks in the camp. Then he went back into the jungle to find a place where he would be left in peace. Since then he hasn't let anyone tell him what to do.

Tommy used to visit Saw Per Kaw often.

Tommy shares his dislike of authorities.

Now and then Saw Per Kaw would give Tommy a bottle of whiskey. Sometimes Tommy gave that bottle to me.

I say, 'It must be here on the left somewhere, a shabby house next to a shop that sells candy and sweet drinks.'

You say, 'There's a strip of silver paper hung up over the door with the words HAPPY NEW YEAR on it in red shining letters.'

I say, ' That's it. That's where Saw Ner Tha and Snowflake live.'

I will introduce you to them but you won't see her until she has brought the child into the world. She believes that the presence of a stranger in the house of a woman in labour will bring bad luck down on the child. Don't expect any conversation from Saw Ner Tha, he is a man of few words – and today he will be even less talkative than usual. Two years ago he was the proud father of a son, who was called Pway Doh, 'the precious one'. One day Snowflake was working for a Thai farmer as a day labourer – illegal and badly paid, but a refugee has no choice. She had taken little Pway Doh with her to the field. When the day was at its hottest she laid him down to rest on a hammock in a worker's shack. When she came back an hour later to check on him, the hammock was empty.

Ner Tha and Snowflake couldn't report the disappearance of their son. That would have put them at risk of being deported for violating the labour laws. Even worse, the Thai landowner had threatened to have them killed if they got him into trouble. A few weeks later a rumour did the rounds that Thai customs had arrested a Burmese woman who was trying to cross the border with a dead baby. A large quantity of drugs were hidden in the baby's body.

No one knows if the rumour is true. No one knows if the baby was Ner Tha and Snowflake's child. But I know that, in their thoughts, they have seen the horrors that little Pway Doh might have been subjected to repeated a thousand times.

The Buddha said, 'It is easy to do what is bad for you, but doing what is good for you is extremely difficult.' Today we will do what is bad for us: together with Saw Ner Tha we will drink the bottle of whiskey. Life today is difficult enough as it is. When the child is born, Snowflake will ask me to name it because she is afraid of choosing the wrong name.

If it's a boy, he will be called k'Paw Taw, 'the brand new'.

If it's a girl, I will call her Hay Pla Hset Soe, 'she who shines brightly from afar'.

One

It was thirteen minutes' walk from my house to the court, at least, if I wasn't held up on the way by Saw Hsa Tu stopping me to ask how things were going with the case against my client P.D., who was accused of drug trafficking. 'He always seemed such an easy-going boy to me,' Saw Hsa Tu said, shaking his old head in pity. Or, 'If you're dumb enough to get mixed up in that, you're dumb enough to get through a few years in jail as well.'

'The way things are looking at this stage,' I said, 'he'll get ten.'

'Ten years! For such a tiny amount? Isn't there anything you can do about it?'

'I'm talking to a teacher who tutored my client for years. It might help if he declares before the court that he was always an exemplary pupil: not the brightest, maybe, but well behaved. But I don't know whether he wants to. And I don't know if it's actually true.'

'Ah, truth!' Saw Hsa Tu said. Who cares about the truth these days in this country?'

Saw Hsa Tu had once owned a large workshop for delivery bicycles. It was an especially profitable business. He imported sturdy men's bicycles from China and extra heavy wheels from India. The steel tubes and wooden boxes were domestic products. In the workshop they welded a frame on to the Chinese bicycles to hold a solid wooden box and used the Indian wheels to support it and keep it in balance. Saw Hsa Tu had thought it all up and designed it himself, and he welded and assembled the first hundred delivery bicycles personally. He then hired a worker, and later a second and a third, so that he could concentrate on sales. Once he even travelled to China to see whether there weren't any better bikes than the Shooting Stars he had been using since the early fifties. (He did find a better bicycle, and even imported twenty of them, but the price difference with the Shooting Stars turned out to be prohibitive for his impecunious customers and he was ultimately obliged to sell them at a loss.)

At that time there wasn't a rice seller or fishmonger for miles around the town of Pan Thar who didn't use one of Saw Hsa Tu's reconstructed Shooting Stars to transport his wares. The carrier cycle trade was going so well that the bicycle maker himself drove around in a gleaming black Chevrolet, second-hand admittedly, bought from a travelling ruby dealer, but so well maintained that after years of intensive use it still looked like it had just rolled off the production line.

That might be why Saw Hsa Tu's car was one of the first private vehicles to be confiscated in Pan Thar during the period of major nationalisation.

'It happened on 7 March 1964,' San Hsa Tu told me one day. 'I was sitting eating my mohinga at the Golden Dawn, where I used to be a regular. Suddenly one of my workmen came rushing in. 'Boss, boss!' he shouted, 'Come quick!' It had already happened in Rangoon and Mandalay, and everyone knew it was only a matter of time before it was the turn of the smaller towns in the provinces. So on 7 March 1964 it was our turn, mine, the turn of the carrier cycle factory I had built up with my own hands and made a – if I say so myself – a fantastic success of.'

At this stage of his story, Saw Hsa Tu had to stop to swallow something. He had just wiped the sweat off his face and I couldn't help noticing that he was holding the handkerchief so tightly that his knuckles were white. 'On the requisition order it said that my business was now the property of the people of Burma, who, in their infinite wisdom, had appointed Lieutenant General Thun Myint as manager. And of course the Lieutenant General immediately demanded my car. That wasn't actually mentioned in the documents, but it was obvious that the Chevrolet was part of the business property, surely I didn't want to dispute that? There were six of them, and five of the six were armed.'

For three years Saw Hsa Tu tried in vain to force the state to pay the promised compensation through the courts. Then the workshop went bankrupt as a result of incompetence and mismanagement, and he knew that he would never see his money.

'Being a lawyer,' said Saw Hsa Tu, 'is an honourable profession. But I hope you don't feel insulted if I say that justice in this country is mere show.'

I wasn't insulted, but I did my work that day with less pleasure than ever.

What had brought me to the sleepy provincial town of Pan Thar? A woman. Not the woman about whom I would have loved to believe that we had prowled the jungle together in a previous life, two tigers in search of prey. Not the woman who had sent me packing like a bothersome child or a mangy dog. There was no one in my life who knew anything about the existence of Yi Yi Win. That made it possible for me to carry her in my heart despite everything. I could even carry her in my heart after I had met Hser Hser Paw.

I saw Hser Hser Paw for the first time at my grandfather's funeral. Doesn't that have a tragic beauty? And it was Tender, of all people, who introduced us. 'This is my niece, Hser Hser Paw, and I saw this young man as a child standing up to his knees in the ponds to catch catfish and butter fish. He's called Min Thein and you can take it from me that he'll go far in life. He studied law in Rangoon and now he's thinking about what to do. It's an honour to be the one to introduce you.'

And there we stood, Hser Hser Paw and I, both embarrassed by the situation, her a little more than me, so I was the one who spoke first, and she was the one who let herself be put at ease by me and guided through the ceremonies and speeches and prayers that seemed to go on forever, but which she submitted to with deep concentration and a dedication that both impressed and disturbed me. I had developed an intense mistrust of all forms of submission.

My grandfather had died after a short illness, three months after I had returned from Rangoon for good, a degree richer but many illusions poorer. I had visited him once in that time, just before he fell ill, and I had taken the opportunity to spend a long time wandering over his land. I realised that I had reached a point in my life at which I needed to make crucial decisions, saying goodbye to some things in order to welcome others. And although I, standing on the bank of one of my grandfather's ponds, had known without a shadow of a doubt that what I saw around me belonged to my past, I had felt incapable of resolving the impasse at which my life had been stalled since my return from Rangoon. I simply lacked perspective.

There is a passage in *Lady Chatterley's Lover* in which D. H. Lawrence describes Lady Chatterley's mood as 'an inward dread, an emptiness, an indifference to everything'. I remember reading those words to Yi Yi Win one afternoon in the teashop where we spent so much time talking about what we had read and what was happening around us, and about the relationship between those things.

Yi Yi Win said, 'That is exactly what I see so often in other students, emptiness and indifference.'

And I said, 'We've been paralysed by the terrors we have been subjected to.' Yi Yi Win gave me the courage to say things that I would not have dared to think before – Yi Yi Win and *Lady Chatterley's Lover*. I said, 'What we need is what D. H. Lawrence calls "a new hope".'

But Yi Yi Win only laughed scornfully. And the question I have never been able to put entirely out of my mind since the last time we saw each other was whether she had ever cherished any hope or whether, through all the things that happened, she had never been more than an observer. And if she was an observer, the next question was, who for?

I thought about all these things while walking barefoot down the narrow muddy paths between my grandfather's paddy fields. And I didn't know what to do or which direction to take. There was an emptiness in my heart that would not be filled until I met Hser Hser Paw.

If Yi Yi Win was a torrent that knocked me over and dragged me along, delighting and entrancing me, but frightening me and confusing me at the same time, then Hser Hser Paw was a smooth pond of fresh warm water that soothed my body and let me float around without having to fear any danger. The affection that blossomed between us was so calm and natural that at first I didn't even recognise it as love.

She was living in a village near my grandfather's farm, but she wasn't really happy there. One of her in-laws had asked her to help look after his ailing mother and, desperate as she was to expand her horizons after growing up in the small and rather inward-looking provincial town of Pan Thar, she had agreed to do so. Six months later the old woman had died. Ever since her funeral, Hser Hser Paw had been meaning to return home, but she had kept postponing her departure because of a vague sense of uneasiness. Later she would say that it was not until the day she met me that she realised that this wasn't coincidental but a direct consequence of divine intervention. We were predestined by God, according to Hser Hser Paw, and those words sounded so sweet to my ears, while simultaneously grating so harshly over the unhealed wound caused by the loss of Yi Yi Win, that it was impossible for me to resist them.

Less than seven weeks after having met, we consecrated our marriage in the small British-built Anglican church of Pan Thar. It was the first time since the death of my brother that I saw my mother really happy. My father stayed home in Min Won.

A good half of the population of the town of Pan Thar was Karen. The only lawyer who practised there was a Chinese who spoke Burmese but not Karen, and it was obvious that the time had come for me to finally do something with the degree I had obtained from Rangoon University. I told myself that I mustn't disappoint Tender and was determined to justify the way he had praised me to Hser Hser Paw. After all, from that first meeting she had trusted me implicitly and it seemed to me that trust might be the best remedy for emptiness – even better than hope.

As a result, almost every workday now saw me walking from my house, where I kept my office, to the court, where I had to pick up and file documents, and consult with judges, prosecutors, police officers and army officers about the cases I had been assigned to: shoplifting and domestic violence, and minor drugs cases (for big drugs cases you had to be in the cities, or in the northeast of the country, the Golden Triangle where Burma borders on Laos and Thailand, the poppy grows on every hill and the opium trade is rampant in every town and every village).

As a lawyer in the provincial town of Pan Thar it was possible to lead a peaceful and honourable existence. People addressed me with both the Burmese male honorific and the Karen, calling me U Saw Min Thein, as if to emphasise that I was respected by both the Burmans and the Karen. The town's worthies invited us to dinners and parties, and when my practice was five years old, Hser Hser Paw and I organised a dinner of our own for almost a hundred guests. Sometimes I was ashamed by how easy I found it to operate within the structures of the dictatorship, but I pushed that shame aside. What else could we do? I had seen where the path of resistance led. What's more, I told myself, law and justice were the last obstacles to complete terror. By dutifully doing my job and defending all who had a right to a defence under the law, I was making my contribution to the struggle against the dictatorship. The cynicism of people like the former bicycle manufacturer Saw Hsa Tu did not detract from that at all.

Two

The Pan Thar courtroom was located in a large colonial building, which also accommodated the public prosecutor, the local police, regional Military Intelligence headquarters and various other, smaller, government departments. At the entrance of the complex a large green sign with white lettering announced, 'If the country is hit by an earthquake it will not cease to exist. But if the country falls prey to a foreign power, it will be devoured completely.' The slogan was part of a large-scale campaign by General Ne Win's government to discredit critics: the goal was to convince the people that the rebels were in the pay of foreign powers whose goal was not just to over-throw the regime but also to annex all of Burma. This made anyone who opposed the government an enemy of the country.

Besides being displayed on billboards, the same message was presented every day in the government newspapers, on national radio and, from 1980, the year in which I began my legal prac-tice, on national television. Although the state only allowed tele-visions to be imported in extremely limited numbers, it wasn't difficult to acquire one in Pan Thar. One of Saw Hsa Tu's brothers made frequent trips to a fishing island in the south, whose fishermen returned regularly from Penang with holds full of refrigerators, cassette recorders, televisions and other electrical appliances they had exchanged for fish. Dealers like Saw Hsa Tu's brother bought these goods from the fishermen and then distrib-uted them all over Burma. Of course, it was the responsibility of the local authorities to suppress these activities, but those same local authorities were generally the ones who profited the most from the smuggling. The very first television set arrived in Pan Thar exactly two days before the national TV station went on the air; Hsa Tu's brother delivered it personally to the home of Brigadier General Aye Thung, commanding officer of the Central Division of the Burmese army. It was common knowledge that Aye Thung didn't pay a penny for it, and it was clear to everyone that as long as he was in charge of the region, the smugglers would not find the slightest obstacle put in their path.

A natural consequence of the endless repetition of the propaganda slogans was that no one took them seriously, not even – or perhaps especially not – the leaders of the regime that had concocted them in the first place. The only exception to this rule was formed by the people I came, during my years in Pan Thar, to call 'the little men', the ones who were responsible for carrying out the reign of terror at the local level, the military bureaucrats. Many of these little men were deadly serious about every instruction they received from their superiors about the struggle against the elements that were undermining the state. They saw no difference between propaganda and reality: propaganda *was* reality. Every doubt filled them with existential fear and was suppressed immediately. After all, if they were not servants of Absolute Truth, what were they? Petty criminals at best, but more likely racketeers, looters, murderers . . .

The apparatus of a dictatorship cannot function without the little men with their deeply repressed guilt feelings and their mortal fear. The dictatorship could not get by without Captain Shwe Ya.

He was standing by the window, next to the cumbersome steel desk, which for fourteen years had been the fortress from which he exercised his cruel and unbending rule over his own little kingdom, the provincial town of Pan Thar and a dozen surrounding villages and hamlets. Captain Shwe Ya, head of the local section of Military Intelligence, held a plastic lighter up to the sky and shook it to see if it was empty.

He ran his thumb over the wheel a few times without getting it to light. Then he put the cheroot that had been in his mouth the whole time back in his breast pocket and turned his attention to me. He was a thin, somewhat lanky man, with a pale face with two very small eyes that were a little too close together. There was a downy moustache on his upper lip.

'Please sit down, Mr. Attorney,' he said. The captain rarely if ever called me by name. 'The case I would like to discuss with you,' he continued, 'is of an extremely sensitive nature.' While speaking he had walked over to his desk and opened a dossier, from which he now removed a form. 'It concerns,' he said, while studying the piece of paper, 'the detention of three suspects under the Unlawful Association Act.'

'Yes, exactly,' I said.

What the captain didn't know was that I had been aware of the case for quite some time and even had a copy of the dossier which was lying on his desk. In the nine years that I had had my practice here I had built up good relationships with various officials within both justice and police departments. I even had contacts among Captain Shwe Ya's own subordinates, the sneaks and report-writers of Military Intelligence. The more sensitive the case that was going before the court, the greater the chance that I would be informed about it at a very early stage. And Unlawful Association cases were always sensitive. The law, which was part of the Emergency Provisions and dated from the days of British rule, related to citizens having contact with prohibited organisations such as the various ethnic liberation movements active in Burma. In the district around Pan Thar, this almost always came down to contacts with the Karen National Union and its armed wing, the Karen Liberation Army. My being the only lawyer for miles around who spoke Karen made me the logical choice to represent the suspects in these cases.

'What makes this case most precarious,' said the captain, 'is that the suspects are not illiterate peasants, impoverished day labourers, bearers or layabouts, no, we are dealing here with three prominent citizens from the village of Myaing Thar, who have consorted with the enemy, or, as the case may be, the Karen Liberation Army.' The poor fellow never got further than primary school and compensated for his lack of education by using, and sometimes abusing, difficult words he had picked up from the legal jargon he had used over the years.

'*De facto* the situation is as follows,' he said, 'all three of them have confessed.'

'Where are the suspects located at this moment?' I asked, despite knowing the answer.

'They arrived at the police station this morning and are being held there in a cell.'

'Then I would like to see them.'

'Of course,' said the captain. He picked up his telephone and barked several quick orders into the receiver. After hanging up, he turned full circle on the heels of his shoes, as if to assure himself that no one else was present in the room. Then he said, 'You will understand, Mr Attorney, that we not only expect you to be extremely conscientious, but also as reticent as possible in your contacts with the outside world. The case is disturbing enough in itself. There is no reason to cause any more commotion. You realise that many people will be deeply concerned if they discover that ostensibly respectable citizens such as the suspects *in casu* have proved receptive to the temptations of terrorism.'

A quiet knock on the door absolved me of the need to answer. It was the court officer come to take me to the police cell.

'Your discretion . . .' the captain added unnecessarily while handing me the dossier, ' . . . can be taken for granted,' I said, finishing his sentence for him. 'Good day!'

The three of them were sitting on the floor, but stood up as soon as they saw us. The court officer had passed me on to a policeman called Khin Maung Yin and now all five of us were standing by the bars: the three men inside, the policeman and I on the outside. Khin Maung Yin was a nice fellow and a Karen as well, I knew that he would do anything he could to make the case as easy as possible for me. He opened the barred door and let me into the cell.

'How long?' he asked.

'Half an hour.' That was twice as long as officially allowed.

'We can manage that,' said Khin Maung Yin.

He then retreated to the end of the corridor, where he sat down on a small wooden stool. When I glanced in his direction a little later, I saw that he was reading a pocket Bible. God's blessing was on this day. That thought helped me through the first, difficult minutes of the conversation with the suspects. Despite my years of experience, the first exchange with my clients was always an unpleasant moment. As if I had to overcome a certain embarrassment, a sense of shame that was closely related to the question that had preoccupied me all of my conscious life: why someone else and not me?

The first to speak was the oldest of the three, a skinny, bald-headed man who introduced himself as Saw Eh k'Kyaw. I was about to permit myself the luxury of a joke by pointing out that by having a name like that he had really brought suspicion down on himself in a case like this, but he beat me to it. 'I know,' he said, "Love for the Karen" is not such a good name when you're on trial for contacts with the fighters for an independent Karen state. But if they picked up everyone with this name, there wouldn't be enough cells in all of Burma to lock us up.'

I said, 'You're the village headman?'

'That's right,' he replied. 'And this is the village clerk, Saw Ner Tha and Saw Albert, chief of the village militia.'

'U Saw Min Thein,' I introduced myself. The village clerk was a cheerful looking man, who wore glasses with thin, gold-coloured rims that looked distinguished from a distance but cheap from close by. There was black showing through the gold in a number of places and the arms looked as if they had been bent straight several times by hand. The village clerk's eyes were still sparkling behind the dull lenses. The militia chief in contrast radiated a certain degree of prosperity, even if he didn't seem the type to enjoy it – the corners of his mouth drooped too much for that, his skin was too sallow. It wouldn't have surprised me to hear that he occasionally used the special authority that came with his office to enrich himself, and the way he looked at me reinforced that suspicion. In his eyes I saw mistrust and contempt.

'Are you standing by your confessions?' I asked. It was the only question that mattered at this stage. If their answers were affirmative, then there was not much more for me to do as they would undoubtedly receive the maximum, five-year sentence. If they retracted, however, the case would really become precarious.

'They forced us to confess,' said Love for the Karen with a winning smile. I knew from experience that nine times out of ten a smile like that meant that it was a matter worth pursuing. But the speed with which the smile disappeared from his face told me to be careful.

I said, 'Let's leave the confessions for the time being and concentrate on the events as you remember them.'

'Perhaps,' said the village headman, 'it would be best for the clerk to speak. Of the three of us, he not only has the best memory, he is also the best at sticking to what really matters.'

Now it was the clerk's turn to smile. And although the issue he went on to delineate was serious enough, he would break into laughter several times during his story. It's a Burmese habit, which, as I would discover later in my life, can seriously confuse foreigners: the more horrific the stories, the more often we have to laugh about them.

This is the story of the clerk, the village headman and the chief of the village militia.

You live in a small Karen village at the top of a valley that is enclosed by thickly wooded hills. In the mountains beyond the village the struggle for an independent Karen state has been raging for decades. In that time more and more troops have been sent to the region to battle the rebellious Karen. The soldiers have set up their headquarters in the nearby provincial town of Pan Thar, but they regularly set up camp in your village as well. For a while now the government troops seem to have been gaining the upper hand and that has encouraged the soldiers to become more and more brazen in their treatment of the Karen population, who they see as accomplices of the enemy. And of course there is contact between the fighters of the Karen Liberation Army and the inhabitants of your village. Contacts like that are unavoidable, even if you wanted to avoid them. Sometimes a patrol of independence fighters crosses the path of men who are hunting in the jungle, sometimes fighters come to the village at night to ask for food and drink. But are those contacts punishable by law?

And then there are the family ties: sons and daughters who have joined the rebels and return home now and then for a party or a funeral or just because they happen to be in the neighbourhood. Of course, you could call that Unlawful Association between villagers and insurgents, but the contacts are informal and incidental, they spring from life itself. How could you condemn someone for that?

There is another, more important source of friction between the army and the people in the village. More and more often the soldiers impose on the villagers: to share their food stores with them by slaughtering a few chickens or a cow, to help them set up camp, to carry supplies and ammunition during their treks through the jungle, or to build a road.

This started out as small favours, work that could be done in a couple of days at the most, but the small favours became unbearable burdens, the days turned into weeks and the weeks into months. Sometimes the villagers are away from home for more than three months at a time and all they get for their efforts is something to eat (rice with sand or the boiled pulp of banana trees) and a place to sleep. More and more villagers complained to their leaders about not having time to work their land, about disrupted families, about forced labourers being mistreated for not working hard enough, about people being wounded and even killed by landmines and ambushes. 'We don't want this war,' the villagers said, 'this is a war of the powerful against the powerless. We want to be left alone!' And the village leaders – the headman, the clerk and the militia chief – went to the army command post to complain. They demanded compensation for the villagers' work, they asked for more respect. Harsh words were spoken. Bitter accusations were made. In the weeks and months that followed the situation did not improve.

Then, one day, they were arrested.

The village headman, the clerk and the chief of the militia were dragged out of their homes by soldiers. They were taken to an army camp and locked up – each in a separate cell. They were interrogated. They were mistreated.

You're standing in a room you cannot see. You are blindfolded with a piece of dirty, coarse material that makes your eyes sting. The blindfold is pulled so tight your skull feels like it will crack at any moment. You hear the soldiers' voices. In front, behind, to your side. How many of them are there? They walk around you. You hear their footsteps, heavy boots on a bare concrete floor. You stand there barefoot, naked from the waist up, wearing only a longyi, and around your head that cloth, that stinking, head-crushing cloth. Your hands and feet are chained. Someone removes the cuffs from your wrists. You let your arms droop beside your body, you don't dare to move. Silence falls around you.

'Is that better?' A powerful, not unpleasant voice.

'Yes.'

'Freer?'

'Yes.'

'Would you like to be free soon?'

'Yes.'

'What were you doing at that meeting in Saw Nay Kaw Moo's house?'

'I don't know what meeting you're talking about.'

'What did you discuss?'

'I wasn't there.'

'You weren't there?'

'No. The last time I was at Saw Nay Kaw Moo's house is more than a month ago. I took him two chickens.'

'Saw Nay Kaw Moo works for the Karen Liberation Army. Why did you take him two chickens?'

'I've known Saw Nay Kaw Moo his whole life. He stays out of politics.'

'What was discussed at the meeting held on the twenty-third of March in Saw Nay Kaw Moo's house?'

'I wasn't there.'

'You weren't there?'

Your hands are cuffed again. In front of your body this time. You feel the sweat from the soldier's hands on your wrists. Someone pulls up the handcuffs. Someone grabs you from behind and lifts you up. Someone screams, 'Lift up your arms! Higher! Higher!' Someone grabs your arms and moves them forward and to one side. You feel cold steel against your hands, against your forearms.

The soldier who is holding you up lets go.

Ha-ha!

'Our confessions are a pack of lies,' said the militia chief. 'In court we will retract it all.'

'We will declare,' the clerk said, 'that we were put under pressure, that they forced us to confess. After all, we are innocent until proven guilty. And there isn't any proof. How could there be any proof? If we are convicted we'll leave the courtroom with our heads held high.'

The village headman said, 'We won't let them humiliate us.'

And the militia chief said, 'We won't crawl, we won't buckle. We are simple people, with simple lives, but we know the value of self-respect.'

You're hanging with your full weight from a hook on the ceiling.

'Maybe you should think it over,' says the powerful, not unpleasant voice. You hear a door open. You hear footsteps going away. The door closes. You listen to the silence. You try to bring your feet up to your hands. You can't – but more to the point, what could you do with your feet there anyway? Your body swings on the hook. You feel the muscles in your shoulders stretch and stretch and stretch.

Ha-ha-ha!

'To start with,' I said, 'I will object to the use of these confessions. What else do they have, besides the confessions?'

'Statements from witnesses.'

'Which witnesses?'

'Villagers.'

'That's not good,' I said.

'No,' the village headman agreed, 'that's not good either.'

'Will they stick to their statements before the judge?'

'We don't know.'

'Only God knows.'

'And maybe He doesn't even know!' said the clerk.

You're terrified they might come back.

It's what you want more than anything.

They come back.

Ha–ha–ha–ha!

Three

I needed to go to the district court in Pegu for the appeal in the case against P.D. The teacher who used to tutor my client had decided, after long hesitation, that he was willing to testify, but in the meantime the case had been heard and my client had been given twelve years. Theoretically a declaration as to how diligent and dedicated he was as a student could help us to reduce the sentence by a few years on appeal – but I thought the chance of that happening was very low. Like almost all judges, the judges in Pegu see appeals in drug cases as a waste of their time. Two years ago, however, my trips to Pegu gained another goal, or perhaps I should say, another meaning, because there isn't really a goal – a goal is no longer possible. There is a teashop in Pegu that is run by a young woman, the mother of two children. The teashop is called the Lady C.

I first saw the Lady C from the train. There are two ways of travelling from Pan Thar to Pegu: by bus, or by bus and train. Although I am the proud owner of a car (a right-hand drive Toyota Corolla), the roads have deteriorated so much that I now only use it for short distances. The trip by bus and train takes longer, because there are large sections of the route where the track is so bad that the train can only go at walking-pace, but the train is a little more comfortable than the bus.

If I hadn't taken the train I would probably have never known about the existence of the Lady C and remained ignorant forever of Yi Yi Win's return to the birthplace of her mother. On the other hand, if I had slept less during my train trips and looked out of the window more often, I could have discovered the teashop much sooner. Now it happened on an exceptionally hot day in July of the year 1986. The rails had expanded so much in the sun that the points had jammed. The stoppage that resulted was as abrupt as it was definitive, and the train ground to a halt half a mile before Pegu Station, just where you could see the Lady C teashop. Aren't the courses our lives take always decided by coincidences like that? You could interpret them as the hand of God, like Hser Hser Paw and my mother, at least when she was younger, or, as a good Buddhist, you could take them as evidence of the eternal laws of karma, or you could reduce everything to products of a totally indifferent chance, like my father in the last years of his life – it made no essential difference. It seems to me that we all choose the explanation we find most consoling. At that stage of my life, I myself refused to choose, perhaps because I didn't want to be consoled. You could tell yourself that your identity was decided by what you had achieved in life, but who was to say that the opposite was not equally valid: why shouldn't I define myself by what had passed me by in my life?

I remember laughing when I spotted the sign on the teashop. I was standing on the bottom step of the train, unsure whether to jump down into the thorny weeds growing alongside the track. People behind me jostled and shouted for me to get a move on, saying we'd all be boiled alive if we didn't get out of there in a hurry. Now that the last cooling breeze had disappeared from the carriage, the temperature was rising fast. And just then I saw the sign with the stylishly written 'Lady C' and under it the words, 'Meals all day'. And immediately I thought of Lady Chatterley – and how could I think of Lady Chatterley without my thoughts going straight to *her*?

I jumped down. Should I go and have a look? Should I investigate whether Lady C referred to Lady Chatterley, and whether that had anything to do with Yi Yi Win? It was an absurd idea.

More than that, it was a childish idea. But would I have any peace of mind until I had personally assured myself that there was no relationship between the name and her? And so I pushed my way through the high, prickly bushes. I crossed the road that separated the restaurant from the track; the air was thick with diesel fumes. I paused for a moment before the door of the restaurant and looked in, but I couldn't make out anyone in the gloomy interior and decided to wait outside, at one of the small tables set up under an improvised awning made of the bright blue plastic sheeting farmers use.

It said 'Lady' on the somewhat grimy menu lying on the table. Had I been mistaken? The sign on the roof of the restaurant had clearly said Lady C. Was the C all that was left of some other word?

A woman emerged to take my order. I could hardly breathe. She recognised me when she came back out with my tea.

Since then my trips to Pegu had followed a fixed pattern. I never travelled all the way by bus. I always looked out of the train window as we passed the Lady C. After arriving I went to a small but clean hotel diagonally opposite the station. I freshened up, went downstairs and took a trishaw to the Lady C. There I ordered tea from Yi Yi Win and, depending on the time of day, maybe something to eat. Then we exchanged the latest news. Unusual things that had happened in Pegu or Pan Thar. Which case had brought me to the city. What we had read in the paper. Very rarely, Yi Yi Win would tell me something about a book she was reading. We never talked about politics, student dissent or any kind of disturbances. From my very first visit it had been clear to me that those subjects were best avoided.

She was putting the tea down in front of me, the mug full of scorching liquid was midway between tray and table, when she suddenly froze – a little bit of tea splashed over the rim and a drop fell down on to the dusty paving stones. 'Min Thein?' she said.

'Yi Yi Win?'

She put down the mug, mumbled an apology, turned and disappeared inside. Minutes passed before she came back out again. I had no idea what she had done. She came and stood by my table as if nothing had happened.

'Did you want something to eat as well?'

I wanted something to eat.

'It doesn't matter what,' I said. 'I'm quite hungry.'

And she was gone again.

'Were you in there?' she asked after returning to my table. She looked across the road at the train, still motionless behind the bushes.

'Yes, I was in there.'

'And then you started walking, because that was as far as the train was going. You saw a restaurant called the Lady C and then you thought, I'm hungry?'

' I thought, does that C stand for Chatterley, and does Chatterley stand for Yi Yi Win? That's what I thought.'

'You thought right.'

'I thought it rather childish of myself. It seemed to be too much of a coincidence.'

'It is,' she said. 'Coincidences like that only happen in very bad books – and in real life.'

'What brings you here?'

'I should ask you that.'

'An appeal before the district court tomorrow morning. I'm a lawyer. And what brings you here?'

'My husband,' said Yi Yi Win.

'Your husband. What does he do?'

'He works for the Ministry of Inland and Religious Affairs. He provides my uncle with information, the uncle you met in

Rangoon.' She looked at me. 'He is very good at what he does, my husband. He thinks his work is important.'

'No doubt it is,' I said. I felt ill at ease. Suspicion reared its ugly head once again, the suspicion that had never disappeared, despite my burying it deep within myself. Why did she say that? Why did she look at me like that? Could it be true after all that she . . .

'And you?' asked Yi Yi Win. 'Are you married?'

'What?' I said. 'Yes . . . yes. Married.' I looked at her, but she turned her face away, gazing across the road at my train, which just in that moment began squeaking and grinding forward. 'Children?' I asked after a while.

'Two. And you?'

'None yet. Unfortunately.'

After a long silence in which there was nothing to hear but the sound of steel wheels on steel rails, she said, 'You'd be a good father.' I wished she hadn't said that.

Four

All things considered, my life as a lawyer in the provincial town of Pan Thar, with its population of thirty thousand, was very privileged. Each year I did around twenty-five cases. If my clients were poor, I charged them one thousand kyats. If they were wealthy, ten times as much. It was true that the majority of my clients were poor, but I still earned three to four thousand kyats a month without difficulty. That was at least three to four times as much as a teacher. And a farm labourer who did heavy physical work every day from early in the morning until late at night got five hundred kyats at most. Burma was nominally socialist, but it was far from being a workers' paradise.

Having my office at home also helped to make life pleasant. And Hser Hser Paw worked at the local hospital as a nurse, giving her an income and a life of her own – which is a blessing for any marriage. Only one thing was missing from our lives: children. That one lack made Hser Hser Paw deeply miserable. In Burmese, the language we all learn to speak, whether we're Karen or Shan, Mon or Kachin, a man talks about his wife as *thet-htar* or *thet-nhin*, *thet-pan* or *thet-le*: 'entrusted with life' or 'given life', 'life as a flower in her hair' or 'life shared'. A wife is not only the fulfilment of her husband's life, she also watches over life, she gives life, she is life.

Our childlessness made Hser Hser Paw feel like a failure as a woman. The sorrow about not becoming pregnant was like a malignant virus that multiplied in her blood, slowly but surely poisoning her body. In the ancient Buddhist books children are referred to as 'the golden hills', 'the golden eggs' and 'the golden reeds'. Buddhists speak about the Buddha, the sangha (the monks) and the dharma (the teachings) as the three gems. We Burmese use the word *yadana* for our children in exactly the same way: the son gem, the daughter gem. In our hearts we carry the words of the great poet Shin Maharahtathara, who wrote: 'The faces of children, like cool clear water; if just one drop falls, the parents' hearts leap with joy.'

Hanging in our bedroom was a framed print of a Biblical scene: Jesus of Nazareth, the Son of God, seated on a boulder and surrounded by a host of children, devoutly looking up at his serene face. Under the picture there was a verse from the Gospel of Matthew: 'Truly, I say to you, unless you turn and become like children, you will never enter the kingdom of heaven.' (It now hangs in my house in the camp, which is something I can only bear because I can't see it.)

Hser Hser Paw prayed to her heavenly Father three times every day and I knew that her greatest wish did not go unmentioned in any of those prayers. Yet after nine years of marriage, she was still childless. In those nine years I saw what had happened to my mother in a single week, the week in which Ngar Yoo was laid out in our front room, happen gradually to Hser Hser Paw: a grey veil descended over her, her hair became lanker, the twinkle went out of her eyes, her tread grew heavier, her smile wearier . . .

And me? What did I do? I attended to my cases. Cases of drug users and drug dealers, cases of thieves and swindlers, sometimes of murderers and once of a rapist. Several times a year I travelled to Pegu for an appeal and to visit the Lady C teashop. Twice or sometimes three times a year I did a case of someone accused of Unlawful Association. Sometimes I won, sometimes I lost. Sometimes it led to a sentence of three years' imprisonment for supporting a prohibited organisation, sometimes my clients were given five years for active involvement. And every now and then the suspect got off because of lack of evidence. Such was the order of the day. And I resigned myself to that order.

We are all responsible for our own lives. I had to defend my clients within the possibilities afforded to me by the law. The judge had to weigh my arguments up against those of the public prosecutor. And my clients had to answer for what they had done, not so much to the judge, but to themselves, their loved ones and, if they were believers, to God. It made no difference to me whether or not they were guilty, or whether they showed remorse. I did my job. I fulfilled my conjugal duties. I lived a half life, as if my one eye was unable to admit enough light to make a complete life possible.

'Do you think they have a chance?' asked Yi Yi Win.

I had told her about the village headman, the clerk and the militia chief. I was the only customer at the outdoor tables and rain was splashing down on the awning over our heads. That had given me courage.

'It mainly depends on the witnesses,' I said.

'The times are not good,' she said.

'No, the times are not good.'

'Things haven't been quiet since September. Not even here in town. And apparently it's really bad in Rangoon.'

'I hear things now and then,' I said cautiously.

'Yes,' she said. 'You hear things now and then.'

We listened to the rain for a while without speaking. 'I hope they get off,' Yi Yi Win said finally.

'Yes,' I said. 'I hope so too.'

Five

I heard things now and then.

Everyone heard things now and then. In every country where the government exercises total control over the media a rumour mill develops and eventually becomes a much more important source of news than the newspapers, radio or television. Burma was no exception to this rule. And since September 1987 the rumour mill had been operating at full capacity. On the fifth day of that month, U Ne Win, the General who acted as if was no longer a general, did something that only he, of all the demented rulers the world has known, could have come up with. He introduced two new bank notes: a forty-five kyat and a ninety kyat. And why? The General's lucky number was nine and it seemed that the old man was worried that he was running short of luck. Parallel to the introduction of the new notes, three old notes were withdrawn from circulation: more precisely, the regime announced that twenty-five, thirty-five and seventy-five kyat notes (the last-mentioned having been recently introduced to commemorate the dictator's seventy-fifth birthday) were no longer legal tender and hence worthless.

Of all the people who suffered from this measure, the students were hit the hardest. In a country without electronic transactions, cash was a basic requirement for anyone who was going to spend any length of time away from home without an income. As a result, students' parents, uncles, aunts and grandparents would give them a big pile of banknotes at the start of each academic year so that they could pay for their stay at the university. The sudden cancellation of these notes, so early in the academic year, plunged tens of thousands of students into major financial difficulties. Immediately after the measure was announced there were disturbances at various universities. And, just as immediately, the regime responded by closing the universities for two months.

While smothering resistance, this move simultaneously increased dissatisfaction. Students passed articles from foreign magazines like *Time* and *Newsweek* from hand to hand. They read about the reforms that were being carried out in the Soviet Union and about the fall of the dictator Marcos in the Philippines. They said to each other, 'If there, why not here?' And those words were repeated so often – in corridors and in lecture theatres, in dormitories and teashops, under the tall trees of the university gardens – that they gained the power of a mantra: if there, why not here; if-there-why-not-here; if-there-why-not-here . . .

It stood to reason that in the driest and hottest months of the year a few sparks would be enough to make the parched dissatisfaction burst into flame. And although there wasn't a word about the riots in the newspapers, and although the newsreaders on radio and television acted as if there was nothing out of the ordinary going on, we knew better, thanks to the rumour mill. Thanks to the rumours, everyone in the whole country knew what was referred to as the Red Bridge incident.

Someone said, 'It started in a teashop in Rangoon. With an argument about a cassette tape.'

Someone else said, 'A cassette tape? What? How?'

A third person said, 'Some students had a tape of the singer Sai Hti Hsaing. They asked the owner of the teashop to put it on.'

The second, 'And then?'

The first, 'There was someone in the teashop, the son of a party member, who objected to the music. He went and got his friends. They told the students, "This is our neighbourhood, this is our teashop, what are you doing here?" They came to blows, things got out of hand. The police arrived and arrested all of the brawlers. And, of course, the first person released was the son of the party member.'

'And the students didn't accept that?'

'No, of course not. They went to the station to have it out with the police. Why were their buddies still behind bars if that guy was already out on the loose? It turned into a big march. The riot police arrived. Shots were fired. Someone got killed. Phone Maw.'

'Phone Maw?'

'Yes, this Phone Maw became a martyr. A hero.'

'Phone Maw?! I know him! I know his sister, I know her very well. She smuggles cassette recorders and radios and all kinds of stuff in from Thailand. She sells them in Rangoon. Phone Maw is an informer!'

'No, he's not, he's a hero, a martyr!'

'But he worked for the regime, I'm sure of it! I know him! I know his sister! He must have been at the riots to see who was taking part. To report to . . .'

'They shot him dead. He's a hero!'

'Madness!'

'There were more demonstrations. The students demanded that the newspapers publish the truth about the riots. About the fatality.'

'The truth?! That Phone Maw was an informer?'

'No, that he was dead! That the police had shot him dead! He was a hero, a martyr!'

'The Rangoon University students wanted to hold a protest march. They wanted to go to the Institute of Technology to consult with other students. They came to a bridge, at a lake, a bridge over a lake, I don't know where exactly . . .'

'That must have been Inya Lake, the Prome Road bridge. I

went to university in Rangoon. I know it. I know where it is!'

'Soldiers were waiting for them on the other side of the bridge. And behind them, riot police were pushing forward. There was a student, Min Ko Naing . . .'

'Min Ko Naing? I don't know him.'

'Min Ko Naing tried to convince the soldiers to let the students through, but it was no use. The riot police attacked from behind. The soldiers from in front. The students were trapped.'

'And then?'

'They beat them. They shot them.'

'They say the soldiers were shouting, "Kill! Kill!"'

'People jumped into the lake. People who couldn't swim. They threw people into police vans. They shot people dead in the middle of the bridge. The bridge turned red with blood.'

'Forty-one people suffocated in a police van.'

'In a van? Forty-one?'

'Yes, forty-one! There was no air.'

'They say . . . they say that . . .'

'They say that female students were raped. Gang-raped. By soldiers and policemen.'

'The next day there was a demonstration for Phone Maw's funeral.'

'Phone Maw was an informer!'

'Phone Maw is a martyr!'

'They had already buried his body in secret.'

'Who?'

'Who?! The police of course!'

On appeal my client P.D. was sentenced to fourteen years' imprisonment for the possession of drugs. According to the court, the quantity of drugs found in his home was too large to be for personal use. To be on the safe side, they sentenced him for trafficking as well. The judge fell asleep while the teacher who had once tutored him was making his statement.

On returning to Pan Thar I found a letter on my desk. 'Dear Mr Attorney,' was the salutation. ' I hereby inform you that *in casu* Case 047.999R, concerning a breach of the Unlawful Association Act, the prosecution has been transferred to Lieutenant General Thun Myint.' Signed Shwe Ya.

This could only mean one thing: the village headman, the clerk and the militia chief had to be found guilty. The army was getting nervous. I called Hser Hser Paw and showed her the letter.

She shook her head. 'These are bad times,' she said.

'Yes,' I nodded. 'They're bad times.'

Six

It was a tremendous idea. A brilliant move. A hilarious joke. It was even more audacious than the theft of U Thant's body fourteen years earlier. In late July of 1988, on the Burmese Language Service of the BBC, the station everyone listened to who wanted to know what was really happening in the country, a student from Rangoon had called for a national protest on 8th August. On that magical day, at eight minutes past eight in the morning, the dockworkers of Rangoon signalled the start of the biggest uprising in the history of Burma: they stopped work and walked out on to the streets.

For the superstitious General Ne Win it must have been as if the people were dancing on his grave before he was in his coffin.

You're a university student in Rangoon, the son of a family full of high-ranking army officers. You know the stories about the General. You know about the student uprisings in 1962 and 1974. You have heard about the dead on the Red Bridge. Two weeks ago you read in the government papers that the General has resigned as leader of the Burmese Socialist Programme Party and that he has been succeeded by General Sein Lwin, the former Minister of Inland and Religious Affairs. Your father has said that the party will reform and might even introduce a multi-party system – when the nation is ripe for it.

You don't believe your father, even if that's something you don't say to his face.

On 8th August you stand outside Convocation Hall with your friends. Thousands of students are gathered there. Together you listen to speeches. You chant slogans. In the afternoon you march through the streets. You have never felt this strong. Never before have you been so sure that you are doing the right thing. In the evening, in the golden light of the setting sun, your body wet with perspiration, your head and your heart full to bursting with rage and joy and courage and despair, you stand before a soldier who is pointing his rifle at you. You seize the front of your shirt and bare your chest in one powerful movement. Buttons go flying, rolling over the dirty asphalt.

'Go on, shoot! Go on, shoot!'

Is that your voice? Are you the one who is shouting or is it someone else, someone who has awoken within you, who has taken control of your body and pushed it forward until you feel the steel of the barrel pressing against your chest?

'Shoot, you coward!'

Blood splatters over the soldier's uniform. Your blood.

You are a Buddhist monk in Mandalay. You lead a life that is entirely devoted to the teachings of the Great Sage. Every morning and every night you kneel before the statue of the Mahamuni Buddha, which was made as a likeness of the living Revealer of Truth. You say, 'I honour him, the Guide to Immortality, the Most Noble Sage, the Unequalled, whose curls fall in dark clouds around him. A radiant aura surrounds him, enveloping the world in a golden glow.'

Early in the morning of the eighth day of the eighth month of the year 1988, after prayer, you go out begging for alms, like every other day, and you and the other monks eat what the faithful in their goodness have given you. This is the start of the last day of your life.

In the afternoon you and dozens of other monks take part in a demonstration against the regime. In the afternoon a bullet penetrates the left side of your head, just behind the ear. At the hospital a doctor records the time of your death as 7.45 p.m.

You are a lawyer in the provincial town of Pan Thar. In the morning you close the door behind you and walk to the court. It takes you seventeen minutes. You know, today it is going to happen.

'Let me repeat the question one more time,' says the judge. In his voice you hear the weariness of someone who has witnessed all too often the way trivial misunderstandings can lead to major consequences. 'Did you, on or around the 23rd March, see one or more of the three suspects on trial here today go into the building described by the prosecutor, where, at that moment, a delegation of the Karen National Liberation Army was located?'

'No, Your Honour. I did not.'

'Is it correct that you previously told representatives of the Burma National Army the opposite?'

'Yes, Your Honour. That is true.'

'And could you, perhaps, like those who preceded you in this place, be so good as to explain why the two declarations differ so much?'

All this time the man has mumbled his answers with his back bent, but now he stands up straight and looks the judge in the eye while saying what he has to say in a clear voice, 'Because the representatives of the Burma National Army, as you call them, forced me to confess.'

His eyes flick to the side, to the tall chair on the left of the small court, where the public prosecutor is sitting, Lieutenant General Thun Myint. The lieutenant general's face does not betray a single emotion. He seems to be staring into an infinite distance, completely unaware of where he is or what has just been said in that place by the impoverished farm worker, the last of the three witnesses for the prosecution. The farm worker – a bony man in a faded longyi and a faded shirt, with a faded base-ball cap on his head, which he only took off for a moment when the judge entered – is hanging his head again, his back is bent as if he is expecting a beating.

The judge says, 'And how were you coerced into making this incriminating declaration?'

'For three days I got nothing to eat or drink. Meanwhile they expected me to keep doing my daily tasks.'

'What did those tasks consist of?'

'In the morning I had to empty the camp latrines. And in the evening I had to do the dishes in the mess.'

'And then?' The question floats into the courtroom on a loud sigh.

'On the afternoon of the third day, I had to appear in the office of the local lieutenant colonel. I didn't know him and I don't know his name. He put a glass of water down in front of me. And then he asked, "You're sure you didn't see them?" If I said yes, he tipped out the water.'

Again he straightens his back and lifts up his head, this time to half turn toward the spot where the three suspects are sitting, the three men he has undoubtedly known for many years and has now put in such a terrible position. He says, 'I'm sorry.'

He is the last of the public prosecutor's three witnesses and now he too has done what the other two did before him: he has withdrawn the incriminating statement he made earlier. He has apologised to the suspects, who have forgiven him with a nod, because they know from experience how easy it is to break someone's will.

The proof against my clients has evaporated like a raindrop on a petal in the morning sun.

The judge looks at the public prosecutor, but Lieutenant General Thun Myint is still staring into the Great Nothingness, with an expression on his face that could be interpreted as disgust or mortal fear. I wonder what has shocked him the most, the testimony of his witnesses or what he saw that morning in front of the court: hundreds of civilians, including a large number of monks, screaming anti-government slogans and demanding the resignation of General Sein Lwin, advancing perilously close to the entrance of the large white colonial building that housed so many of the organisations that turned these people into prisoners in their own town, their own country, even their own homes.

The rage and frustration of years, the fear and irritation; it all erupted – and it is hard to imagine that the lieutenant general did not have a momentary vision of what would be in store for him if the people decided to cool their anger on the little men who represented the great evil of the dictatorship in the provinces.

'Lieutenant General Thun Myint, do you have any further questions for this witness?' The judge's piercing, nasal voice breaks through the public prosecutor's shield of fear and disgust. 'No, Your Honour,' he mumbles, scarcely audible. 'No . . . nothing . . .'

'I then declare this trial closed. I will give my judgment in two weeks.'

On 17 August 1988 two of the regime's 'little men' were murdered by an angry crowd. One was Captain Shwe Ya, head of the local branch of Military Intelligence. The other was Khin Maung Yin, the police officer who had allowed me to spend twice as long as officially allowed with my clients. Captain Shwe Ya was stabbed to death with a *jinglee*, a weapon made by sharpening one end of a bicycle spoke until it's as sharp as a needle. Khin Maung Yin was beheaded with a sword. I saw his head being paraded around the streets on a stick.

Five days later the judge delivered his verdict in the Unlawful Association case against the village headman, the clerk and the head of the militia. All three were acquitted due to lack of evidence. Lieutenant General Thun Myint listened to the verdict in silence.

On 26 August several hundred thousand people gathered at the base of the Shwedagon Pagoda in Rangoon to listen to a speech by a woman who had just returned to the land of her birth from England. Daw Aung San Suu Kyi was the daughter of General Aung San, the father of the nation, the man who had led Burma to independence and been murdered on 19 July 1947, when Aung San Suu Kyi was still a child. At an early age she had become familiar with death, not just through her father's murder, but also because her oldest brother drowned in a swimming pool. And although it was completely irrational and a sign of a seriously inflated ego, I felt a special tie to her because of that tragic event in her past.

To the hundreds of thousands who came to listen to her, Aung San Suu Kyi said: 'It is true that I have lived abroad. It is also true that I am married to a foreigner. These facts have never interfered and will never interfere with or lessen my love and devotion for my country. Some people say that I know nothing of Burmese politics. The trouble is that I know too much. My family knows best how complicated and tricky Burmese politics can be and how much my father had to suffer on this account.'

Aung San Suu Kyi said: 'I could not as my father's daughter remain indifferent to all that was going on. This national crisis could in fact be called the second struggle for national independence.'

Her words floated away on the wind and spread over the whole country. She gave her downtrodden people new hope.

'We must show that we are true successors to the ideals of my father, who founded the Burma National Army to protect the people, not to oppress them,' said Aung San Suu Kyi in Myitkyina and in Sittwe, in Pathein and in Pan Thar. 'We must seek change in a dignified and peaceful manner.'

The Buddha said: 'Someone who speaks a lot about what is good falls short if he does not put his words into action, like a herder counting someone else's livestock. And someone who rarely speaks about what is good is true if his actions are guided by truth.'

It was time to be guided by truth.

Seven

He was on the other side of the street, leaning on the brickyard fence. His camouflage trousers were torn at the left knee, above them he was wearing a threadbare, greyish-white T-shirt. It took me a while to figure out why his face looked so familiar – the drooping right eye, the long teeth, the yellowish skin – not that long ago, he had been sharing a police cell with one of my clients. Now he was hanging around on the other side of the street and watching my house.

'Lieutenant General Thun Myint is angry at you,' they said at police headquarters.

'The lieutenant general has got you in his sights,' they said at the Public Prosecutor's offices.

'He feels humiliated, shown up. And in such a delicate case!'

'He didn't have any proof,' I said. 'He didn't *have* a case. That's not my fault, is it?'

'Maybe not, but he'd rather blame you than himself.'

'What can he do to me?'

'Nothing. As yet. That's why he's watching you. He's not in a hurry. He's patient. He'll wait for you to make a mistake. And then he'll strike. He's as patient as a heron in a rice field. And just as merciless.'

I had decided not to be afraid. For all that he was a lieutenant general, that rank no longer gave him the status it once conveyed – not since the muggy day in September when the army moved into the streets of the towns and cities where people were still protesting against the government. Not since they used force to clear away the last barricades. Not since they shot dead the last rebellious students and monks, murdering men and women, children and the elderly. Not since a new government took power, led by a new general, a government that went under the euphemistic name of State Law and Order Restoration Council.

No one trusted the new government. No one trusted the little men who had taken on the task of restoring law and order. Lieutenant General Thun Myint knew that as well as I did.

'Stay calm,' Saw Hsa Tu told me after I explained about the man on the other side of the street. 'They're trying to upset you. And scare you. They want to throw you off balance.'

'I have nothing to hide,' I said.

Saw Hsa Tu couldn't restrain a laugh. 'Don't be so sure of that,' he said.

'I have something to ask you,' said Yi Yi Win. 'I have something to ask you on behalf of my uncle and my husband.'

She had taken me off guard. During my visits to the Lady C, I had generally found it easy to forget about the life Yi Yi Win led when she wasn't serving customers. Occasionally I had asked her about her children, and twice I had seen the two girls in the restaurant: the first time playing with sand under one of the tables; the second time dressed up in silk with bows in their hair. An older woman arrived to take the girls to a party. Later, Yi Yi Win told me that the older woman was her mother-in-law. That was as close as I had come to a confrontation with the man who had taken my place in her life, and I was more than happy to keep him at that distance.

'My uncle and my husband are working for the new party,' Yi Yi Win said.

'The . . .' Quickly, I looked around. 'Her party?' I mumbled, just to be on the safe side.

'Yes. Hers. And they want to ask you to set up a branch in Pan Thar. You have the contacts. And the ability. The question is . . .'

I didn't let her finish. 'Of course,' I blurted. But in the meantime, I didn't dare look at her, terrified as I was that she would see the panic in my eyes. Aung San Suu Kyi's party! The National League for Democracy! Her uncle and her husband?! Me?! Set up a branch?!

I said, 'I'm surprised that your uncle, and your husband . . . I mean . . . The ministry . . .'

She said, 'Of course, the work they do for the party is secret. But who wants to stand by this government now? Who wants to be part of a regime that impoverishes the country and then murders its own people when they rise up against it?'

I asked, 'Did you think it would succeed this time? That it wouldn't be drowned in blood like before?'

She said, 'Yes. Yes . . . I think this time I really believed in it. Partly because people like my uncle . . . And it's still possible! If we persevere . . . If we now . . . They say there are going to be elections. The Old Man has become an old man. His party's been dissolved. Have you noticed that nobody uses the word "socialism" any more? It's been scrapped, rubbed out, painted over . . . We need something new, but no one knows what. Except *her*.'

'Yes,' I said, 'Yes, you're right.'

She had charisma, that was what people said. She was as wise as she was fearless. And most importantly, she was the daughter of General Aung San, they wouldn't dare to touch her.

'I . . .' I began. 'I'd like to do it, of course I would! I just need someone to . . .'

'My husband,' she said. And now she looked at me. I looked at her. For a moment our eyes were linked together, like the hands of trapeze artists, before I let go and sent her swinging back to her own life.

'Can you come here tonight? After dark?'

'Yes.'

'Good. Then come back tonight. And now you should go.

No, I don't want you to pay today.'

She turned and walked into the kitchen.

It took a long time before I trusted my body enough to dare to stand.

Yi Yi Win was right. Who wanted to be part of this regime now?

A letter went around the country, a letter that was read and copied, and passed from hand to hand, like the books the regime didn't want people to read. It was an open letter from an army officer, Brigadier Aung Gyi, to his old comrade in arms, General Ne Win. The brigadier and the general had worked closely together in the late 1950s and early 1960s. In the first few months of 1987, for the first time in twenty-five years, the brigadier had visited a number of countries outside Burma – and it had come as a terrible shock. How was it possible that the tempestuous economic development that had transformed countries like Thailand and Malaysia had passed Burma by entirely? How was it possible that nations that forty years earlier had been dependent on rice imports from Burma – not to mention the import of precious metals and stones, fuel and hardwood – how could those same nations have left the Burmese behind in every way?

There was only one possible explanation and, in his letter, Brigadier Aung Gyi told General Ne Win straight out what that explanation was: the economic policies of the Burma Socialist Programme Party had been a fiasco. According to the brigadier, it was not only high time to recognise the errors of the past, but essential to ensure that such errors not be repeated in the future. And how better to do that than by transforming the one-party state into a multi-party democracy? It was a letter that astonished everyone who read it: the fact that such a high-ranking officer, a man who beyond any shadow of a doubt was part of the establishment, a member of the country's political elite – that such a man dared to openly state his opinion! It was unheard of.

My first, small act of resistance, my anxious, timorous echo of the courageous words of Aung San Suu Kyi, was to have the letter delivered to the office of my tormentor, the man who had set his spies on me because he blamed me for ruining *his* case, and getting *his* suspects released: Lieutenant General Thun Myint. I made sure that he could never establish who had sent the letter, but at the same time there was no doubt that I would be his primary suspect. And that suspicion would undoubtedly become much stronger if he found out that I was engaged in setting up a branch of the National League for Democracy in Pan Thar.

Did I dare to risk that confrontation?

Did I have any choice?

I only had to turn my thoughts back to that bus ride through Rangoon, when Yi Yi Win told me about the years her uncle had spent in prison, I only needed to think back for a second on the painful conversation with Yi Yi Win's uncle that followed, and I knew that the answer to that last question could only be 'no': I had no choice, I had to do what Yi Yi Win's uncle and husband asked – not for them, but for her.

That night, around eight o'clock, just after the moon rose, I was welcomed into the Lady C by U Tin Pe, Yi Yi Win's husband.

What should I say about him? That he was a handsome man? He was. Pale skin. A face that betrayed both pride and a certain degree of gentleness. A tall, lean body – he was at least a head taller than me and clearly much fitter.

Should I say that his behaviour towards me was particularly polite and friendly? It was. That he was meticulous in explaining what was expected of me, how I should seek out the right people, and how I should respond to the intimidation that would certainly follow? It was all true. In another place and in other circumstances, Tin Pe was a man I could have easily warmed to. But that night, in the hot stuffy office above the kitchen of the Lady C, I found it impossible to bring myself to see Yi Yi Win's husband, the father of her children, as anything more than 'polite' and 'correct'. He gave me a number of names and telephone numbers of people in Rangoon I could keep in touch with about the progress of my work for the party. He told me how to contact the party leadership and Aung San Suu Kyi. I took notes, just as I took notes when I was being briefed on a new case. I asked some questions and told him a little about Pan Thar and my position there as a lawyer for its Karen inhabitants. It turned out that my ethnic background had been an important reason for his approaching me. U Tin Pe himself was three quarters Burman and one quarter Kachin. As a result he sympathised with the ethnic cause, while agreeing wholeheartedly with Aung San Suu Kyi that there was no alternative to the single Burmese state. And surely someone like me, half Burman and half Karen, took exactly the same line?

I nodded but thought, I've never asked myself these questions, for the simple reason that there was no necessity. What was the sense of thinking about questions like this under a government that only allowed one answer to any question at all? I realised in a flash that I was totally unprepared for the changes taking place in my country, let alone for helping to precipitate them. Of course U Tin Pe was right when he said that I couldn't possibly be in favour of dividing Burma up into ethnic states; I might just as well advocate cutting myself in half. But was it possible that the Karen National Union would surrender the territory under its control if a new, democratic government came to power in Rangoon? Would a democratic government be able to provide sufficient guarantees for the Karen to start finally feeling at home in Burma? I had no idea. And if I didn't have any idea about things like that, subjects that I had a reasonable insight into by virtue of being constantly confronted with them in my day-to-day practice, and even in my own family, how much worse would it be with all the other problems facing the country, problems a new government, whatever kind of government it might be, would have to try to solve? Suddenly I was convinced that there was no future for me in politics – not even in a party like the National League for Democracy. But there was a problem: I could admit that to myself, but admitting it to U Tin Pe, of all men, was clearly impossible.

'It seems to me,' I hesitated, 'that the new party has a duty to make non-Burmans feel that they too are full citizens, in every way.'

In the circumstances, I thought I had come up with quite a decent sentence.

'Exactly!' said U Tin Pe. 'That's why it's crucial we have prominent ethnic members. And that's why it's so fantastic to have you on board!'

I nodded politely, but couldn't help feel a little more confident. I drank my tea, and then, at his insistence, a small glass of Karen whisky, distilled by one of his wife's relatives.

I did my very best not to let anything show, and I believe that I actually succeeded.

When I came home the next day, the man with the yellowish skin was standing on the other side of the street. He looked me straight in the eye and sneered.

Eight

'Of course it's none of my business, U Saw Min Thein,' the lieutenant general said, 'but if you are so anxious to play a role in the
changes our country is currently going through, your behaviour
will need to be irreproachable, don't you agree?'

He clamped a pencil between his two index fingers: one
finger on the freshly sharpened point, the other on the flat end.
He held the pencil up to face level and stared at it intently, as if
the letters on the side were some kind of secret message instead
of just the brand name and the hardness of the lead.

'After all, where would we be if the people's leaders, or those
who aspire to that role, no longer wished to set a good example?'

'You mustn't believe everything you hear on the street,' I
began, with more confidence in my phrasing than in my heart,
'You must know better than I that gossip lends wings to the
smallest of words.'

'I am not talking about gossip, U Saw Min Thein!' He said it
in the tone of voice he undoubtedly used to address subordinates,
and the sweat that broke out on my skin told me that this scared
me more than I cared to admit.

I said, 'In that case I don't know who or what you might be
referring to.' But my voice was shaky and betrayed the falsehood
of my words – I knew that he knew that I was lying.

Lieutenant General Thun Myint had summoned me to his office
to lecture me on the changes to the judicial system that had been
announced by the new regime. In an open letter to the country's
new leaders, the Burma Bar Council had raised serious objections

to the way the government was changing the law to suit its requirements. The lieutenant general had a copy of that letter on his desk when he received me in his office.

'U Saw Min Thein,' he said at the start of his long monologue, 'I can safely assume that you are familiar with the contents of this letter, and I won't ask you whether you subscribe to them, because that is a total irrelevance. What *is* relevant is that you realise that these exceptionally difficult times require the government to sometimes resort to exceptional measures to preserve the country from anarchy. What *is* relevant is that you realise that the government is forced to take such measures by certain elements in society who allow themselves to be led astray by characters who are devoid of all sense of responsibility, people who don't even have a bond to this country. Individuals who have given themselves over – I will not mince words here – to the agents of foreign powers whose only goal is the destruction of Burmese independence.'

Here, he raised his hand briefly as if to admonish me to silence, even though I had made no show of wishing to interrupt. I wasn't that foolish. I was more than familiar with the endless litany of insinuations against Aung San Suu Kyi, insinuations which, in varying forms but with constant maliciousness, were standard fare in the official media.

'Naturally, I am aware,' the lieutenant general continued, 'that you have for some time been engaged in activities on behalf of the so-called National League for Democracy. You have every right to do so – the organisation concerned is not illegal – however, at the same time, I would like to point out that the government is keeping a very close watch on the leaders of that party. They are constantly abusing the liberties offered to them by the new government to provoke the population and incite them to anarchy and disorderly behaviour. To my sorrow, I cannot avoid the impression that you too are incapable of offering sufficient resistance to the dark temptations of freedom.'

He stood up and walked over to the window, where, with his back turned to me, he took the opportunity to relish in the inevitability of the legal reforms planned by the new regime by summarising them one after the other, knowing full well that I had, through various channels, already been thoroughly informed about all of these measures. The introduction of military tribunals, expanded possibilities for long-term preventive detention, trials in camera: all steps the government had been compelled to take because of the perniciousness of the enemy.

For me, personally, the changes would undoubtedly lead to a drastic reduction in the number of appeals cases requiring me to travel to Pegu. 'And that,' the lieutenant general added while turning around and stepping closer, 'brings me back to my previous point: how difficult you seem to find it to resist the temptations of our newfound freedom. I expect that travelling to Pegu less often will do no harm at all to your reputation, both as an upstanding citizen and as an honest husband.'

He was now so close that I had to tilt my head back to look at him. I wanted to stand up, but for some reason I couldn't bring myself to do it. Was it fear? And if it was fear, was it fear of him, or fear of myself, of what I would feel if I looked him straight in the eye from such close proximity?

'Of course, it's none of my business,' he finished, turning away again. He walked to his desk and sat down without specifying what exactly was none of his business. But I knew from that moment that Yi Yi Win had become a pawn in the game the lieutenant general was playing with me.

Looking back on those days – even if 'looking back' is an expression I can no longer use without a sneer on my face – it feels as if my life was constantly swinging from one extreme to another, just as the whole country was swinging between extremes.

I travelled to Pegu on the pretext of an appeal, but only went there for Yi Yi Win. I took a trishaw to the Lady C in the early afternoon and didn't leave until long after sunset. And all that time I had her serve me and watched her serving others. I imprinted every detail in my memory: her face, her hands, the way she kept using the fingers of her left hand to push a troublesome lock of hair back behind her ear, the way she swayed on her heels when a customer couldn't decide what to order, the way she smiled at me, the tired look on her face when she stared into the distance when she had nothing to do. I compiled a catalogue of Yi Yi Win, never doubting that I would be able to leaf through it for the rest of my life, stopping at this or that picture, reviewing this or that recollection – what did I know about the fragility of the visual memory?

I sat at my table in the Lady C and ate and drank, but more than either of those, I got drunk on Yi Yi Win. When I finally settled up and looked into her eyes for the very last time to say goodbye, I was hardly able to stand.

Back in my hotel room I wrote a letter to Daw Yi Yi Win and U Tin Pe, explaining that, owing to the 'special circumstances' and 'our particular social obligations', it seemed to me that it would be better if I avoided the Lady C during any future visits to Pegu. I thanked them for their friendship and hospitality. I wished them wisdom and happiness. I had the letter delivered by a court officer whose reliability and loyalty I had seen proven over the years. I never visited the Lady C again.

At home in Pan Thar I worked carefully and conscientiously at building up a local branch of the National League for Democracy. BBC radio reported the establishment, somewhere in the Karen-controlled border regions, of the Democratic Alliance of Burma, in which ethnic resistance groups, student organisations and the National League for Democracy were represented.

The man on the other side of the street was relieved by another, who, in turn, was relieved by another.

The state media showed images of exhausted, dishevelled students who, with the assistance of the Thais, had been rounded up along the border and were now being repatriated.

Rumour had it that many of them were executed as soon as they arrived in Rangoon.

The censorship grew stricter.

More independent illegal magazines, pamphlets and newspapers appeared than ever.

The State Law and Order Restoration Council put Aung San Suu Kyi under house arrest. Dozens of party leaders and active members were arrested. I went to my father-in-law's house, just outside Pan Thar, and lay low for three weeks.

I no longer did any cases involving breaches of the Unlawful Association Act. Those cases were now heard by military tribunal. Unless they were dealt with immediately in a torture chamber or an open field, where a soldier carried out the sentence with a pistol shot or a burst of submachine gun fire.

The chairman of the National League for Democracy, Tin U, was sentenced to three years' hard labour.

Aung San Suu Kyi was excluded from participating in the elections on the grounds of an old, almost forgotten law from the colonial period that banned anyone who was married to a foreigner from holding public office.

Hser Hser Paw got pregnant.

In the first free elections since 1960 the National League for Democracy gained an absolute majority of 392 of the 485 parliamentary seats.

The State Law and Order Restoration Council resorted to a new wave of arrests. Instead of taking their seats in the parliament, the elected representatives of the people ended up in prison.

The repression intensified. The fear grew.

My father died.

Nine

There was something wrong with his face. My father was in bed, propped up on pillows. His jaw was drooping and there was a trail of saliva running out of the right hand corner of his mouth and down his neck. That wasn't the most disturbing thing. The most disturbing thing was that the saliva was dribbling out of the other corner of his mouth as well. His face had become symmetrical.

'*Koko*,' my mother said, 'Min Thein is here!' It had been a long time since I had heard her call my father that: '*koko*', older brother. As a pet name it expresses both affection and respect and it is quite common for Burmese women to use it for their husbands. I remembered my mother calling my father *koko* often when I was a child, but she must have stopped doing it over the years without my noticing. It was only now that she did it again that I realised with a shock how long it had been since I had last heard that word from her mouth.

Had she already stopped using it when *I* was suddenly unable to use it any more because I no longer had an older brother? I didn't know, and this was no time to ask her.

My father didn't react. His eyes were open, but they didn't seem to see anything. His hands were resting, pale and limp, on his stomach. I sat down on a chair next to the bed while my mother rearranged his pillows. My father's right hand slipped down.

'Has he said anything?' I asked. 'Can he still talk?'

My mother took two steps back and studied the man in the bed before her – did she see it too? Of course she did, she

167

couldn't possibly have missed it. Maybe it had been the first thing she noticed when she came into the room that morning: the fact that he no longer had two faces.

My mother said, 'Last night he said he was thirsty. Those were the first words he's said since regaining consciousness. And this morning he said something to the doctor. Something about his head hurting. It's not easy for him to talk, he's almost impossible to understand. But I think he can still hear you and understand what you're saying.'

She left the room. I looked at my father, at what was left of him, and I tried in vain to think of something to say, something meaningful.

'Hser Hser Paw sends her love,' I said at last. My father didn't reply.

'She's praying for you.'

I was suddenly convinced that her prayers wouldn't help, that nothing anyone could do would save my father now. I looked at the left side of his face. He had given up. The battle was over. He wouldn't say another word because he didn't want to scare off death, his death, which had stepped out of the shadows and was creeping closer with growing self-confidence, ready to carry him off.

Did that disappoint me?

Did I want him to put up a fight, refusing to give in?

Those were questions I didn't dare to answer.

My mother came in with a cup of tea, two glasses and a carafe of water. She filled the glasses. Watching her stop and stare at my father again, I saw the look in her eyes change, her attention drifting off to another time, another place. Maybe she was seeing him in his army uniform: back straight, chin up, a look in his eyes that said, 'I'm ready for whatever life throws at me, the world is my oyster.' Did she believe him or was she just attracted by his youthful recklessness, knowing full well that he was overestimating himself?

They had loved each other deeply, my mother and my father, I had no doubts about that. People like them, who stand up to prejudice, mistrust, mocking and outright rejection, can only be motivated by love. 'Love is patient and kind,' my mother had taught me. 'It does not rejoice at wrong, but rejoices in the right. Love bears all things, believes all things, hopes all things, endures all things. Love never ends.' These words of St Paul's were on a painted sign on the wall of the Baptist church my mother and I attended every Sunday for years. I learnt them off by heart long before I appreciated their beauty and wisdom. I learnt them because my mother had told me that they were the most beautiful words she had ever read.

My brother Ngar Yoo did not come to church with us – on Sundays he stayed home with my father. No one ever told me why. As a child you accept things as they are. And later, you don't ask about them because they no longer seem relevant.

My mother drained her glass and put it back on the tray. She asked me how Hser Hser Paw was doing. She had to ask twice before her words got through to me.

'Well,' I said. 'Very well. She wakes up every morning as sick as a dog. I've never seen her happier.'

That night, while I was asleep in the room my mother still called 'Min Thein's room' even though she had used it as a guest room for years, death took my father by the hand and led him off. My mother told me in the morning after setting my mohinga down on the table in front of me.

I telephoned Hser Hser Paw that afternoon. She said she wanted to be there with me when they buried him. 'We're not burying him,' I said.

'That's not the point.'

'I don't want you travelling,' I said, 'not in your condition.'

She asked to speak to my mother and I called her. She came downstairs in a red silk dress, the dress she wore on the day of Ngar Yoo's funeral. 'Hser Hser Paw would like to speak to you,'

I said. It was a trivial sentence, but I found it extremely difficult to get out in one go.

I walked out into the garden, where I lay down under the acacia.

'There's someone here to see you,' said Hser Hser Paw, 'a woman from Pegu.'

It was like a downpour from a clear blue sky.

'A woman from Pegu,' I said.

'Yes, she came yesterday.' Hser Hser Paw explained with a piercing look in her eyes. 'She waited.'

So that was why the man on the other side of the street had grinned at me like that! The pawn in the game his superiors were playing with me had come to Pan Thar. That must have immediately made good all of the annoyance he had felt about my unexplained absence.

Eight days had passed since my mother called me. 'Your father has had a stroke,' she said. 'The doctors say he's stable now, but I'm not so sure.' Of course I was shocked by my mother's sudden call, just as any child is shocked when suddenly confronted by the mortality of their mother or father. I told her that I would come at once. After hailing a trishaw and riding off in the direction of the train station, I saw the man watching my house. This time it was an older man, with a right leg that bent out at an unnatural angle below the knee. I said goodbye cheerfully. The thought that he would have nothing to do in the coming days and that his superiors would have no idea where I had gone made my departure light-hearted after all (I had told Hser Hser Paw that if anyone asked she should tell them that I was away for a few days for personal reasons and leave it at that).

When I came home he greeted me as cheerfully as I had said goodbye to him when leaving.

'She slept here?!' I asked, as if I couldn't bear the thought of Hser Hser Paw offering a bed to someone who had made a long journey from Pegu to speak to me. But it *was* an intolerable thought – Yi Yi Win sleeping in my house, under my roof, in the room next to my study, and me away from home.

Hser Hser Paw said, 'I'm sorry about your father.' Her tone of voice suggested that her thoughts were somewhere else entirely. I almost said, 'It's nothing', but recovered just in time. I said, 'It's nothing I won't get over.'

Then I followed her into the living room. Through the open French windows I saw a woman on the verandah. She was sitting with her back to me. I felt like turning on the spot and going upstairs to my study as if she didn't exist.

Why had she come here?

And what had she discussed with Hser Hser Paw in my absence?

I stepped out on to the verandah. She turned to face me. There was something wrong with her face. It was the face of the owner of the hotel opposite the train station in Pegu – it wasn't Yi Yi Win's face at all.

Four of them had shown up at the crack of dawn – she had just washed and got dressed. They told her to come at once. When she asked what was wrong, they told her to keep her mouth shut – they asked the questions. Two army jeeps were parked in front of the hotel. They made her sit in the back of the rear vehicle. They raced out of town, heading for Rangoon. That was when she knew it had something to do with Aye Lwin, her youngest son, who was studying at the Rangoon Institute of Technology.

She thought, He's dead. I have to identify the body.

All the way to Rangoon she looked out of the window. She tried to name everything she saw. The birds flying over the paddy fields in long graceful lines. The flowers growing in the garden of a run-down colonial mansion. The colour of the clouds that caught the morning sun. She read the billboards on the side of the road: 'Combat hostile elements!' 'Long live the army that watches over national unity!' She counted the passengers in the buses they overtook. She counted the potholes. Anything to avoid thinking about what lay ahead.

In Rangoon they got stuck in traffic. The soldiers cursed and shouted. Children selling newspapers, sweets or cigarettes pressed their noses up against the windows, staring defiantly at the soldiers and shooting off between cars the moment one of them made a move to get out.

Finally they stopped in a street she was sure she had never seen before. Getting out, she saw more army vehicles. Armed soldiers were standing in front of the door of a house. Someone shouted an order. Five young men came out, followed by two soldiers, guns at the ready. The youths lined up on the verandah. Aye Lwin was not dead. He was the one in the middle.

'Point out your son,' said one of the soldiers, a man she hadn't noticed before, but whose face she would never forget. She felt an icy calm descend over her. Her eyes glided over the faces of the five young men. They all looked back – except Aye Lwin. Her son stared into the air beside her. His face showed no emotion at all.

'Point out your son!' screamed the soldier.

She looked in his direction. She wanted to look him straight in the face. She wanted him to read in her eyes that she would rather die than betray her own child.

The next moment she heard someone bellow, 'That's him!'

I listened to her story without taking my eyes off her. Her voice grew softer, she huddled over more and more. She avoided my gaze.

She said, 'They threw him down on to the ground. They tied his hands together with nylon cord. I could see it cutting into his skin. When they pushed him into the police van, he looked back at me for a moment.'

She was silent for a long time. Then she told me about the weeks of uncertainty that had followed. She had no idea where he was being held or what they were planning to do with him. Finally she heard that he was at Insein Prison. She was allowed to visit him. There was a hatch near the gate. The hatch opened. He was standing on the other side, just a couple of feet away from her. His face was swollen. His hair was matted with dried blood. When he smiled she saw that he was missing a few teeth. He said, 'Tomorrow I go before the court, together with eight others. They've accused us of sedition and conspiring against the government.'

Two days later she received notification. Her son had been given a ten-year sentence.

She said, 'I don't know what to do. He'll die there. They're murdering him. I thought, I have to find someone I can trust. Someone who understands the law and justice. That's why I'm here.'

I closed my eyes and said, 'I'll do what I can, but you mustn't get your hopes up. There is probably very little I can do for your son. Maybe nothing at all.'

After I had shown her out, Hser Hser Paw was waiting for me in the living room. She asked, 'Was it for her that you went to Pegu?'

It took me a while to find the words to answer her, 'No, it wasn't for her that I went to Pegu.'

Three weeks later I posted the following letter.

Dear Daw San Dar,

At your request I have immersed myself in the case of your son, Aye Lwin. I have contacted the authorities in Rangoon; I have spoken to fellow lawyers who are involved with similar cases in that city; and I have passed information about the case on to the leadership of the National League for Democracy, as you requested. Attached, please find a copy of a letter that Daw Aung San Suu Kyi recently sent to the responsible minister and the other members of the government. In her letter, as you can see, she considers the current state of lawlessness and the way in which the government treats people who criticise the military authorities. She has not yet received a reply of any kind. This, unfortunately, is entirely consistent with the experiences of fellow lawyers involved with cases similar to your son's. They, too, keep coming up against a wall of silence. None the less, I have found one of them who is prepared to exert himself for the release of Aye Lwin. You will find his name, address and office telephone number below. He is expecting your call. Once again I would like to emphasise that you must not entertain too great a hope regarding the results of his mediation. Unfortunately, the current government does not have a great respect for the law. I deeply regret my inability to do more for you, and can only wish you strength. My wife has asked me to tell you that she prays every day for the release of your son.

With the greatest respect,

Yours faithfully,

U Saw Min Thein.

Ten

For me rain is first and foremost a noise; I have felt like that ever since I was a child. I remember one morning when my brother and I got caught by the rain on my grandfather's farm. We were out in the middle of the rice fields, where we were spying on fishing egrets. The elegant white birds had an almost magical appeal. The way they left their sleeping places in the nearby forest just after dawn to come sailing through the sky in long elegant ribbons before landing and taking control of the rice fields. The way they stood bent over the water, entirely motion-less and with infinite patience, improbable white patches in the equally improbable green of the rice shoots. And then the fatal precision with which they stabbed at their prey: a frog, a small fish or maybe a large beetle. It was enchantingly beautiful.

That morning we were so absorbed by the birds that we hadn't noticed the dark clouds gathering overhead. When the first drops started to fall, we sought out a hiding place as fast as we could, because in the rainy season it's never long before it's pouring. Just before getting soaked, we managed to reach a hut that had been built on the edge of the rice field for the workers. The bamboo construction consisted of four poles, an elevated floor a couple of feet off the ground, and a palm-leaf roof that, although somewhat leaky, provided sufficient protection from the deluge that seemed to consume the world around us. Soon the rain had reduced visibility so much that we could no longer see the edges of the fields. Thirty or so feet away from us, just visible in the mist of falling and splashing drops of water, stood an egret. For a moment it had stretched its neck in concern as we

175

clambered into the hut, but now it had pulled its head back under its feathers to wait for drier times.

We sat imprisoned in a cage of water that was, for me at least, also a cage of sound. I looked for a dry spot, sat down on the bamboo floor in the lotus position and closed my eyes. The world became a sea of noise.

I was reminded of that moment late on a Sunday afternoon towards the end of August when we were eating on our verandah while the rain poured down around us in a torrent that showed no sign of stopping or even abating. The Karen call the lunar month that corresponds more or less to August *la hkü*, meaning 'the locked-in month'. It is an appropriate name. Hser Hser Paw's sister and brother-in-law had come to dinner, and Hser Hser Paw had decided to cook early, so that we could sit out on the verandah while it was still light, safe under the roof but outside at the same time, and therefore a little less imprisoned. We didn't speak much during the meal, which was unusual, as we generally had a lot to say to each other – not just Hser Hser Paw and her sister, Naw Tamla Paw, but also her brother-in-law, Saw Ta Doh, and I. Ta Doh had spent years working as a clerk at the public prosecutor's office – although he hadn't been my brother-in-law at the time. He married Naw Tamla Paw just before I was assigned to the case of the village headman, the clerk and the militia chief. When I won it, he was fired on the spot. Now he did odd jobs for the brother of Saw Hsa Tu, the bicycle maker, and helped me with the organisation of the party branch. Naw Tamla Paw, lovingly called Diamond by Hser Hser Paw because her name meant 'diamond flower', had a great deal in common with her sister, including a fascination for the more mystical sides of Christianity. Not long before Hser Hser Paw became pregnant, we had attended a meeting where a faith healer took the stage. It was only natural for the sisters to link this event to Hser Hser Paw's pregnancy and Ta Doh and I knew better than to try to change their minds.

But all of those subjects, which would normally have kept us talking for hours, remained undiscussed that afternoon because the monsoon drowned our words: the heavy drumming on the roof, the gurgling streams of water shooting off the roof and splashing down into the muddy garden, the rustling of the rain on the trees and shrubs further away. Now and then, lightning lit up the sky and the thunder that followed momentarily overshadowed the din of the rain. According to the ancient wisdom of the Karen, thunderstorms result from the struggle between the forces of the *Law hpo*, which are responsible for the rains, and the forces of the *Hku de*, which control the dry season. Switching seasons is like a changing of the guard, something that always involves violence and a show of arms. The flashes of light are caused by the glittering spears of the *Hku de* and the furious beating of the wings of the *Law hpo*, gigantic demons that live high in the heavens. The thunder is the flight of the arrows and the thuds of the blows the combatants inflict on each other. My brother-in-law said that all those stories were nothing but superstition. And according to Hser Hser Paw and her sister they were inventions with which the devil had long succeeded in keeping the Karen from the narrow path of Our Lord Jesus Christ. I myself had always been terrified by stories about the ghosts and demons, primaeval creatures and witches that the Karen had once believed in – a fear that was undoubtedly closely connected to the mysterious death of my brother Ngar Yoo, who believed that he was a fish and possibly wanted to become as one with the climbing perch he thought he knew so well.

I now take the line that those stories are an artistic interpretation of reality, just as surrealist painters impose their will on reality in paintings that are often as bizarre as they are fascinating. It is too easy for us to judge the products of others' imaginations, from fear of our own imagination perhaps, or from an inability to empathise with those others, which in itself demonstrates a lack of imagination. That's how I think about those things now, but I didn't think about them like that on that rainy afternoon in August, I didn't *dare* to think about them like that then, encaged as I was in my own fears.

When it finally stopped raining and the roar became a whisper, Hser Hser Paw said, 'Isn't it time we left here, all of us, for good?'

PART IV

A Thousand Shades of Black

It rained last night, did you hear it? That's unusual for this time of year. We'll have to be careful going down the hill, the paths can be treacherous when they're slippery, even if it's no comparison to what we go through here in the rainy season.

In the rainy season the river smells like soil and the soil smells like river. Everything is so soaked there's only one smell over: the smell of mud. In that regard, this is the most beautiful time of year: the months of December and January, when the countryside is starting to dry out, but hasn't got dry enough to be dusty. In April everything smells the same as well, but then it's not the presence of water, but its absence that makes all smells blend together. In April and May everything smells like dust.

It's good to walk here with you. We have got so used to being invisible that we get suspicious when someone says, 'I want to know who you are.' For a long time we believed that our invisibility was our salvation, that it was the only thing that kept us alive. I no longer believe that. Our invisibility is our greatest enemy. You can treat the invisible any way you like: you can rout them out like game, you can shoot them and exterminate them, you can chase them out of the country. And we are not safe in this new country either, because who will protect us? Every day we fall victim to violence and arbitrary decisions. We are climbing perch in a trough of water high in a tree, and every night the fish owl comes to gorge on us – and no one notices.

On the bank of the river, I ask you how high the mist is, and you say, 'About halfway up the mountainside.'

I say, 'Then it will be a while before we see the sun today. The higher the mist in the early morning, the longer it takes the sun to break through. I don't know why, but that's how it works.'

On the far side of the river we follow our ears. The Bible school students are singing one of the Psalms of David. Their voices weave together to form a carpet of sound. They bring colour to my darkness.

Pastor Marcus has asked me to interpret today. Yesterday an Australian evangelist arrived, and not all of the students have enough English to understand his sermons.

It was the pastor who first took Tommy and me under his wing. The pastor is one of the people I have put my hopes on. If there is anyone who might be able to do something for Tommy, he is the one.

We sit down on the stairs to his office and he greets us the way he greets all his guests: with aloofness approaching indifference. For a long time I mistrusted the pastor because of that quality, but now I believe that it is shyness — shyness and the suspiciousness that comes from disappointment.

I introduce you to each other and the pastor sends someone to the kitchen to fetch us some coffee.

'Do whatever it takes to get through it,' the pastor tells me.

And to you, in English, he says, 'A brother from Australia is visiting us, a most respected preacher.'

To me, 'He's a stupid man, with stupid opinions.'

To you, 'It is very enriching to feel the solidarity of our overseas brothers and sisters.'

To me, 'He was here before, years ago. I don't think you met him then, but he's not a man you would forget in a hurry. As much as you'd like to.'

To both of us, 'Ah, there he is.'

The first thing I notice about the Australian evangelist are the vibrations, no, the shock waves he creates. The bamboo floors and walls sigh and groan and creak under his weight. He's not a tall man. When he greets us from the doorway with a jovial 'Howdy!' I notice that his voice doesn't come from very high up, so he must have a considerable girth.

Once we have all been introduced to each other and Marcus has sent someone off to get some more coffee, he says in Karen, 'He is about your height, weighs at least twenty stone, and is wearing shorts and a traditional Karen shirt. He has long grey hair tied in a ponytail and his nose is peeling.'

In English he says, 'Saw Min Thein is the best interpreter we have. He never lets the pretty girls in the class distract him.'

I feel a little guilty – guilty and slightly embarrassed. About your having to listen to this. For more than an hour now you have been subjected to a lecture on Joseph and the Pharaoh, Egyptian beliefs regarding the divinity of their leaders, and the unimaginable and therefore highly significant fact that this divine Pharaoh asked Joseph for advice.

'Because what exactly was Joseph when you come down to it?' asks the Australian preacher. 'A poor slave from the land of Canaan! Sold by his own brothers to a bunch of spice merchants! Who sold him on to an officer of Pharaoh's guard! Joseph was oppressed! Joseph was . . . a refugee!'

The Australian preacher likes talking in exclamation marks.

'And yet Pharaoh made him master of his household! Yea, he made him ruler over all of Egypt! He gave him his most expensive ring and his finest robes! He gave him a chariot and horses! And he commanded his subjects to kneel before him and kiss his hand!'

The Australian preacher preaches and I interpret. The students listen or doze off, their minds on other things. And you sit on a wooden bench at the back of the classroom and wait for me to finish. What choice do you have?

By the end of the double lecture the Australian preacher is out of breath. I smell the sweat patches on his traditional Karen shirt. He puffs and pants his way to a conclusion. He says, 'We may differ from each other in many ways, in language, in culture and in habits, but we have one thing in common, we are all children of the same Father, we believe in the same God and in His Son, who died on the cross for our Sins. Hallelujah!'

I use the freedom Pastor Marcus has given me and translate his words as 'We may differ from each other in many ways, in language, in eating habits and in weight, but we have one thing in common, we are all people, with the same human desires: we long for freedom and independence and the warm embrace of our loved ones. Hallelujah!'

From the back of the room I hear the voice of Pastor Marcus, 'Amen!'

From the back of the room I hear a happy sigh of relief.

One

I would have loved to look down on us from above. I would have enjoyed the clouds of mist draped over the hilltops like veils and the last red glow of the fire that had burnt all night and was now warming the hands of two young women. I could have smiled at our clumsy attempts to get my father-in-law, U Hla Shwe, into his hammock. The hammock was attached to a long bamboo pole that would be carried by four men, with another four walking along to relieve them. I would have looked at the faces of the ones who were leaving and the ones who were staying behind, and I would have mumbled words of consolation to assuage their grief. But for those of us who were caught up in the event there was no room for such tender emotions. For us there was only worry and nerves, and beneath them fear, like a cold undertow in warm water.

Did we have all the luggage?

Had we forgotten anything?

Were we trying to take too much, clasping to too many things in a last desperate attempt to hold on to the past? Or was it the other way round and would we discover that we had left things behind that we actually needed?

Would we survive?

None of us had any experience of long jungle treks, let alone any idea of what it meant to cross territory in which a hopeless war had been raging for so long. We didn't say a word to each other. Every now and then our guides and bearers exchanged short sentences in voices that were restrained but confident. Around us the forest seemed quieter than it had been for hours and even the cocks, which earlier had seemed to crow constantly, fell silent. The sky above us was slowly paling. An enormous eagle flew over the valley on silent wings. Somewhere far away a dog barked. The moment of departure had arrived.

Fear, as I now know, has a colour and a taste, fear is something you can smell and feel. The colour of fear is yellow – that's not just an expression – and the taste is like stagnant water. Fear has a sour smell, like a leaking battery, and it feels like coarse sand-paper. Of all emotions, fear is the most treacherous, because its purpose is to save our lives and it can just as easily cost them.

After we had decided to flee, I asked the help of Saw Hsa Tu, who called in his brother. The former bicycle maker had assured me that we could not want for a more reliable travel agent. We would start with a bus journey, after which we would be met by someone who, it was agreed, would introduce himself as Jimmy. In a rattling Datsun pick-up, Jimmy would drive us to the village where our foot journey would begin. We would stay there for three days, until our group was complete. Besides Hser Hser Paw, my sister-in-law, my brother-in-law and me, the group included my father-in-law, three students from Rangoon (two youths and a girl), twelve bearers and two guides. Together we were lugging a fairly bizarre collection of domestic items, clothes, books and trinkets. To be able to transport my father-in-law, we had to leave part of our already quite limited baggage behind in the village. That didn't improve our mood.

For the first few days we walked every morning until the sun was directly overhead and it had grown so hot that nothing seemed to be moving except the toughest of insects. We looked for a shaded spot, preferably near running water, and rested for a few hours. Hser Hser Paw had trouble with her feet, her hips and her pelvis.

'Softening of the bones,' said Tamla Paw. 'Because of the

pregnancy.' Tamla Paw was in a position to know, she had spent years working at a maternity clinic.

For myself, I had blisters on both feet and after a couple of days they were badly infected. Tamla Paw had brought some ointment for just such a situation but it didn't help, or hardly. One morning, while pulling on my shoes, I saw something moving in one of the sores and was so shocked that I let out an embarrassingly bestial screech and hurled my shoe away with a wild gesture. Tamla Paw was not impressed by the minuscule maggots crawling around in the wound. Her small travelling first aid kit included a pair of tweezers, which she used to remove the creatures one at a time. With a triumphant gesture, she brought the first one up close to my face to give me a good look at the insignificant, harmless things that had terrified me so much.

'I should actually leave them in there,' said Tamla Paw. 'Maggots keep the wound clean.'

Although I didn't discover any more vermin in the days that followed, I suffered from visions of armies of gnawing insect larvae consuming me from the inside out. The only thing that helped against the pain and fear was the stupor of deep sleep, but that was something I struggled to resist. The jungle was too full of noises that were impossible to place for an unpractised ear and trying to interpret them only set off a whole new range of fears.

How could our guides be so sure that the snapping and swishing of branches were caused by a troop of monkeys and not by soldiers?

How did they know that that strange coughing noise was a pig and not a tiger choking on a big chunk of meat?

And why did they keep saying that everything was safe, while constantly maintaining a four-man guard around our camp, even in the middle of the day?

When the worst heat was over, we resumed marching until sunset. We slept on mats on the ground and in hammocks between trees. When darkness began to fall, some of our guides and bearers would climb trees and sleep on branches – half sitting, half lying, in a frighteningly precarious equilibrium. As the trek progressed, we penetrated deeper into the territory of the Karen National Union and more and more often we were offered a place to stay in a village or hamlet, miserable settlements of ten or twenty bamboo huts and a church. We spent a couple of nights at Buddhist monasteries. No one ever asked us who we were, where we came from or where we were going. The students from Rangoon spoke only in whispers and even then very rarely.

Our guides turned out to be experts at gathering food. For those with sufficient knowledge, the jungle of eastern Burma is a well-laid table. They found countless edible plants among the lush vegetation along the dozens of streams and brooks we passed. By using the mosquito nets we had brought with us, it was also easy to catch enough fish for the whole group almost every day. Hser Hser Paw had to steel herself to eat the small fish, which we generally threw live into the hot oil in the pan, and two Buddhist bearers refused to eat fish at all on religious grounds, but for the rest of us the catch of the day provided a welcome boost to our strained bodies.

The same applied to the snake that one of the bearers managed to kill one morning by beheading it with a single, well-aimed blow of his *dah*. All of the men accompanying us insisted that they were experienced hunters and could have easily provided us with fresh game every evening, except that they had decided to only use their guns in emergencies to avoid attracting the attention of army patrols or people who might betray us.

Once, when we had been delayed for a while in the morning after Tamla Paw had been stung by a scorpion (she had an ointment for that too, but first she had to cut the wound open to remove the poison and then she needed to staunch the bleeding), we walked on until long after sunset. More than anything else I remember the astonishing ease with which our guides and bearers moved through the darkness and Hser Hser Paw's sigh of despair after a thorny branch had left a bleeding slash on her face, 'Oh Lord, teach me how to see in the dark!'

It was no doubt completely unrelated, but that night she had her first attack of malaria.

A strange mechanical clicking slowly roused me from my sleep. The sound belonged in an urban environment and it was hard to reconcile it with a bamboo hut in a Karen village that had been left untouched by progress. It sounded like the ticking of a kitchen timer or the marching of tin soldiers. I lay on my back with my eyes open and listened. The sound was close at hand. I turned over on to my side to hear it better and, in that same instant, the clicking was interrupted by a deep, animal groan.

'Hser Hser Paw?! Hser Hser Paw, is that you?' I bent over towards her, seeking her face with my fingers. 'What's wrong!?' Her forehead was wet and felt strangely cold, as if the life had drained out of her. Hser Hser Paw was lying with her knees pulled up to her chest, her arms wrapped around her legs. Her teeth chattered and she groaned and sighed and wrestled with something that seemed to have taken possession of her body.

I need some light! I have to give her something to drink! I have to find some medicine to lower the fever! The baby! The baby in her womb! I have to calm down! Calmdowncalmdown! Calm . . . down.

Suddenly Hser Hser Paw sat up. Strands of hair were stuck to her face. She looked around wildly, her eyes big with fear. She shouted out a couple of incomprehensible words, then curled up again.

'Hser Hser Paw,' I said nervously, 'you've got a fever. You're sick. You have . . . I'm going to . . . Don't be scared! We'll make you better soon. I'll get you something to drink. Are you thirsty?!' (Calm, I thought, stay calm!)

Hser Hser Paw groaned.

'Saw? Saw, what's wrong?' A woman's voice.

'My wife is sick!'

I heard rummaging and then suddenly there was light. A young woman I couldn't remember seeing before was walking towards us with a kerosene lamp. She hung it up on a hook in the wall and squatted next to Hser Hser Paw. Gently she took Hser Hser Paw's hand, felt her pulse expertly, laid three fingers on her throat, then shook her head slowly. 'Does it hurt?' she asked quietly.

Hser Hser Paw nodded and groaned.

'Where? Your head?'

Again she nodded her head weakly.

'Where else? Your knees, your pelvis, your bones?'

Yes, Hser Hser Paw nodded, more intensely this time.

The young woman bent forward. 'You've got malaria,' she said. 'I'll look after you. It will pass, but it might take a while. I'll get you some water. Then I'll make a warm drink for you, you'll have to drink it all up.' Then she turned to me. Her face was as round as the full moon, without a single blemish. 'I'll take care of her,' she said gently. 'Try to get some sleep.'

I looked around. I was in a bare room, a barn perhaps. I tried to think where I was, but I could only find vague recollections of reaching a village late at night. There were mats around the sides of the room. People were lying on the mats under thin blankets. I recognised my sister-in-law, my brother-in-law and my father-in-law. I recognised the other members of our group. Everyone was asleep. Everyone, except Hser Hser Paw, the young woman and me. The woman was right, I had to get some more sleep. Tomorrow would be another long, hard day. But I didn't go back to sleep that night. I was kept awake by regiments of marching tin soldiers.

The next day we decided to stay in the village until Hser Hser Paw had recovered enough from her malaria. Someone said that we could use the rest. Someone said that the village was the safest place for miles around. Someone shot a dog, a black dog with white legs and two white spots above its eyes, like eyebrows on a negative. An old woman gutted it and skinned it. She pointed at the white spots. 'A dog with four eyes,' she said. 'The meat of four-eyed dogs is good for malaria fever.'

And so, for the first time in her life, Hser Hser Paw ate dog – without knowing it.

Two

This is how the Buddha described the first, happy years of his marriage to Yasodhara: 'I had three palaces, one for the cold season, one for the hot season, and one for the rainy season. During the four rainy months, I was entertained by female minstrels and never left my palace.'

The palaces that King Suddhodana built for his son were a delight to the eye, each more lavishly decorated than the other. At any hour of the day or night the young prince and his consort could indulge themselves in the arts of musicians, storytellers, jugglers and dancing girls. The trees in the palace gardens were full of exotic birds, the waters sparkled with glittering silver fish. When the young couple went for a walk, they were followed by dozens of servant girls, virgins who carried trays of delicacies, played musical instruments and cooled the royal couple with gorgeous fans. And still the king felt uneasy. Had not the sages and fortune-tellers foretold that his son, tormented by the suffering of mankind, would one day turn his back on his regal existence to live as a beggar among beggars? Unable to forget the prophecies, Suddhodana made sure that the young Siddhartha never heard bad news and was never confronted by the dark side of life: sorrow, decay or mortality. Whenever a dancer tired, another immediately took her place. As soon as a servant got his first grey hairs, he was removed from the prince's household. And every morning, before the prince awoke, gardeners picked up all the withered leaves that had fallen in the night.

And still the king felt uneasy.

One night he dreamed that his son left the palace wrapped in the shabby robes of a monk. The king woke with a start and immediately had the palace checked to make sure that the prince was still there. Siddhartha slept the calm sleep of the unknowing. The next day the king consulted a soothsayer. The soothsayer told him that he needed to go even further in his attempt to shield the prince from the suffering of the world. 'Make a pleasure garden that is so beautiful and so enchanting that the prince will never want to leave it again.' The king set to work immediately. He ordered his best gardeners and landscape architects to make a garden that was far superior to all other gardens, with hundreds of lookouts with beautiful panoramas and thousands of pools and streams that gleamed and glittered between shrubs and flowers like so many jewels; the trees bore the sweetest of fruit; the meadows were sown with the most fragrant flowers; and wherever you went you heard sweet-sounding birdsong. The garden was rightly called the Garden of Happiness.

There was only one problem: the Garden of Happiness lay just outside the royal city of Kapilavastu. To reach it the prince would have to leave his palace gardens and go through the streets of Kapilavastu, and then pass through the fields that surrounded the city. Because of this the king ordered that every house and every street be repaired and cleaned before Siddhartha went to visit the new pleasure garden. Things that were ugly were concealed behind large plants. All the houses were decorated with flowers and colourful silk ribbons. People were ordered to dress in their best clothes, and all those who were ugly, old, handicapped, ill or imperfect in any way were instructed to hide themselves so that the prince would not see them. Everything was prepared. On the great day, the prince drove out in his carriage through extravagantly decorated streets that were lined with cheering subjects, who strewed flowers out before him and sprinkled the road with precious perfumes. He left the city by the East Gate, and still nothing had woken him from his princely slumber.

But the king's efforts were not enough to foil the plans of the gods. As soon as the prince left the city he saw a man by the side of the road who was unlike anyone he had ever seen before: his hair was grey and his skin was wrinkled, his back was bent and the veins in his emaciated limbs were swollen and blue; a bestial growl issued from his lips.

'Who is that man?' the horrified prince asked his coachman. And the gods moved the coachman to tell him the truth. He said, 'That is what people call an old man, my lord.'

'Why is he called old?' the prince asked.

'Because he does not have long to live.'

'But does that mean that I too will one day grow old?'

'Yes, my lord,' answered the coachman, 'as will we all.'

The prince ordered him to turn back immediately.

Back in his palace, he said to himself, 'It is a scandal, this thing we call birth, if old age manifests itself like that in all who are born!'

The story goes that, after hearing what had happened, the king organised even greater festivities, with even more dancing girls, new magicians and jugglers who were skilled in the most miraculous of arts. But when the prince left for a second time to see the Garden of Happiness, something similar happened: after driving through the scrubbed and decorated streets, his coach left the city by the South Gate. A little later the prince saw a man lying by the side of the road, shivering from fever, with blood-shot eyes and groaning with every breath he took.

'What is wrong with that man?' the shocked prince asked his coachman.

And the coachman answered, 'That man is ill, my lord.'

'What does that mean, ill?'

'That means that a disease has taken control of his body and he is suffering great pain.'

'Can I also become ill?'

'Yes, my lord, you too, as can we all.' And again the prince returned to his palace disillusioned. And again his father tried to console him with even greater festivities.

On the third attempt the coach passed a funeral ceremony and the prince learned that he too, like all of us, would die. The fourth time the prince saw a man with a shaven head, dressed in simple robes. The man seemed completely unimpressed by the princely pomp and circumstance. He stood on the roadside untouched, in total peace.

'Who is that man?' asked the prince.

'That is a monk,' answered the coachman, 'someone who has gone away.'

'Gone away?'

'Gone away from home and hearth to lead a simple and virtuous life, to find peace of mind by doing good deeds and being gentle and kind to all living things.'

The prince then returned to his palace for the last time. He had discovered the truth about life: that everyone grows old, that everyone can fall ill and that everyone dies. And he had seen a man who did not seem to be affected by that knowledge, who had somehow found salvation. That night he saw the world around him with different eyes: he saw the dancing girls asleep, one snoring and groaning, the other with an open mouth and a trail of saliva running down her chin. He looked at his wife and saw her perfect beauty, but he knew that that too would be lost. Growing in his heart was an awareness that he would have to say goodbye: goodbye to all his princely riches, goodbye to his loved ones. He went to his father's bedroom and when the king woke up he heard his son say, 'Do not try to stop me any longer and do not be sad, because the hour of my departure has come.'

The king burst into tears and begged Siddhartha to stay. Siddhartha replied, 'I will stay if you can fulfil four wishes for me.'

'Wish anything you like!' exclaimed the king.

'Ensure that old age does not affect me, that my body is never ravaged by disease, that I will never die, and that you and Yasodhara, and all those I love, will never change.'

'That is beyond my power,' sighed Suddhodana mournfully. And Siddhartha told him that he would be gone before the full moon.

Of course we had not left without first visiting our parents. When we went to tell Hser Hser Paw's father, who had been a widower for many years, he cut his daughter off in mid-sentence. 'I'm coming,' he said, and we knew that nothing and no one could make him change his mind because the old man was as stubborn as an elephant. We would need to find a way to transport him because he was eighty-seven and no longer able to walk long distances.

'God will help us,' said Hser Hser Paw.

We arrived at my mother's late one afternoon. The golden glow from the setting sun moved me to look at our house closely for one last time. Only then did I notice how grey and rundown it was. The house next door, where Maung Maung Aye and his parents had once celebrated Id ul-Fitr with us, was empty; they had moved away a few years earlier. An early bat fluttered out through a windowless frame. I felt the full burden of life under a dictatorship pressing down on me. There was no more room for doubt: if we wanted to survive, if we wanted our child to have a life that was worth living, we had to go. Nothing my mother said would make me go back on our decision. That thought did not make the last few steps to the house any easier.

We found my mother in the front room, sitting at the long wooden table. Before her on the table lay a magazine, open at a photo of the Mahamuni Buddha in Mandalay. My mother was sitting bolt upright in a chair, eyes closed. She is dead! I thought for an instant, but in the moment that followed a deep sigh escaped from her chest and she opened her eyes.

How had I expected her to react to our plan? I don't know. I think that I had succeeded in banishing it from my conscious thoughts until the moment I stood before her. But what I hadn't taken into consideration, the thing I was not prepared for in any way at all, was her not reacting. She looked at me and from me to Hser Hser Paw. Then she nodded twice, almost imperceptibly, and said, 'I'll put on some tea. You must be thirsty.'

Later that night, long after it had grown dark outside, when the streets were silent except for the occasional bark of a dog, I raised the subject again. Again the only reaction was a slight nod of her head.

'My father is coming with us,' said Hser Hser Paw.

'Would you like that too?' I asked, unsure which answer would worry me the most, denial or agreement.

My mother smiled. At least, the thin lines of her mouth moved up a little in the corners. Then she shook her head. 'No,' she said. And again, 'No.' She straightened her back, held her chin proudly upright for a moment, and said, 'Don't worry about me. There are good people who look after me. They bring me food and when my time has come they will bury me. Go, and may God protect you.' That was all she said, until the next morning when we said goodbye.

'If your child is a boy,' my mother said, 'call him k'Paw Taw, 'the brand-new', so that everything in your life can be new and different. And if it's a girl, call her Hay Pla Hset Soe, 'she who shines brightly from afar'. I will watch out for her at night.'

Three

He introduced himself as Thra Kay Nay and invited me into his house on the edge of the village. An old man with a skinny, leathery body, he was wearing a colourful longyi, woven according to the traditions of the Karen, and a yellow T-shirt with a green collar. Stitched on to the left breast was a blue circle with the words ORDEM E PROGRESSO embroidered on it in white letters.

Thra Kay Nay noticed me looking and said, 'The shirt of the Brazilian football team. From a smuggler who goes to Thailand a lot. He says the Brazilians play the best football in the world.'

'It's a nice T-shirt,' I said.

He said, 'The butterflies love it.'

It was our fourth day in the village where Hser Hser Paw had come down with malaria. For three days I hadn't left her side, but today she seemed a little better. There had even been talk of moving on tomorrow morning; the rainy season was coming and once it started the trek through the jungle would become very hard, and probably too hard for us. To kill time and take my mind off things, I had gone for a walk around the village. Boredom fed my fears too much.

'Don't go into the forest alone,' they had told me. 'The village is protected by landmines.' Thra Kay Nay's house was as far as I dared to go.

The old man made tea for me. We sat down on the bamboo floor of the larger of the two rooms that made up his hut and he told me the story of his life, the way old people do when they meet strangers.

'I was born seventy-four years ago in this same village,' Thra Kay Nay said. 'And in all those years virtually nothing has changed. Except that people are a bit kinder to orphans these days. You wouldn't think it from my name, but I was an unwanted child.'

Kay nay means 'wished for and received', *thra* is the term of address for a teacher. Besides being wanted by the person who gave him that name, he must have also, at a later stage of his life, won the respect of the community as a teacher. I nodded and smiled encouragingly. Go on, I want to know it all! The thought that this man had already survived the perils of the jungle for seventy-four years reassured me a little. If he could do it, why shouldn't we?

'My father,' said Thra Kay Nay, 'was a married man; my mother, a young widow who had lost her husband in a hunting accident.'

One night, when the boy Kay Nay had reached an age at which he could form his own opinions about his life, an old woman from the village called him to her to tell him the tragic story that had preceded his birth. 'According to that woman,' Thra Kay Nay said, while blowing on his tea, 'my mother was already secretly in love with the man who would become my father before her husband died.'

The old woman told him that it was an untamed and untameable love that sprung direct from her heart and coursed through her veins like a hungry animal, like a dog that had gone wild. Until the evil day, just a few months after the death of her husband, when that love broke out and sunk its teeth into the weak flesh of its object, a man who was married with children but had decided to put that out of his mind for a moment. Then her womb, which had remained dry and barren through seven long years of marriage, bore fruit after all, and she knew that as soon as the swelling of her belly became visible, not just to her but to others, a great calamity would come down on the man she loved so deeply.

'In a village like this,' Thra Kay Nay said, 'the unwritten laws of the Karen are infinitely more important than the paper laws of the Burmese penal code. Amongst other things, those unwritten laws state that a married man who commits adultery deserves the death penalty.'

At university I had read about the customary law of the Karen, and in Pan Thar I had once defended a client who had been involved in a violent conflict in a village. The background to that case included the murder of an adulterous husband. Then, too, the customary law of the Karen was raised, but as the murder itself was never solved, there was no resolution as to the true motives of the murderer.

Thra Kay Nay said, 'It is possible to make an exception for a woman who is breastfeeding small children, but for a man the law is implacable: the only choice he has left is between dying at the hands of others or killing himself. After my mother told the adulterous husband that she was pregnant, he went home to get his *dah*. He told his wife that he was going to cut bamboo to make a new basket for the gamecock he entered in fights in the surrounding villages, and the next day his body was found, without the head. And no matter how thoroughly the villagers searched, that head was nowhere to be found.'

Kay Nay's mother carried him to term, but died from a broken heart seven weeks after his birth. 'In the end the call of my father's *k'la* was irresistible,' Thra Kay Nay said. 'And that had great consequences for the rest of my life.'

In the old days, long before the birth of the little Kay Nay, a Karen child that was orphaned would have been immediately chased away by the villagers, who were afraid that the evil spirit that was responsible for the misfortune that had befallen the child would go on to harm the rest of the village as well. Later that changed, and orphans were attributed with special powers, perhaps because some of them had managed to survive on their own in the jungle – something that could only be possible with the help of magic.

'When I was small,' Thra Kay Nay said, after slurping down the last drops of tea in his mug, 'the villagers held orphans in awe, but that included being afraid of them. My childhood years were very lonely. I fought that loneliness for a long time, until the day I realised that I would never defeat it. From then on, I was reconciled to my fate and, slowly but surely, I gained a place for myself in this small community. A place on the edge, it's true, but inside it, not outside it.'

The old man's flood of words was interrupted by the entrance of a pig. The animal rubbed its rough skin on the doorpost and snorted loudly. Thra Kay Nay jumped up with a speed I hadn't thought possible in such an old body. 'Get out, you!' he shrilled. The shocked pig turned tail and fled. 'Come with me,' said Thra Kay Nay, 'I'll give that beast something to eat, then I'll show you the village.'

The village had been built in a large shaded opening in the forest, a place where years before the undergrowth had been torched and the small trees cut down, leaving only the ancient giants of the forest. At eye level their trunks were bare and marked with the scars of old fires and it was only high above that they branched out into green crowns. Between the tall trees were hardwood and bamboo houses, with roofs made of branches and leaves, a few dozen structures with no two exactly the same, each made according to the needs and wishes of its inhabitants. Planted around the houses were fruit trees like mango, *nayji* and kapok, and flowering shrubs that offered protection from evil spirits. The biggest tree in the village, a magnificent fig that had far outlived the much smaller tree on which it had once began its parasitic life, was hung with garlands of flowers. In the many hollows of its trunk were candle stumps and pots with incense sticks, bottles of water, dishes of fruit and other offerings.

'This is where the spirit that protects our village lives,' Thra Kay Nay said, 'at least, as long as we look after it.'

Outside the village were the fields where the villagers grew their rice and their beans. As we walked down the narrow muddy paths that connected the fields, the old man told me about the years in which he had earned a living as a messenger, trader or representative for people from his own or neighbouring villages who needed someone they could trust who knew his way around the jungle. The medicine men he met on his travels taught him a great deal of traditional wisdom about medicinal plants, the uses of the organs of certain animals and the meaning of chance encounters with animals in the jungle.

'But I was never a naive believer,' Thra Kay Nay said. 'I took it all with a grain of salt and only embraced the things I considered useful and true.'

To his mind there was no doubt that the plant called *k'thi baw tho* offered protection from a great many diseases (although malaria was not one of them). 'But I would never recommend anyone to attack a tigress with cubs without any weapons in the belief that the power of *k'thi baw tho* also protects against the mightiest of wild animals, as some medicine men claim.'

He considered it nonsense to claim that the gallbladder of a wild swine could tell men anything about the future, but thought it true beyond a shadow of a doubt that the flight of certain birds had prophetic value. 'The birds,' he said, 'have saved my life many times, particularly in times of war. But take care! There are many misunderstandings about how to read signs from the animal kingdom. You can only draw reliable conclusions after a long study with lots of practical experience.'

'And what about four-eyed dogs?' I asked. 'Does eating the meat of four-eyed dogs help against malaria?'

He stopped at the edge of a field and stared intently at the young rice plants. After a while he said, 'If you believe that people are really concerned about you, trust their good advice.'

When he stopped suddenly for a second time a little later, I asked him about the landmines. He shrugged and said, 'Ah, those mines. They were laid so long ago that I would be very surprised if a single one of them still works. No one has ever fought over this place, people have good reason to call it the Forgotten Valley. Long after the big war, during my wanderings, I once met two Japanese soldiers who didn't know that their emperor had surrendered in August 1945. And a few years ago I met a bunch of Americans who were armed to the teeth with weapons I had never seen before. They were together with two fighters from the Karen Liberation Army. I watched them for a while from a hiding place, but I was too scared to approach them. Their weapons looked too dangerous.'

He turned around and we started back to the village.

'People always have to choose between two kinds of life,' he said when we were back at his house, 'a life of being visible or a life of being invisible. Sometimes it's good to choose the first and sometimes it's better to choose the second.'

By evening it was clear that the worst of the malaria attack was over. Hser Hser Paw's eyes were shining again and she ate the large piece of meat on her plate with gusto. She didn't ask what kind of meat it was.

When I told the others about visiting Thra Kay Nay, the girl with the full-moon face who had been looking after Hser Hser Paw said, 'Thra Kay Nay has learnt from the birds how to let his spirit rise up past the tallest trees and the mountain tops, so that he can look down on the world from above.'

When our guides decided to resume our journey in the morning, I was, for the first time since leaving Pan Thar, unafraid.

Four

You wake up from a dream only remembering the smells: mud, wet leaves, burnt flesh . . . It takes a while for you to find the pictures that go with the smells. Now you try to link the pictures together to make a story, the story of your dream, but you can't. They remain meaningless, without any context.

Mud.

Wet leaves.

Burnt flesh.

You are lying very still on your back and only vaguely aware of your body. Everything is happening inside your head. But because the dream keeps eluding you, refusing to be captured by your consciousness, you turn to the world around you for help: you want to bring the dreamed reality back by turning to the outside reality for help. You open your eyes. At least: you do your very best to open your eyes. Your brains send impulses to the muscles around your eyes that would normally make them open. And again. And again. But nothing happens. You feel yourself sinking back into dream. Except: now you don't want to! You resist, but that too fails. The dream is stronger than your fear, you are dragged back into night. It's not until hours later that you wake up again. All you remember of your dreams are the smells.

Sometimes you hear voices, distant but close. Sometimes you feel a gentle touch. You want to say something, but you can't move your mouth. Very gradually you become aware of a nagging pain in your face. It starts as an uncomfortable tingling, but gradually grows more intense, piercing. You try to raise a hand to your face to feel what's wrong. After a great struggle, you manage to move your hand, but you can't get it up past your chest. Now you discover that your chest is wrapped in bandages. You fade away again. Under your hand, your chest comes alive. You feel throbbing and wriggling, you hear a quiet gnawing. You try to move your hand away but it's too late. Hundreds of maggots and worms are creeping out through the bandages! They immediately start gnawing at your hand!

You call for help, but no noise comes out of your mouth.

With an extreme effort you succeed in moving your hand up to your face. Your face too is bandaged. Gingerly, you feel it. No worms. No maggots. You hear a woman's voice. The voice says your name, 'Saw Min Thein! Saw Min Thein?'

I lift my hand as a sign that I have heard her and recognise my name.

'Ah, you've come to, you've come to at last!' says the female voice.

Now I hear a second voice. Much weaker. It's like the voice of a young boy or maybe an old woman. The voice says something. I can't make out the words.

'That's good, Tommy,' the female voice says. 'I'll get it for you in a minute.'

Tommy . . . Do I know a Tommy? I don't know any Tommies.

'Saw Min Thein?' The female voice is very close now. I turn my head towards the sound. 'Lie still,' the woman tells me. 'Move as little as possible. There was an attack, Saw Min Thein. You were hit by shrapnel. Your face is covered with bandages. But the operation went well. You were terribly lucky.'

Again I hear the boy's voice from further away.

'I have to see to Tommy. Don't go anywhere.' She laughs for a second and for a moment, just for a moment, I think I recognise her voice.

I drifted off again. For how long? An hour? A day? A week?

A boy's voice woke me up, close to my ear. The voice was singing a song, 'Come on, come on, come on out. Come on, come on . . .'

I asked, 'Who are you?'

I asked, 'What happened to me?'

Tommy said, 'You're blind. They don't want to tell you yet, but you'll never see again.'

Tommy said, 'I lost two fingers from my left hand. I was lucky.'

Tommy said, 'I thought they'd shoot me. That would have made more sense than this.'

Tommy said, 'Don't be angry at me.'

It was hot, unmercifully hot. The bandages around my head and upper body were drenched with sweat. I was itchy everywhere, but I couldn't scratch. A fly landed on my leg, let me chase it away, landed again, let me chase it away again, landed, walked around a little.

I said, 'Is it true?'

'Yes, it's true.'

'Tommy, there was a pregnant woman. Do you know where she is?'

Tommy didn't answer.

At night sounds get paler: first the red drains out of them, then the yellow, and finally the blue as well, so that in the depths of the night every sound, whether it's the slightest rustling of a leaf or the distant cry of a wild animal, is a chilling white, like the light of the stars.

Why do we populate the nighttime sky with mythical creatures and tell each other stories about the people of the stars? To reassure ourselves, to dispel the terrifying idea that we might actually be alone in the cold black infinity of the universe. For a similar reason we sit around campfires and kerosene lamps at night to tell each other stories about lives: our own and the lives of our loved ones.

One night, in the quietest, whitest hour, the hour before the first cockcrow, I heard a voice, close to my ear. '*Saya* . . .' whispered the voice. 'U Min Thein!'

'Tommy?'

'It wasn't my fault, *saya*, I couldn't . . . I didn't have anything to do with it.'

'Anything to do with what, Tommy? What didn't you have anything to do with?'

'With the woman with a baby in her stomach.'

'What happened, Tommy? Can you tell me what happened? Come and sit on my bed.'

I felt him climb on to my bed. He didn't seem very big, just a child, ten maybe, twelve at the most, judging from his weight and the way he was talking to me.

'I knew something was going to happen all day,' Tommy said. 'When something's going to happen, they don't talk as much as usual, they leave me alone more.'

'Who are "they", Tommy?'

'The soldiers, my . . . I was with a battalion from the Fifth Division.'

'Which battalion?'

'We called ourselves the Black Tigers.'

'How long had you been with the Black Tigers?'

'I don't know exactly. More than a year, I think.'

'Tommy?'

'Yes.'

'How old are you?'

He didn't answer immediately. Then he said, 'Fifteen.'

I could tell from the way he said it that he was lying. 'Fifteen,' I repeated.

'Yes.'

'And what happened then?'

207

'When night fell everyone got nervous. I was ordered to stay near Kyaw Win. I was glad of that. Kyaw Win is a nice man, even if he is a soldier. Kyaw Win used to be an oozie, an elephant driver, like my father. My father was the best oozie in all of Burma! And he taught me everything he knew. I was already a pejeik when I . . .'

'A pejeik?' I asked.

'Yes, don't you know what that is, a pejeik?'

'No, I don't.'

'That's the assistant, he helps the oozie and gets to ride along on the back of the elephant.'

I could tell from his voice that he was relieved about being able to talk about the elephant and his father instead of what happened on that fatal night. I let him. Maybe I would rather talk about elephants as well.

'When I was still very little,' Tommy continued confidently, 'my father would take me with him in the morning when he went out to look for his elephant. At night we let the elephants wander free in the jungle, did you know that? So they can find their own food.'

'Don't they go away?' I asked.

'Oh, yes! You have to find them again.'

'How? How on earth do you track down an elephant in the jungle?'

Tommy laughed. He had shrugged off all reticence. 'The main thing is knowing your own elephant. How does it put down its feet? What kind of prints does it leave in the mud? On which side of the path does it throw away the branches after eating the leaves off them, left or right? And the dung is important. The dung is maybe the most important of all.'

'Why?'

'If there's bamboo in the dung, that means it ate bamboo in the night and it will be looking for something else, like sugar-cane. Then you have to look in the sugarcane. They love that, elephants, wild sugarcane. When you get to the sugarcane you have to wait patiently. You can't just walk into the cane and start looking for your elephant, that's way too dangerous. There could be tigers in there, and bears. You could scare your elephant and make it do something unexpected. First you have to listen and see if you can hear it. All tame elephants wear a bell and every bell is different. That's how you recognise your own elephant.'

'And once you've heard it?'

'Then you have to lure it, with a song.'

'A song?'

'That's right. So the elephant can recognise your voice and feel at ease. My father had a beautiful singing voice. Come on, come on, come on out!' The soft thin sound of a child's voice. 'Come on, come on . . . Until it finally appeared, the elephant. And then you have to call "*Mek, mek!*" and see whether it'll go down on its knees for you. Because you've taught it to do that, to kneel down with its front legs when you call "*Mek, mek!*" But sometimes a tame elephant has met wild elephants in the jungle at night and then it won't listen. You can't just saddle it straight away, that's too dangerous. You have to tame it again first.'

'You really know a lot about it, Tommy,' I said.

'I would definitely have become the youngest oozie in the camp if it hadn't been for them.'

'The Black Tigers?'

'Yes, the Black Tigers.'

We had to talk about it. I needed to know exactly what had happened, how it had happened. There was a big black lump in my head, clotted blood, clotted fear . . . It was blocking everything. That lump had to go. But the boyish voice was luring me – I let it lure me.

You are a child in an elephant camp in the jungle. Your mother died when you were three years old. She died giving birth to your younger brother. Your baby brother lived for a week, then he died too. Your father is your everything, your father and his elephant. One day a buzz goes through the camp. Someone's spotted a herd of wild elephants, a herd that includes a few calves that could be tamed. Six men are chosen to track the herd, one of them is your father. He takes his tranquilliser gun and a small backpack. While he's gone, you will be in charge of his elephant. Someone is designated to help you, but it will be your responsibility, you know your father's elephant better than any other oozie there is!

You are so proud and excited that you can hardly wait to say goodbye to your father.

How could you know that it would be the last time you would ever speak to him?

For eight days you look after your father's elephant. For eight mornings in a row you successfully track him down in the jungle, even though it takes so long one morning that the sweat is running down your back and you are about to burst into tears. And just then you hear the quiet tinkling of the bell, the bell you would recognise out of thousands! You almost rush into the bushes to find the animal and hug it, that's how grateful you are, and proud.

Late at night on the eighth day, two of the six hunters return to the camp. You are already asleep, but they wake you up. 'For three days we were close on the heels of the herd, but they kept slipping away from us,' the hunters explain. 'Then we bumped into an army unit. We were polite to them. We gave them some of our water to drink and shared the meat of a monkey we had shot that morning with them. Then they wanted to know where we were coming from and what we were doing there. They wanted our guns. We said they were tranquilliser guns, that we needed them to shoot elephants and that they wouldn't be any use to them anyway. They didn't agree. Whether we wanted to or not, we had to give them our guns. There was an argument, then a fight. Shots were fired.'

They glance at you, for just an instant.

'Your father was wounded,' they say. 'The soldiers rounded us up. "You're coming with us," they said. "You can carry our gear and do other work for us. You can even tame an elephant for us, if you're that good at it. We'll shoot anyone who tries to escape." That's what they said. But we still escaped, us two. We don't know what happened to the others.'

They glance at you again.

You walk back to your father's hut. You look through his things. You find an old pocket-knife and a rusty *hkyun*, the first elephant hook your father ever owned, the one his father gave him, the grandfather you never knew because he was crushed against a tree by his own elephant before you were born. You wait until everyone is asleep and then you sneak out of the camp.

You're going to free your father.

Five

I knew this much: the village had been attacked; I had been hit by shrapnel; one of the pieces had ended up in my good eye; I would never see again; and Hser Hser Paw had been killed in the attack, Hser Hser Paw who was carrying my child. I was sure that I felt terribly sorrowful about this loss, but the sorrow couldn't get past that clot of fear.

My sister-in-law, my brother-in-law and my father-in-law were only lightly wounded. The three students from Rangoon disappeared – no one knew what had happened to them. Seven villagers died, among them two small children. Everyone who could run fled into the jungle and stayed there, terrified of another attack. Whether or not Thra Kay Nay had survived was unknown.

I knew this too: a boy had fought on the side of the government troops, a child soldier called Tommy; he was left behind wounded when his battalion withdrew; he had lost two fingers from his left hand; he had come through it better than me. But I was thirty-five and already had half a life behind me; Tommy's life hadn't yet begun. He was supposed to become an oozie, like his father and his father before him. He would have been the youngest oozie of all. He had sung at the edge of the sugarcane field and his father's elephant had heard him.

And now he was lying here, on a camp bed in a field hospital in the jungle, being cared for by a nurse called Magdalena who came to his bed three times a day to sit and pray for him, just as Hser Hser Paw had prayed for years for a child . . .

Standing by the door day and night were two fighters from the Karen Liberation Army, soldiers Tommy didn't know, men he had never seen before, who, a few days earlier, had been his enemies – the enemies of the Black Tigers.

While lying on my camp bed and staring at the patchy blackness before my eyes, I made a decision: as long as Tommy was still in the clinic, I would do everything in my power to give him the courage to live on. After that I would wait until I was strong enough to leave. There was a river not far from the hospital, in the still of night I could hear it gurgling and splashing, especially after heavy rain. I would grope my way through the darkness, heading for the sound. I would throw myself in the water.

I don't remember the moment as a child that I first became aware of the existence of elephants as a species, but I do remember the very first time I saw one in the flesh. We were sitting in the back of the car, my brother and I – my father was driving and my mother was in the front passenger seat. We were on our way to my grandfather's farm. It was raining. It was raining so hard that my father had to drive at walking pace, even in those places where the road wasn't full of potholes and cracks. The side windows of the car were misted over; if we wanted to see anything, we had to look through the windscreen. My mother kept it clean with a cloth. We jostled for position in the middle of the back seat, with me holding tight to the back of my father's seat to stop Ngar Yoo from pushing me aside. My father grumbled for us to calm down. My mother said, 'As soon as it clears up, we'll stop somewhere for tea and something to eat.' In a tone of voice as if she was doing us a big favour.

Ngar Yoo said, 'Hey, what's that?!'

In that instant my father stamped on the brake and, although we were only driving slowly, we both shot forward, my brother and I, between the two front seats. If our bottoms hadn't jammed together between the sides of the seats, we would have definitely bashed up against the dashboard. Now the damage was limited to a sore spot just under my right ear, where Ngar Yoo's hard head had banged mine. Almost immediately a big purple bump started to come up on his forehead.

My father said, 'It's your own fault, Ngar Yoo!'

And my mother said, 'Look, boys, look what's coming.'

While my father tried to restart the stalled engine, an elephant emerged from the grey curtain in front of us. The massive animal was gleaming wet and seemed to be swathed in a fine mist of raindrops, splashes, and clouds of evaporating elephant sweat. A trickle of water was dripping from the end of its trunk. Seated on the elephant's head was a man in a torn shirt and brightly coloured shorts. He was holding an umbrella over his head, but it didn't really help. As the elephant swayed closer, my father grew more and more impatient, as if afraid that the enormous animal would crush our Morris Minor, my father's prize possession, with a single sweep of its tusks or mighty trunk. And that fear might not have been entirely unfounded – in the eighteen months he had left to live, Ngar Yoo would regularly shove newspaper reports under my nose about the damage caused by elephants to crops, houses, cars and what-not.

'An elephant!' shouted Ngar Yoo, immediately forgetting his sore head. 'An elephant!' I repeated. The engine started. My father moved the car as far as he could to the side of the road and drove on in a hurry.

'We wanted to see the elephant!' Ngar Yoo shouted indignantly.

'Yes!' I shouted, trying to cram as much indignation in that one word as my brother had put into a whole sentence. But my father was implacable. Ngar Yoo and I were able to catch a glimpse of the elephant's impressive backside through the misted rear window, but the curtain of rain soon hid the animal completely.

Tommy thought about it. Tommy said, 'An oozie with an umbrella . . . Maybe it was a circus elephant?'

Tommy asked, 'What's a Morris Minor?'

Tommy asked, 'Why was your brother called Ngar Yoo?'

Tommy asked, 'What does your brother do now?'

The afternoons. The afternoons were the worst. Especially when it rained in the morning. Then the air got so hot and muggy, so damp and dirty, that it was like gagging on filthy rags. We didn't talk on afternoons like that, Tommy and I. We lay on our beds in silence. Now and then I heard him sigh. Now and then he turned over. Swatting away an insect. Wiping his face. Sitting up. Lying down again. I listened tensely to every noise he made. The more I concentrated on him, the less I had to think about myself.

Self-pity is addictive.

Why didn't they leave me there, lying in the mud between the burning houses? Why didn't they let me bleed to death, leaving my body behind for the ants and termites, the vultures and the other scavengers?

What made them think they were doing me a favour by saving my life?

For days I had been trying to remember what preceded the attack. Where was I when it happened? Why wasn't I with Hser Hser Paw? Hser Hser Paw believed in a righteous God, a loving God, the God of Abraham and King David. Hser Hser Paw also believed in the love and mercy of Jesus Christ, the Nazarene. What help was that?

What use is your God to me, Hser Hser Paw? What kind of God takes you and our unborn child and leaves me lying in the mud so that the brave fighters of the Karen Liberation Army can find me and take me to their field hospital, where they operate on me and save my life, so I can say, I am blind, but at least I'm not dead? What did I do to deserve that? How did I offend Him?

How did you offend Him?

There is no mercy, no love, no charity, there is no loving God, no God that brings light into darkness, no salvation or forgiveness, there is only the mud from which we are born and to which we will return, and in between there is our miserable existence, full of meaningless suffering, inflicted by our fellows, full of meaningless loss, by drowning or disease, by unnecessary attacks that were unpreventable and have no deeper meaning, that serve no higher purpose, that only make you desperate and numb, that make you realise that we are surrounded by a thousand shades of black, yes, that everything is futile and purposeless, as meaningless as the life of a moth that sputters out in the flickering flame of a candle that gutters and is blown out by the wind a little later.

Tommy said, 'U Min Thein, do you speak English?'

'Yes.'

'Will you teach me English?'

'It's very difficult, Tommy. You need books for that. And time, a lot of time.'

'We've got plenty of time, haven't we?'

'But we don't have any books. And if we had them, I wouldn't be able to see them. Can you even read? Tommy? Can you read? Someone could teach you how to read, Tommy. Maybe someone can even teach you English. Of course someone can teach you English! When you're better, you can go to Manerplaw. They've got schools there. They'll teach you English. Have you heard of Manerplaw? Do you know where that is, what it is?'

'Manerplaw is a stinking cesspit full of rats and flies that carry diseases that make you rot away,' said Tommy.

'Did they say that? Is that what the Black Tigers said about Manerplaw? Don't believe them, Tommy! They said that to scare you. To get you to fight the Karen with them. Manerplaw is the base camp of the Karen National Union, it is the capital of

Ka-Thoo-Lei, that's what the Karen call their land, *ka-thoo-lei*, the land of the burnt earth. Because that's how the Karen lived for centuries, and some Karen still live like that even now: they burn part of the jungle and plant their vegetables and rice there. And when the soil is exhausted, they give it back to the forest and move on. And the forest embraces the exhausted ground and gives it new strength, making it fertile again, so that after a while it will once again be suited to serving as a field for the Karen. It was like that for thousands of years and it can be like that again, if the Karen are free to live the way they want, if the Burmans leave them in peace, if they . . .'

'I'm not Karen. I don't want to go to Manerplaw. They'll kill me because I'm not like them.'

'No, Tommy, no! I'm not Karen either!'

'You speak their language! Don't tell me you're not Karen!'

'My mother is Karen, Tommy, but not my father. I'm just a poor half-blood. But that doesn't matter. There's a place there for me. There's a place there for you too!'

Oh, the unbearable heat! The itch that's driving me mad! The pain in my bones and muscles!

Let's not talk any more. Let's be quiet. Just listen to the crickets. Quiet, Tommy, please, be quiet. You're right, it's not true, they won't receive you with open arms in Manerplaw, you don't speak their language, you're a Burman, you're the enemy. You've been lucky, this time, they let you live, they even saved your life. You see, there are good people and bad people. The good ones save your life, the bad ones shoot you dead, or worse: they use you as a beast of burden, a mule, they make you slave until you drop. And then they push you to the edge of the path with their boots and give you a nudge to send you rolling down the mountainside, cutting open your face and hands on thorny shrubs, breaking your bones on boulders, and then they leave you to lie in the scorching sun or the pouring rain, they leave you lying there as live bait for ants and termites, and at night the wild pigs will come and tear your ravaged body to shreds and no one will shed a tear.

'Tommy? Tommy, I've got a plan. Shall we go to Manerplaw together, you and I? Then I'll teach you English on the way, and Karen. And we'll . . .'

'You're blind, U Min Thein! You're a blind old man! And I don't know the way to Manerplaw. We'll get lost. We'll starve. They'll find us, the Black Tigers, or the troops of the Karen, and they'll shoot us! If only they'd done that before. They should have finished me off straightaway. And you too! Why did they kill my father but not you? You're a useless blind man! And I'm a useless boy with one good hand and it's not even the right one!'

'Tommy? Tommy?'

'I wish I was dead.'

Not being able to go to him then, that was the worst of all.

Six

One morning I woke up with a head full of thoughts about the last days before the attack, as if my memories had been on a secret journey and returned home in the night, under cover of darkness. I heard an old man called Thra Kay Nay speak comforting works about a Forgotten Valley. I saw Hser Hser Paw lying pregnant and sweating on a mat in a gloomy room without windows. Her eyes were closed, there was spit in the corners of her mouth and now and then she made quiet noises that suggested intense pain and high fever. I saw her elderly father bending over her anxiously and trying to console her, and I felt again what I had felt then: a pang of jealousy about the bond between them and sorrow about the death of my own father, whom I hadn't seen at all in the final two years of his life – that last time excepted – but had been estranged from for so much longer.

How ill was Hser Hser Paw by that time? How great was her chance of surviving the disease? And what were the baby's chances?

A woman's voice called me back to the present – and again, for a moment, it was as if it was her voice, the voice of Hser Hser Paw.

But Hser Hser Paw was dead.

I said it to myself, I said it to the woman standing next to my bed, a nurse called Magdalena: 'Hser Hser Paw is dead. Hser Hser Paw is dead.'

The Burmese army assault on the village where we were

stranded because of her illness had made all questions about her chances of surviving the malaria superfluous.

'Saw Min Thein?' said Sister Magdalena.

'Yes?'

'There's someone here for you, Saw Min Thein. Someone has come to fetch you.'

'To fetch me? But I don't want to go anywhere.'

'It's Pastor Marcus from . . .'

'What did you say? A pastor?' I laughed. 'Has a pastor come to fetch me?'

The laughter was like a soothing flood of warm water, lifting me up and carrying me off. Soon I gave in to it completely, laughing without measure or restraint, like a little girl. I was fully aware of how odd, and even inappropriate, my behaviour was, but I didn't care. What difference did it make what this minister thought of me, or this nurse in a godforsaken field hospital in the jungles of eastern Burma? I'm going to die! Hooray, I'm going to die! And they've sent a minister to fetch me, how thoughtful! Ha-ha-ha-ha!

'Saw . . . Saw Min Thein?'

I got a grip on myself, reluctantly. 'Yes, sister, go ahead and introduce me to the pastor. I'm sorry, I . . .'

I heard her footsteps moving away from me. I was still hiccupping a little. In a quiet voice the nurse exchanged a few words with someone who must have been the minister. Then I heard heavier footsteps coming towards me.

'Saw Min Thein? Marcus, Pastor Marcus. I have come from Manerplaw to get you.'

Strange, I thought, suddenly Rangoon and my years at university popped into my mind. And her, of course . . . Yi Yi Win.

'Your father-in-law sends his fondest regards,' the minister continued. 'He is well, given the circumstances.'

I realised that it was his accent. He spoke Karen, but it was the kind of Karen I had heard in the bus in Rangoon, from workers from Insein.

'You come from Rangoon, don't you?' I asked.

'That's right,' he said. 'Do you know Rangoon?'

'I went to university there.'

'I taught at the Theological College, on Missionary Hill in Insein.'

'But now you live and work in Manerplaw.'

'I'm based there, you could say. My wife and children live there. And I travel from village to village to speak to church leaders and the faithful.'

'My mother is a Baptist,' I said.

'Where is your mother from?'

'Min Won.'

'Ah,' he said, 'I used to go there often! There was a minister there, come now, what was his name again . . .'

'My father-in-law is in Manerplaw, you say?'

'Uh, yes . . . I'm sorry. He is doing reasonably well. Physically he has made a full recovery, but emotionally, the loss of his daughter . . . your wife, and the child . . .'

'The child hadn't been born yet,' I said. 'There wasn't any child, only the promise of a child.' (I was speaking to myself more than to him, but he wasn't to know that.)

'Really?' He sounded genuinely surprised. 'Your father-in-law spoke about it as if he had already held it in his arms, as if . . .'

'There were two other people in our group, my sister-in-law, Naw Tamla Paw, and her husband, Saw Ta Doh . . .'

'They were taken to Manerplaw first as well, along with your father-in-law. But afterwards they left for Thailand. Your father-in-law didn't have the energy for that. How they are now, I don't know. But it's not that far from Manerplaw to the border and the area is firmly in KNU hands. So I expect they would have arrived safely. In Thailand there are big camps where . . .'

'Why have you come to fetch me? What is there in Maner-plaw for me? Or in those camps?'

'You can't stay here, Saw Min Thein. It's much too dangerous. And there aren't enough doctors in this district. When was the last time a doctor came to see you?'

'What use is a doctor to me? Listen, Pastor Marcus, I appre-ciate your good intentions, I realise that you've made a long and dangerous journey to visit me here . . .'

'I was already in the neighbourhood,' he protested.

'But it's better for you to leave me behind. What kind of future do I have in Manerplaw? What kind of future do I have anywhere? I'm blind and I'm going to stay blind.'

'I know that.'

'But you don't know what it means to be blind. You don't have any idea! I scarcely know myself . . .'

And suddenly she was there again, in my thoughts. The picture was crystal clear, sparkling in the morning light: Yi Yi Win! Why was I thinking of her now? Why was I tormenting myself with that image, those eyes, that smile . . . I should have been thinking of Hser Hser Paw, my poor dead wife, I should . . .

'To keep it short, pastor, and please don't take it personally, but I'd like to ask you to leave. Give my regards to my father-in-law, may God give him strength in these sorrowful days.'

The problem was that the pastor wouldn't be dismissed. He stated simply that there was no question of his leaving without me. I said that I could only shuffle along, that up till now I had only walked a hundred feet at most, and never unaided. He said that we would travel by river until we could find somewhere with bearers and maybe an elephant.

'An elephant?' I said. 'Did you hear that, Tommy? The pastor wants to travel by elephant!'

'Where are we going?' asked Tommy.

I only have vague memories of the journey that followed. The one thing I can recall clearly without effort is the fear, the fear that didn't leave me for a moment, almost suffocating me, paralysing me. How could my feet find their way in the darkness that surrounded me? Where could I find something to hold on to? I sat in the narrow boat that took us downstream, further and further from the sea. ('The rivers here don't flow to sea, the rivers here flow to the north,' echoed through my thoughts.) I was too scared to move. The boat carried us through a tunnel of cool, shaded air that was only occasionally pierced by a ray of sunlight, which I felt on my skin but didn't see, although I did seem to detect a difference in the colour of black before my eyes. For hours no one spoke. The only sound was the humming of the motor, the splashing of the water, and now and then the call of a bird. When we finally reached the place where we would continue by elephant, it took four men to lift me out of the boat: I couldn't move a limb.

We spent the night in a house which smelt of dried tobacco leaves. I didn't sleep. I waited for the first shot, the whistle of an incoming shell, the cries of soldiers, the shrieks of women and children. I waited for salvation.

During the journey on the elephant's back they had to tie me to the seat – without sight it was impossible for me to keep my balance. The descents especially were hellish. Often the elephant leaned so far forward that I felt like I was hanging upside-down. Eventually I lost all sense of direction. I didn't know up from down, I couldn't say whether we were moving forwards or backwards. It was like being rolled down a mountain in a barrel. I vomited bile.

They say that the journey took four days, but when we arrived in Manerplaw, I was an old man.

They say that Tommy didn't leave my side the whole trip. But if someone were to claim that Tommy was picked up from his hospital bed by a gigantic bird that flew to Manerplaw with him in its claws, I could just as well believe that. I don't have a single memory of Tommy's presence – not even of the moment that he was reunited with his precious elephants.

They say that I met my father-in-law in Manerplaw. I believe it, but I don't remember. My father-in-law is buried in Manerplaw. He died during a Burmese air force bombing raid, two days after Tommy and I had travelled on to a refugee camp in Thailand.

The bad news followed along behind.

'Pastor Marcus is here!' I heard Tommy call. 'U Min Thein, Pastor Marcus has arrived!'

He shouted it from a distance. It wasn't like him to raise his voice. We had been in the camp for three months, but Tommy hadn't felt at ease for a single moment. We were sharing a hut on a hillside. It wasn't a convenient location for a blind man, the path to get there was steep and slippery. But Tommy had rejected all suggestion of moving. When I kept on insisting, he finally told me why. 'U Min Thein,' he said, 'We can get away from here. The forest starts just behind our hut.'

I stopped insisting.

I was teaching him Karen and he was an apt pupil, although ashamed of his accent. And he didn't trust anyone. At night I often heard him creeping around the hut. I suspected that he was looking out on all sides to make sure no danger was approaching. Sometimes I woke with a start to the sound of his screams – he had terrible nightmares. When they came back he stayed in his room for days on end and refused to talk to anyone. On days like that I was glad that Tamla Paw and Ta Doh were there. They made sure I didn't die of hunger or thirst.

Tommy rushed into the hut. 'Come on!' he shouted, grabbing my arm. 'Come on!' He was so excited that going down the hill I had to do my very best to keep up with him – and avoid falling.

'I didn't know,' I said, wading the river that splits the camp in two, 'that you were so crazy about Pastor Marcus.'

Tommy hesitated for a moment, then said, 'He saved our lives.'

'Pastor Marcus?'

'Yes,' he said, 'without him we would never have got away from that hospital. Not alive, anyway.'

I thought about that while Tommy led me to a part of the camp I hadn't been to before. Now I was the one who felt ill at ease.

'What if I'd listened to you?' said Tommy as he led me down a path that was buttressed with nylon bags full of large pebbles. 'And gone to Manerplaw with just the two of us? How far do you think we'd have got?'

'You're right,' I said, feeling miserable and, more than that, useless. The next instant I was angry at Tommy. Ungrateful dog, I thought.

The pastor had arrived with his family: his father, his wife and his two daughters. He introduced them to me one at a time and suddenly I thought I knew why Tommy was being so enthusiastic. The second girl laid a hand on my arm to greet me and for a moment I was no longer in the office of the head of the camp – where newly arrived refugees have to register – but in a stadium in Rangoon, where the body of the great U Thant was lying in state, I felt a hand on my arm.

Was it possible that Tommy was in love with this girl? He had just turned thirteen, a great age for puppy love. One glance at the two of them would have been enough, a single glance! But that was futile to wish for.

How could I live among so many riddles?

How could I ever learn how to cope with such an enormous lack?

I had to do something! I had to enlarge my world, my *knowledge*. I told Tommy, 'Come here.'

Tommy stepped towards me. 'Closer.'

He did what I asked. He was standing in front of me. I took him by the shoulders. Then I raised my hands and put them on his head. I felt his hair. Shoulder length. I felt his ears. Small, close to his head. I felt his neck. Broad, strong. His shoulders. His arms.

No one spoke. I bent my knees and felt his legs, his feet. He had the broad, callused feet of someone who has grown up without shoes.

'I suddenly had to know who you were,' I said, standing up again. 'Pastor Marcus?!'

Everyone laughed. It was a liberating laugh.

When we had stopped laughing, Pastor Marcus said, 'I have bad news for you, Saw Min Thein, and even worse news for your sister-in-law.'

That was how we heard about the bombing of Manerplaw and the death of my father-in-law.

There is a story the Karen tell about themselves, a story I heard Pastor Marcus tell Tommy not long after he arrived to settle in the camp with his family and founded the Bible school where Tommy would learn to read and write and where he would learn English from the King James Bible.

'The Karen,' said Pastor Marcus, 'have a historical role to play in Burma. We were the first inhabitants of this land, did you know that? We, the Karen, were here before the Burmans and the Shan and the Kachin, we were the first. And where did we come from? We came from the land of Abraham, Mesopotamia, the land of the Euphrates and the Tigris. We are descendants of Abraham, the patriarch!'

Pastor Marcus said, 'What is the Hebrew word for God? Yahweh. And what do the Karen call their god? Y'wa! And which qualities do we attribute to him? We call him, our father. We honour him as the creator of all that lives. We say, "When the earth was made, it was Y'wa who made it; when the earth was populated, it was Y'wa who populated it." Y'wa is eternal. He existed long before the beginning of time and he will exist long after this world has passed away. Y'wa is immutable, omnipotent and omniscient. That is how we think of our god – and Abraham thought about Yahweh in exactly the same way.

'Can you imagine how surprised the first missionaries to Burma were? In between millions of Buddhists and animists they found one tribe that believed in the same god as they did: the Karen. And what stories did the Karen tell about their god? This story for example. One day the god Y'wa spoke to the first human couple he had created, saying, "I will make a garden for you, and in that garden there will be seven kinds of trees that will bear seven kinds of fruit. And you will eat of all those fruits, except one. You will not eat of that one fruit. If you do, you will become sick and old, you will die. And once every seven days I will come to you to see how you are and whether you honour my word."

'Not long afterwards they were visited by the devil, who came to them in the form of a snake. And what did he tell them, after they had told him about the seven fruits of which they were only allowed to eat six? He said that God had deceived them. That if they ate of that fruit they would be able to fly to the highest heavens and descend to the bowels of the earth! That was what the devil said. And who believed him? The woman! She let him talk her into ignoring the word of God and eating the forbidden fruit. And once she had done that, the devil laughed and said, "Convince your husband to eat this fruit now as well, because if God is right, you will fall sick and grow old and leave your husband behind alone, and if I am right, you will soon be flying through the heavens and descending to the bowels of the earth, but you will be there alone, without the man you love. You must give him the fruit out of love for him." The woman did what the snake asked of her and finally managed to convince her husband, and so they left the straight and narrow path of Y'wa, just as Adam and Eve left the path of Yahweh.'

Pastor Marcus said, 'The story goes on. From the moment that the first people trusted the word of the devil, they were at the mercy of his whims. Not only did they become sick and old and mortal, they also had no choice but to turn to him to avert all those calamities. When their first child fell ill, the devil killed a pig and cut out its gallbladder. "If the gallbladder of a pig is round and firm," the devil said, "that is a favourable omen and the child will recover. But if the gallbladder is flaccid and shapeless, there is no hope." When the child made a miraculous recovery, the parents thanked the spirits with a ceremony, just as the devil had taught them. And thus the Karen became more and more entangled in the web of idolatry and the occult. But the hope that they would one day return to the straight and narrow path was not lost entirely. Because a story that was passed down from generation to generation spoke of a Golden Book, *Lei Htoo*, in which the will of God was recorded. The Karen had once possessed that book, but it had been lost. One day, the story promised, it would be returned to them by someone called "the white brother". And that white brother came! And he brought us a book with gilt-edged pages! And that is why so many Karen have converted to Christianity since the arrival of the first missionaries in 1813.'

Pastor Marcus taught Tommy these words of Jesus, whom the believers call the Son of God, 'Truly I say to you, all sins shall be forgiven the sons of men.' And Tommy wrote those words down, in Karen, and stuck the piece of paper up above the door of our house on the hill on the edge of the camp.

And Tommy became a Christian.

Eight

One of the many disturbing discoveries I made in the first year of my blindness was that I had almost no sense of smell. I had never stopped to think about whether or not I had a good nose. As a child I breathed in the smell of the oil my mother rubbed on her skin, as an adult I liked to bury my nose in Hser Hser Paw's hair at night and smell the flowers she had worn in it during the day. And, like everyone else, I hated the acrid smell of fish paste. It was only after being blinded that I noticed the lack of subtlety in my sense of smell, how crude and hopelessly limited the perceptions I was able to make with it were. I wished I had a nose like a dog. I think my sense of smell has improved a little since then – I'm better at distinguishing one smell from another, I can read them – but I still reproach myself for having neglected smell for so many years. I can't help thinking that my nose would have been more use to me if I had paid more attention to it earlier.

I also reproach myself for not having looked at things more carefully – for never looking at them properly. Rather than being like a finished painting, most of the pictures in my memory are like the sketches my Uncle Thet Tin used to do before he started painting. There are so many blank spaces, so many details that haven't been completed. Strangely enough, the sharpest images are the oldest. I can see my mother's face very clearly, at least, I can see my mother's face as it was when I was still a child. But what did she look like the last time I visited her? She had gone grey and there were deep lines in her face. But how exactly did those lines run? Did she have a single line over the bridge of her nose, or were there two? And how had her eyes changed? How was it possible that I didn't know whether the brown and yellow petals were still there, fanning out from the black of her pupils? How could it be that I couldn't picture her throat and her hands, that I wasn't even sure what she was wearing the last time we were together?

That was the other big shock: discovering that so many years had passed since I had lost the knack of looking and realising that I would have to make do with incomplete and therefore unreliable memories.

Sometimes I woke with a start in the middle of the night, convinced that all the images had disappeared, that I couldn't remember anything any more. Then I would sit for hours on end doing my utmost to summon it all up, everything I had ever seen, from my brother's ears to the flight of an egret, from Yi Yi Win's toes (she had lovely feet, but why exactly had I found them so beautiful, and what exactly had those feet looked like?) to Hser Hser Paw's hands, the hands she ran over her belly again and again when the fever had her in its grip and the cold sweat was pouring down her face.

What I have had to learn more than anything else, the thing I have found most difficult of all, is that I have to rely on an image of reality that I know to be incorrect. Of the people I have met since losing my sight, there is not one I have got to know as well as Tommy. The first time he took me by the arm and led me through the darkness, he was half a head smaller than me, now he is an inch taller. I know that he has a muscular body, with strong, slightly bowed legs. His hands are rough and callused like his feet, but his features are fine: he has soft, smooth cheeks and a smooth forehead. I know all of that. And based on what I know and what I suspect, what I have felt and smelt, and what others have told me about him, I have formed a picture of him. That picture undoubtedly corresponds to aspects of reality, but I can be just as sure that it doesn't match reality. If I could see again tomorrow and someone held up a photo of Tommy, I doubt that I would recognise him.

That knowledge, the certainty of not knowing, constantly undermines my self-confidence.

Even now there are days when I can't bring myself to get up, when I stay in my hammock and send away everyone who comes to see me. On days like that I feel like a helpless child, no, less than a child, an animal, a beetle that has fallen in the water and is drifting helplessly downstream. At times like that the concerns of the people around me, their homesickness and their loneliness, their boredom and their lack of hope, their loves and their longing, all seem like folly, like so much affectation.

Tommy is caring.

Tommy is a thief.

Tommy is an exemplary student at Pastor Marcus's Bible school.

Tommy is quick with his fists.

Tommy leads me and supports me, his patience is inexhaustible.

Tommy can go missing for days on end.

Tommy said, 'I was visiting a man who lives in a cave. It's not far from here.'

'Who is he? What's he called?'

'He's called Thra Kay Nay.'

'Thra Kay Nay?! Are you sure?!'

'Of course I'm sure.'

'Where's he come from? Do you know who he is? Did he tell you . . .'

'I know,' Tommy said. 'I know where he's from and that you met him there. He remembers you too. He asked me to say hello.'

'Can you take me to him? How far is it to walk? Is it possible, for me?'

(What a way to live! Always dependent! Always unsure, powerless, incapable!)

Tommy said, 'I'll take you.'

Thra Kay Nay was silent. He had been talking for a long time. He had told us everything: about the raid on the village in the night and how he survived it. About his wanderings afterwards. About his return: 'More than half of the houses had been razed. All the livestock stolen. Fields and gardens destroyed.' About his decision to leave. 'I spent three days in my house. The silence drove me mad. Then I gathered up my things and left.' About his journey to the Thai border: 'Of course I met other people. There are so many dispossessed, desperate people wandering through the forest. It was impossible not to meet them. But I noticed that I had absolutely no desire to talk to anyone. I acted as if I was deaf and dumb. That helped. People let me be.' And about the cave: 'The swallows showed me where it was.' But when I asked him if he knew why the village was attacked – after all, it was in the Forgotten Valley – he fell silent for a long time. I heard the twittering of the swallows nesting deep in the cave. I heard the steady dripping of water. I wondered how the old man could stand it in this musty, damp place. And just when I was about to ask him why he didn't come to live in the camp – somewhere on the edge, of course, there were plenty of remote places – just then Thra Kay Nay ended the silence.

He said, 'You were followed, from the very first day of your flight. They waited until you were somewhere that would be poorly defended, somewhere that had never been fought over. They knew they would take us by complete surprise. Your guides did what they could, they tried to defend the village, but they didn't have a chance. They were completely outnumbered.'

Another long silence fell. Then Thra Kay Nay said, 'They say that the order for the attack came from someone in Pan Thar.'

'Who told you all that?' I asked.

'Me,' said Tommy.

Nine

I think that Tommy was happy in the camp for a while – I really believe that. Tamla Paw took him under her wing like a mother. And although Ta Doh could not possibly take the place of his father, he did everything in his power to help the boy to feel at home. Tommy, in turn, looked after me. And while he taught me to see in the dark, I taught him the language of our people. When his Karen was good enough, he went to the Bible school to learn to read and write and to master English.

In 1995, when Manerplaw finally fell as a bastion of Karen resistance and the camp's population shot up to over forty thousand (our house was no longer on the edge, but Tommy could now live with that), the pastor asked me if I would maintain contacts between his school and the many refugee aid organisations based in the nearby town of Mae Sot.

'You're good with languages,' he said. 'You know our problems, the problems of the Karen as well as the problems of the students who have fled Rangoon, you know the stories of the dispossessed, the banished, the desperate ones, the people who have been driven out of their homes and those who have washed up here by chance. You know Tommy's story. Take Tommy with you when you go to Mae Sot. I'll register you with the Thai Authority, so you can leave the camp unhindered. In Mae Sot itself you'll need to be careful for the time being, because a refugee outside the camp is always illegal – even if I'm able to arrange things for you here at the gate. But will you do that for us, Saw Min Thein? Will you go out into the world for us and tell people what we need?'

I didn't want to. Or more accurately, I wanted to, but I didn't dare.

I didn't dare to once again step into an unknown world. It had taken me years to familiarise myself with the camp, years in which I had fallen into countless deep depressions, unable to accept my blindness. I didn't dare to show myself outside of the camp. I knew that my face was hideously scarred, I could feel it under my fingertips, I heard it in the catch in people's voices when they met me for the first time, I had heard it in the timid sobs of Tamla Paw when we were first reunited. But finally I accepted Pastor Marcus's proposal after all – I did it for Tommy. I would never escape the prison of my blindness, but I could help Tommy to escape the boredom and hopelessness of the camp.

It turned out to be my best decision in years.

I will never forget the first time that Tommy and I drove from the camp to Mae Sot. We were sitting in the back of a car that belonged to the Bible school (donated by an American Baptist church) and was being driven by one of Pastor Marcus's students, and the experience was nothing like any of the car rides I had ever had in Burma, which had been in old, worn-out cars on roads that were even older and more worn out.

In Thailand it was like floating.

The road rolled and rose and fell and the car followed. It took the sharpest corners smoothly, climbed effortlessly, slid downhill with a sigh and conveyed us to our destination without any problems at all. I sank into the soft upholstery of the back seat and listened to the quiet hum of the engine and the zoom of the tyres on the undamaged asphalt. And I praised the king of Thailand and Jesus of Nazareth and the Buddha and Allah and His Prophet, peace be on Them, and all the gods and devas of the Brahman heavens. I praised man, the unlikely creature that had made all this: the car and the road, and the busy streets of Mae Sot, with its shops and teashops, its restaurants and offices, its markets and temples, and parks and houses and motorbikes, motorbikes, motorbikes! If only I could see that beauty one last time with my own eyes!

Tommy, tell me, what do you see?

What's that we hear? What's that noise?

What do the people look like?

What kind of jewellery are the women wearing?

What kind of trousers do the men wear?

What are they reading?

How do they look around them?

How do they smile? Are they smiling?

Tell me! Tell me everything!

In Mae Sot life seemed so light and so . . . liveable! I couldn't find a better word for it – I still can't. Burma was like a swamp sucking down life, and the camp was like stagnant water: everything dies in stagnant water. But Mae Sot was like a bubbling brook, a clear splashing stream. Even *I* could be cheerful there. And Tommy, the hurt child, the wounded soldier, the elephant driver who had been banished from the paradise of his childhood . . . In Mae Sot, Tommy learnt to live again.

We bought Thai English-language newspapers that Tommy read to me and we were astonished at their open criticism of the Thai government. At my insistence, Tommy started a scrapbook with unusual articles about escaped elephants, miraculous cures and, of course, anything to do with Burma. We read about the links between the military regime and the drug barons, and we read about foreign criticism of the human rights situation. We read about the Nobel Peace Prize for Aung San Suu Kyi. Sometimes the reports gave us hope, hope of change, hope of being able to go back. But more often, they depressed us, because every small step forward seemed to be followed by two determined steps backwards. Then we would turn to the pages with Thai news or Tommy would read the sport section out loud.

We became Manchester United fans.

In a bookshop next to a hotel where a lot of foreigners stayed we found cheap paperback editions of classic English and American novels. We bought *Lady Chatterley's Lover*, and one afternoon Tommy started reading to me – slowly at first, sometimes hesitantly, but with growing self-confidence: 'And softly, with that marvellous swoon-like caress of his hand in pure soft desire, softly he stroked the silky slope of her loins, down, down between her soft warm buttocks . . .' The tremble in his voice did not go unnoticed.

Ten

Time: the year 2739 according to the calendar of the Karen.

Location: a teashop in Burma Alley in the centre of Mae Sot.

The reason for my presence: the manageress, Daw Wei Wei, a talkative woman who, like me, comes from Min Won and makes the best mohinga this side of the border – by which I mean, her mohinga is most like my mother's.

It is rumoured that Daw Wei Wei's husband is an informer for the Democratic Karen Buddhist Army, which has split off from the Karen Liberation Army. Similarly there are claims that the owner of the teashop next door works on behalf of the All Burma Students' Democratic Front, and that the man across the road is a spy for the State Peace and Development Council – the new name for the State Law and Order Restoration Council, Burma's military junta.

Burma Alley is a snake pit, a hotbed, a cesspool; nowhere else makes me feel so much at home.

In Daw Wei Wei's teashop I sometimes manage to feel happy. I listen to the Chinese kung fu film being shown on two television screens above the bar, or to the ridiculously excited commentary of the All Star Wrestling, a phenomenon that I will unfortunately never completely fathom because I haven't seen it with my own eyes. One of the teashop's regulars, Ko Aye, can list all of the wrestlers' physical characteristics and identifying features by heart, along with their biographies and the greatest achievements of their wrestling careers. Sharing a table with Ko Aye for an hour is something else that makes me happy.

On the morning in question I ate breakfast with Tommy, after which he left me alone to visit some friends he hadn't seen for a long time and do some shopping. We arranged for him to pick me up again around midday.

'There's no rush,' I told him, 'I'll entertain myself.' And Daw Wei Wei called out from behind the bar that she would look after me. 'I'm stricter for him than his own mother ever was!' she shouted in her harsh, grating voice.

That was the kind of morning it was: one of those carefree mornings when life seems to have slipped back into its normal course and Burma Alley is just a place like so many others in the world, where people gather to eat and drink and occupy themselves with the little things in life that make it possible for them to bear the big things.

But Tommy had only just left when a youth rushed into the teashop to warn us about the arrival of the Thai Authority.

'Police! ID check!' he shouted and then he was gone again, on to the next teashop, and from there to the Tangsit family's gem cutting workshop around the corner. In the fluster that followed, I suddenly felt a hand on my shoulder. Someone said, 'Come with me.' I stood up and gave the man an arm. We left the teashop, together with all the others who didn't have the documents that allowed them to be in Mae Sot legally. Suddenly it was very quiet in Burma Alley.

Later I would realise that it was symbolic, us meeting like that, as fugitives. But in the moment itself, fear and relief were all I felt: fear at what might happen if I fell into the hands of the Thai Authority, and relief at being able to get away in time, even when Tommy wasn't around.

'Is there somewhere you need to be?' the man asked.

'No,' I said. 'I have to be back here this afternoon, but otherwise it doesn't matter.'

'I live in a house not far from here. It's safe there. And cool.'

'Excellent,' I said and let him lead me through the narrow

streets and across the market to a neighbourhood that was new to me. I had laid a hand on his shoulder and he led me through the bustling streets as if he had been doing it all his life. We didn't speak much. I tried to picture him from his height (about half a head taller than me), the steps he took (self-assured, energetic), and the sound of his voice (soft, slightly hoarse and with great inner calm). I could only guess at his age: he had the physique of a young man, but the natural authority of someone older. When we arrived at his house, he offered me a chair on a shaded verandah, but before sitting down I stood before him and ran my fingertips over his face. He had a handsome, straight nose that felt almost European; shoulder-length, wavy hair; glasses, a cotton shirt and a longyi; I estimated his age at late twenties, early thirties.

He introduced himself as Aye Lwin. I told him my name.

'Would you like some tea, U Min Thein?'

We talked to each other for hours, days and nights on end, Aye Lwin and I. The two of us on the verandah of his house and later with Tommy in the teashops of Little Burma, in the monastery gardens and parks of Mae Sot. Sometimes he took us to the paddy fields outside the town. That was where he went at night when he was troubled by bad dreams. 'In the fields,' he said, 'I can breathe more freely.'

He had spent eight years in jail for speaking up against censorship in the university library when he was eighteen years old. One thing had led to another and before he knew it he had been labelled an enemy of the regime. He was tortured on innumerable occasions during his imprisonment. The little men of the regime had done all they could to break his will. Listening to his stories, I felt for the first time that I might have got off lightly, and I noticed something similar in Tommy.

Aye Lwin in turn undoubtedly put his own fate into a different perspective after hearing the story of our flight through the jungle and the battle at the village. He was audibly moved by Tommy's description of the way the Black Tigers had opened fire on the village, how the houses had caught fire and how he had seen men, women and little children burning like torches as they ran through the darkness. It was the first time I had heard from his mouth exactly what had happened. It was the first time I cried at the loss of Hser Hser Paw and our unborn child. I cried without tears.

Later that day, Aye Lwin asked us if we wanted to go to the paddy fields with him. He had a regular spot there in a labourers' hut, the kind without walls that are at the mercy of the wind, a place where your spirit can forget the fear of imprisonment. Of course, we agreed to go, because in the monotonous life of a refugee every small deviation from routine is an opportunity to be seized with both hands. But even more than that, because I wanted to hear and understand, I wanted to feel the anguish he had been through. The underlying reasons for that curiosity would fill me, once I was aware of them, with a bitter realisation of my own inadequacy – but that was later.

'They wanted,' he said, 'my own mother to betray me. That was what they wanted.' We were sitting in the hut in the last rays of sunlight on a warm, languid afternoon, but suddenly I felt cold. I knew who he was! I knew his story – at least, the start of his story. Aye Lwin said, 'They came in broad daylight, about ten of them, most of them in uniform and heavily armed, a couple were in plain clothes. They stood outside the house where I was in hiding and ordered everyone out. There were five of us at home and, of those five, I was the only one who had anything to do with the student resistance. We went out and there she was, my mother, trembling with fear or maybe restrained fury, because my mother is someone who can't bear abuses of power. I didn't know what to do.'

Should I interrupt him? Should I tell him that I knew his

mother? That she had sat on the verandah of my house waiting until she could tell me about the fate of her son, hoping that I might be able to help him?

Aye Lwin said, 'A man I would later get to know as the commanding officer of Military Intelligence Unit No. 7 told my mother to point out her son. My mother did not move or reply. The officer poked her in the side with the barrel of his gun and repeated his order. My mother still refused. A second soldier stepped forward, grabbed my mother by the hair, pulled her head back and spat in her face. That was when I betrayed myself. A dog is walking towards us.'

It took me a moment to realise that that last sentence didn't have anything to do with his story. I was still thinking of his mother and how humiliated she must have been to have someone spit in her face.

'It's a scrawny dog with brown and white patches,' Aye Lwin said. 'It's got two black patches above its eyes, like eyebrows.'

'A four-eyed dog,' said Tommy.

'According to the Karen in the jungle,' I said, 'the meat of a four-eyed dog increases your resistance to malaria.'

'We can eat it,' said Aye Lwin.

The dog had come so close that I could now smell it.

'Here, boy,' I said to the dog, but the dog didn't come.

'It's crawling in under the floor,' Aye Lwin explained. And to the dog he said, 'Lie down and relax.'

'So you betrayed yourself?' asked Tommy.

'Yes, fortunately. I mean . . .'

'I think I understand what you're saying,' I said. 'I know your mother. I know what she went through.'

'Yes . . . yes, that's a good dog,' said Aye Lwin. And only then did he realise what I had said. 'My mother?!' he said. 'Do you know my mother?'

I told him about her visiting our house in Pan Thar, of course without mentioning my confusion about who had come. I told him about the letter to the National League for Democracy and about the letters from Daw Aung San Suu Kyi to the military authorities.

He said, 'I got to know that captain from Military Intelligence Unit No. 7, U Si Thu, quite well. Do you know what the drip is?'

We didn't know.

You're standing in a room you don't know, surrounded by men you can't see. Your head is covered by a hood that stinks of sweat and blood and vomit. It is extremely difficult to breathe. Your hands and feet are chained and you are wearing dirty prison clothes. You haven't been able to wash yourself for days, just as you haven't been able to get a decent night's sleep. You don't know whether it's day or night, morning or evening, you no longer have any idea how long you've been in jail, because they keep on waking you up when you fall asleep. Sometimes they wake you up just to stop you from sleeping, other times they have 'a few questions' for you.

They push you back, sit you on a chair. The chair is wet, you feel the liquid and cold seeping up through the thin material of your longyi, through your dirty underpants. They pull the hood tighter over your head. You're scared you're going to suffocate, but when you move to try to free yourself from the fear, the suffocating panic, they hit you on the side of the head with a hard object. You flinch, you clench your teeth from the pain, you stay dead still.

You hear *plonk*.

Plonk.

Something is falling on the hood, on top of your head. It's so light you can hardly feel it, but you hear it very well.

Plonk.

'So.' The dreaded voice. The voice you have come to hate with an intensity you didn't know you were capable of.

'So, maybe today you are finally going to answer our questions.'

Plonk.

'The worst thing,' Aye Lwin said, 'is that for a long time you can tell yourself that it's not actually that bad. You think to yourself, I imagined it worse. If nothing else, it doesn't hurt. Not like the electric shocks on your testicles that set your whole body on fire. Not like the iron bar they roll over your shins until the skin is hanging off in strips. For a long time you even think it's better than the ordinary kicks and punches. But it's the worst thing that ever happened to me.'

The dog had fallen asleep. I could hear it quietly snoring under the floor of the hut. The sun had gone down behind the mountains of eastern Burma. A new night was about to fall over the country we had fled and longed for every minute of the day, yes, even now, while talking about torture and imprisonment, with Aye Lwin evoking the demons that keep him awake at night, the demons he hoped to dispel or at least keep at a distance here in the open field.

'I never gave in,' he said, almost whispering. 'Not even then. That's what saved me.'

It was quiet for a moment. Then he said, 'A guy I knew was shut up in a tank after his arrest, a big rusty tank with a layer of stinking greasy water in the bottom, so that he couldn't sit or lie down, even though he couldn't stand either, because the space wasn't high enough. Then they turned a tap on somewhere, very slowly, so that it was just a trickle. The tank filled up, agonizingly, agonizingly slowly. When the water was up to his chest he started screaming and shouting, he ripped and gashed his hands pounding the metal. He screamed that he would say anything, whatever they wanted to hear, as long as they didn't let him drown in that pitch-black, stinking tank. They pulled him out and threw him in a cell. He cried twenty-four hours non-stop.

Then they interrogated him and let him go. God knows what he told them. He lives in Australia now. I tried to get in touch with him when I first came to Thailand. I spoke to him on the phone, but he refused to have anything to do with me. He didn't want anything more to do with Burma, our struggle, all we'd fought for.'

The frogs had started croaking, their song drowning out the dog's snoring. Aye Lwin said, 'Twenty-four hours. Non-stop. Like a child.'

Eleven

There's a place, not far from the camp, where the Moei River forms the border between Thailand and Burma. There is a shallow stretch where Burmese cattle dealers smuggle cows and water buffalo into Thailand. In the rainy season, when the water is high, the cattle baulk at the crossing. The cowherds shout and swear and hit the animals with branches and sticks until one plunges into the water and swims to the other side. The rest follow automatically.

That's what it's like with the stories we don't dare to tell but can't keep bottled up inside for our whole life either: once one of those stories has been told, more follow.

A story.

You've got an idea, but you don't have a plan. The idea is: look for your father. Beyond that you'll see what happens. You're still a child and what's more you've just proven that you're capable of finding your father's elephant all by yourself. You know that the herd of elephants your father was looking for were somewhere off to the north-east. So you walk that way. The first few days you know no fear. The only thing you're afraid of is arriving too late, that they might do something to your father before you get there. For three days you don't meet anyone. You keep yourself alive with all kinds of edible plants – from your earliest childhood you have learnt to distinguish them from their bitter and poisonous cousins. One time you set a snare at a mouse hole. In the morning there is a lizard in it. You kill it with your father's *hkyun*. It tastes delicious.

One night voices wake you up. You climb into the tree you were sleeping under. A little later you see six soldiers approaching in the moonlight. They talk to each other in subdued tones. You stay quiet on your branch as they pass beneath you. What should you do?

The voices die out again. The soldiers are already out of sight when you suddenly hear something drop, the crack of branches, a muffled bang. Someone swears. Someone retraces his steps a little to relieve himself. You see the dark figure loom up out of the blackness and squat next to a bush. The soldiers aren't going any further. They're setting up camp for the night, just outside your field of vision. You stay sitting in the tree all night. You're too scared to go back to sleep. In the morning you have made your decision: you will go up to the soldiers and tell them that you are lost.

The soldiers take you with them. They're not unfriendly. After two days' march you reach an army base where the commanding officer gives you an old army coat and a pair of camouflage trousers they shorten by cutting off part of the legs. 'We'll make a soldier out of you,' says the officer. 'We'll turn you into someone your parents can be proud of.'

Weeks go by. They train you. They teach you how to handle weapons. How to clean them. How to load them. Aim. Fire. You learn who to be afraid of. One night, after a long march, you reach a large camp, somewhere deep in the jungle. They tell you that the army is regrouping in preparation for an offensive against the Karen Liberation Army. You're busy taking your gear to one of the big tents when you suddenly see your father – though it takes you a while to realise that it's him. He is carrying three big bamboo poles on his shoulder, his back is bent under the weight. He is naked except for an old, torn longyi. His legs are covered with sores. He doesn't see you.

The next day you go looking for him. You maintain a safe distance, afraid that the soldiers will get suspicious if they see the two of you together. After a while he notices you. He looks at you. He looks you straight in the face. He doesn't do anything. He doesn't say anything. He doesn't move. The two of you stand there like that, you in your shabby uniform, him in his dirty longyi.

Then you gesture to him. It's nothing. It means nothing. But you want to give him a sign, you want *him* to give you a sign. Your father turns around and walks away.

He lives for another three weeks. You see each other almost every day. You don't say a word to each other. One day the unit he is working for goes out on patrol. When they come back at night your father isn't with them. You never dare to ask how he died.

Another story.

Four of you are in a six by eight foot cell. There are no beds, no mattresses, no pillows. You sleep on the floor on a gunnysack. You drink from a water pot that all four of you have to share. You have another pot to relieve yourself. You share that with all four of you as well. On one side of the cell there is a door that opens to an outdoor caged area. You are allowed into the cage to air for one hour every morning and one hour every afternoon. Twice a day you get something to eat. Rice, bean soup without the beans, *ngapi*. Once every two weeks you are allowed visitors. A maximum of two people for a maximum of fifteen minutes. The only thing the visitors are allowed to bring you is food. The possession of pens, paper, books, newspapers or magazines is strictly forbidden. The same applies to drinking alcohol or using other intoxicants. You are allowed to smoke.

And there is some slack.

The prison has its own economy. Visiting family members slip money to prisoners. It is possible to pay off guards. 50 kyats will get you a lighter. 200, a book. There is a guard you trust, a simple man who does his job. Your mother pays him 200 kyats to smuggle in *Great Expectations*, a book that you saw for years in your father's bookcase but have never read. Your father died when you were two. You want to read the book because of the title – and because of your father. Every day the guard brings a few pages. After you've read them, you pass them on to others. When there is no one left to read them, you burn the pages. Or eat them. At page one hundred and three it goes wrong. Your cellmates get careless. Another guard catches you.

You get twenty strokes of the cane and two weeks' solitary confinement. Once a day the cell door opens and they beat you some more. They want you to tell them the name of the guard who smuggled in the book. You don't tell them.

Every morning and every evening they make you sit for an hour like a dog: on your knees, back straight, hands in front of your chest. If they don't like the way you're sitting, they beat you again. You tell them the name of the guard.

The man is fired immediately.

You get transferred to a harsher prison.

Another story.

You are attached to a unit called the Black Tigers. The Black Tigers have a reputation. Everyone is afraid of the Black Tigers – even the other soldiers. People say that the members are criminals who have been released on condition they fight for the army. They don't get any pay. They live by robbing and looting. By killing and raping. The Black Tigers have been ordered to prepare the offensive against the Karen by sowing panic among the Karen population. By confusing the enemy: a raid here, an attack there, a massacre three days' march away . . .

The Black Tigers follow orders.

One day your unit spots a small group of guerrillas. There are four of them, no, there are six, or five. You follow them at a safe distance. You have no idea where the guerrillas are, but the Black Tigers know exactly what they are doing. No one says a word all day. They hand out tablets. Everyone takes two or three. You are allowed one, they make you take one. You swallow the tablet and wash the bitter taste down with some water. You walk on. You feel a strange pressure in your head, you start walking faster, your movements speed up. An intense excitement comes over you, an excitement that is completely new but not unpleasant. You look at the Black Tigers. They too are moving more quickly, with greater concentration, more purposefully. Someone grins at you. You can feel from your face that you're grinning as well. You can't do anything about it. It is not unpleasant. It is not unpleasant at all. Suddenly everyone stops. Bodies hunch down. Eyes shoot left to right, exchanging keen hungry looks, eager looks. In a few minutes it's over. Two dead bodies are sprawled under a tree. A few steps away a third body is hanging in a thorn bush. Three Black Tigers have set off after the others. You hear a shot. And another. And again.

You squat next to one of the dead fighters. Someone pushes you aside, you roll over in the wet leaves. You can't get back up. The pressure inside your head is so enormous that you're afraid your skull will burst open. A *dah* swings through the air, splitting a skull. Blood splashes on your face. You still can't move. You grin. You feel the grin around your mouth, you're grinning so hard your jaws are aching. You lie with your head on the wet leaves. A drop of blood is stuck to your eyelashes.

The Black Tigers eat the brains of the dead fighter.

Another story.

A different place. Different light. Different air. Less humid. Dustier. A different cell. Smaller. Just for you. Every morning you get a bowl of water, a shard from a broken pot and a piece of plastic. You have to use them to smooth out the earth floor of your cell. For four hours. A guard comes by regularly to make sure you're doing a good job. If he catches you when you're not hard at work, when you're having a rest, catching your breath or reproaching yourself, he will beat you. You can look forward to the same task in the afternoon. For four hours. Every day. It is a completely pointless activity, and it's meant to be.

Once a day you can leave your cell. To wash. But when they take you to the washroom, you're not allowed to raise your eyes from the ground. If you look up or around, they hit you. And you're not allowed to say anything. If you say anything, they hit you. You're allowed to use three bowls of water to wash. Not a drop more. You wash your clothes by standing on them while you rinse yourself off. You don't get clean. Your clothes don't get clean. That too is intentional.

You now only get visitors once every two or three months. Your family can't afford to make the longer journey any more often. You have to make do with the prison food and sometimes you don't even get that. In another part of the prison there are hardened criminals. As a reward for good behaviour, they are sometimes allowed to take over the duties of the ordinary guards. If they like, they can hit you. Or drink your water. Or . . . They like it very much.

One afternoon you're kneeling down in your outside cage, in the burning sun, with your bowl of water and your piece of plastic and your shard. You have taken your prison shirt off and buttoned it around your head. You look at the shard in your hand. You look at your own bare chest, gaunt and chapped. You scratch your chest from one side to the other with the shard. You do it again, deeper than the first time. You start bleeding. With the palm of your free hand you smear the blood out over your ribcage. You stretch out your legs and pull up your longyi. Both of your shins are covered with torture scars. You start to scrape at the scars with the shard. Your eyes fill with tears that you wipe away with the back of your hand. You keep on scraping until the old wounds are gaping once again. You lay the shard aside and rub both shins with your hands. You raise your hands up to just before your eyes. You study the strange patterns of the lines of your palms. You cover your face with your hands and sniff the sweet metallic smell. Then you roll over on to your side with your legs pulled up, like a little child that's had a bad dream. You stay there lying like that until the guard kicks you up on to your feet.

PART V

People of the Stars

PART V

People of the Stars

Are there any peoples who don't look at the night sky, who don't tell each other stories about the inhabitants of the heavens, those mythical creatures whose fates are bound to ours in ways no man has ever completely fathomed?

You say that at night in your country the stars are drowned in a sea of manmade light, that you have to travel abroad to see a starry night. And I tell you that yours is a poor country. You have wrapped a blanket around your shoulders and poured yourself a glass of the Scotch you brought with you from the airport. I say, 'Do you see, high in the sky, seven stars that form an oblong? And do you see three stars in a row in that oblong?'

'Yes,' you say after a while, 'Yes, I see them.'

'They are the Hsa Yo Ma, the stars that carried off women.'

One day, infinitely long ago, the Hsa Yo Ma were wandering around the universe when they suddenly discovered three magnificent young women. The women were daughters of the Hsa Deu Mü tribe. That's the small group of stars a little to the right of that big oblong. The Hsa Deu Mü are the most prominent of all the peoples of the stars and their women are famed throughout the universe for their exceptional beauty. The three wandering stars felt so attracted to the young women that they decided to force them to become their wives by overpowering them and carrying them off from their people. But they hadn't counted on the wrath and vengefulness of the Hsa Deu Mü. As soon as that noble tribe discovered the brazen kidnap, they dispatched their fastest and most skilled warriors to track down the culprits. And it wasn't long before the villains had been found and vanquished. The triumphant warriors led the women back to their own people. The guilty three were banished to an obscure corner of the universe. There they serve their sentence for all eternity.

'In a sense,' I say, 'the same thing has happened to Tommy.'

255

I need to ask your discretion. More than that, I have to ask you not to be too quick to judge. What I am going to tell you about Tommy is delicate, not just for him, but for the others who are involved as well and, by extension, for all of us here in this camp and for the Karen refugees in other camps and outside them, in the jungles and villages and towns of this country that shelters us – begrudgingly.

Nothing makes people more vulnerable than dependence, and few people are as dependent on others as refugees. The manufacturer or farmer in search of cheap labour can find us just as easily as the detective who wants to gain kudos by arresting illegal aliens. If one of us has managed to make some money, by selling one of the family's gems or thanks to a good harvest on a small piece of land they are tilling just over the border in the Burmese jungle, and if that person wants to spend that money in town on a luxury item they have been dreaming of for years, or on something the family has needed for a long time, it can happen that another inhabitant of the camp informs the Thai Authority. The person departing for town with the money gets collared just outside the camp, and the Thai Authority confiscates the cash. The informer gets a percentage. That is the reward for betrayal.

Representatives of the Thai Authority abuse young girls from the camps and no one can do a thing about it. Women are trafficked, men are exploited, children are seduced with drugs. We have to stand up against these things with little more than our sense of self-esteem, the memory of who we once were, in a time most of us never experienced.

I have told you the story of my life and I have told you about the people who have played an important part in it. Tommy is one of those people. But Tommy's story is unfinished until you know what has become of him, where he is, and why he isn't here, by my side, as my y'meh klee po, *my little eyes. Tommy is in prison. Not in a Thai cell, not in a Burmese army cell, or a Burmese police cell, or a Burmese secret police cell, no, he is locked up here in the camp, in our own little jail. Tommy is imprisoned because of his love for Naw Ta Eh Shee, a woman you met on your first day on our way back from the Monastery of the Silent Wind. She was carrying a child on her back and I asked you whether you had noticed that her left leg was artificial. You hadn't noticed.*

Tommy fell in love with Ta Eh Shee, but Ta Eh Shee was married. It was true that her husband had been missing for two whole years, but that didn't mean he was dead – although Tommy must have hoped he was. I don't know exactly what happened between them because neither Tommy nor Ta Eh Shee is willing to talk about it, from shame or pride, who can say? What I do know is that one night Ta Eh Shee's family burst into her hut and found Tommy there: fully dressed and sitting on the floor at a decent distance from Ta Eh Shee, according to one witness; half-naked and desperately trying to escape, according to others.

There was a fight, people were stabbed, the neighbours arrived just in time to prevent fatalities. Tommy was carted off to prison. He was there for a week, two weeks. He wouldn't make a statement: not to the camp authorities and not to me. He sat in his cell and refused to speak. Ta Eh Shee went into hiding for a week and when she emerged she seemed completely unaffected, as if nothing had happened. She didn't say a word about the night-time clash and she definitely didn't talk about what had preceded it. She didn't ask about Tommy. And as for me, I sat in my hut and waited. Sometimes I arranged to be fetched and delivered, going to this meeting or that consultation. Sometimes I sent everyone away. I hoped that the problem would solve itself in time, like so many family arguments and conflicts do: ultimately emotions cool and everyone gets back to everyday life, which is, after all, difficult enough without problems like this as well.

I hoped things would peter out like that, but that's not what happened.

Just when I was thinking about cautiously approaching k'Pru Htoo, the camp leader, to ask about the possibility of Tommy's release, on that very morning, Ta Eh Shee's husband emerged from the jungle like a ghost: emaciated, wounded and almost crippled, but alive. Within a day, people had whispered in his ear about what had happened, or what people said had happened. I no longer had to go to k'Pru Htoo, the camp leader – he came to me. He said, 'We'll have to try Tommy.' And I knew that I would have to mobilise all the support I could find to save Tommy from the worst.

The case will be heard this evening and Thra Kay Nay and Pastor Marcus have promised to defend Tommy. One of Tah Eh Shee's husband's brothers will take the role of prosecutor on his behalf. Saw k'Pru Htoo, the camp leader, will be the judge. I won't be taking an active role, I am too prejudiced: how could I plead for anything accept Tommy's immediate release? But I will be allowed to be present at the trial, because of my friendship with Tommy and because of my special interest in the outcome.

On top of the Mountain of Salvation and Prayer there is a house. I would like to ask you to wait there until the trial is over. Afterwards we will return to the camp and I will tell you what was said. Again I will ask you not to judge too hastily, but to consider everything carefully in your heart. Because as the Buddha said, 'It is easy to see the faults of others, but difficult to recognise our own faults.'

The path uphill is steep and narrow, branches whip back into our faces, we catch our feet on creepers and almost stumble. We need to concentrate fully on walking. I like that. That way we don't need to talk, and I don't need to think about what is going to happen.

It does me good to feel the cool of the evening rolling into the valley from the mountains. The smells become more pure again, easier to distinguish from each other. When the heat is at its most intense, it is as if the smells have been cooked in a soup. In the heat of the day, hearing is all I have left to perceive the world, but that's the very time when everything stays quiet.

I want you to pay attention to the faces when we get there. There is a cliché in your world about our faces, Asian faces, that dates from the days of colonial rule. The cliché goes that you can't read anything from our faces, that we are closed and inscrutable, full of unknowable secrets – that's it, isn't it? But I am sure the cliché is wrong. The faces in my memory tell me a thousand stories. Later, when it is all over, when the

*court's verdict has been announced and you know what you think you
need to know and are getting ready to leave, I want you to tell me very
precisely how you remember the people you met here.*

*I doubt that your coming here can serve a greater purpose, or that the
stories you will write about us will make any difference to the world; I
hope you don't have too many illusions on that score. But if you will do
me that one favour, then your coming here will have at least been meaningful for me.*

*The path widens, the hill flattens out, we have reached our goal. I
hear the voices of Pastor Marcus and Thra Kay Nay. Will you take me
to them? And then go to the house? There are chairs there and even a
hammock. Be quiet, listen to the nightfall, look at the stars, sleep. When
everything that must be said has been said, I will send for you. We will
walk downhill with the others in the first light of a new day.*

I recognised his voice from the street where the Muslims have their shops.
He runs a restaurant there where they serve mohinga and sweet corn. He
is one of the last non-Muslims left in that street. He once explained it to
me like this, 'We were already living here before the Muslims came.
They're nice enough people, but very noisy. Their children play on the
street long after dark and when a husband and wife argue the whole
neighbourhood gets to listen in. That's why the Karen have left here one
after the other. They build or buy a house somewhere else in the camp
and sell the house they leave behind to a Muslim family. But I have no
intention of moving. I refuse to be driven out a second time!'

He was the brother of the betrayed husband. The husband himself
had come as well, but didn't speak. Only once did I hear him grunt his
approval, when his brother stated the punishment they had in mind for
Tommy.

The brother said, 'What do we have here, in this camp, in this
country that is not our own? We only have one thing, one thing that
saves us from complete destruction, we have each other!'

The brother said, 'What did this fellow have before he came to us in
the camp? He had nothing, he had nobody. If we hadn't taken him up

in our midst, he would have died long ago. An elephant can survive in
the jungle by itself, but a boy of his age, the age he was when we first
took him into our care, cannot – even if he thinks he can!'

The brother said, 'We saved this fellow's life, we, the Karen of this
camp. And was he grateful to us? Did he show his gratitude by sticking
to our laws, by accepting our customs? Not at all! He only thought of his
own pleasure, his own desires, and to satisfy those desires he has
committed one of the most serious offences a man can commit, he has
seduced a married woman, dishonoured her and shamed her in the eyes
of her family! He has shown us the contempt he feels for us, how much
he hates us, we who have done nothing to harm him, we who saved his
life!'

The brother said, 'Our ancestors knew what they were doing when
they passed their wisdom down to us. They knew what they were doing
when they emphasised protecting our people from external dangers. We
are strong when we stand side by side, just as we stood side by side in
1949 during the siege of Insein, when the Karen fighters withstood the
attacks of the Burmese army, and just as we stood side by side in 1988.
This Tommy proves once again that Burmans are not to be trusted.
Those who want to enjoy the achievements of our people – our hospitality and our ability to put others at their ease – must be prepared to do
something in return. That was too much for Tommy. On the contrary, he
has endangered our unity, he has wounded one of our brothers to the
depths of his soul. Our ancestors were right when they told us that there
was only one punishment sufficient for those who break the oaths of
marriage: the death penalty. Because little endangers a community so
much, threatens peace, order and mutual respect so much as breaking the
oaths of marriage.'

The brother said, 'We want to take Tommy to Burma and give him
his just punishment there.'

'And Ta Eh Shee?' asked the camp leader. 'What punishment did
you have in mind for Ta Eh Shee?'

'The wife must look after her children,' said the brother. 'It is bad
enough that she has shamed her family and ours with her loose behaviour

– she does not need to be punished further. No, we must limit the punishment to the man: he knew what he was doing, he did it consciously. Maybe he thought he would never be caught. Maybe he hoped that my brother was dead. But my brother is not dead. My brother is alive. And he must die!'

The brother said all this and much more. He presented the case as dramatically as possible, while simultaneously doing everything in his power to protect his sister-in-law. He was clearly doing this on his brother's urgings, because he repeatedly emphasised how important it was for his brother that Naw Ta Eh Shee look after the children, that she look after him. Naw Ta Eh Shee was the victim of this ungrateful foreigner, this non-Karen, this Tommy. Her sin had to be forgiven her, but Tommy needed to be punished, it was essential to banish evil by destroying it.

When he had had his say, the camp leader said, 'The charge is clear, as is the desired punishment. Thra Kay Nay may now take the floor.'

A very long silence fell. I can only guess at what was happening. Had Thra Kay Nay raised a hand to call for silence, the way guides in the jungle can hush a whole party with a single gesture when danger is approaching? Was he lost in thought, meditation or prayer, and had the others accepted this without demurral?

Just when I was unable to suppress the ridiculous but inescapable thought that they had all left the mountain, leaving me behind alone, so that they could go through the rest of the trial elsewhere without my disruptive presence, just then I heard Thra Kay Nay clear his throat. A little later his voice came, from farther away than I had expected, but clear and distinct for all of that. He said, 'The laws our forefathers passed down to each other were intended for a different era: not for the Karen we have become today. We were a people of small communities, villages with just a few families where everyone was dependent on everyone else. In communities like that adultery could prove fatal to everyone by driving the members of the community apart, pitting them one against the other, so that the things that needed to be done – sowing, harvesting, hunting, maintaining the houses, all the things that can't be done alone and can only be completed as a group – were neglected. That is why the law was harsh, but wise. But we no longer live in communities like that. We live in a camp with a population of forty thousand. We are fed by aid organisations from distant, wealthy countries. We are no longer in charge of our own lives. As a result the law has lost its wisdom. We need to design new laws that take account of the world we now live in.'

Thra Kay Nay said, 'We don't know what it means to grow up in these camps because all of us, gathered here now, were lucky enough to come of age in a world that we could feel to be our own, despite its hostility and oppressiveness – and because we felt that the world was ours, we felt able to shape it. Often we were over-confident, we cherished unrealistic illusions, but that doesn't matter, what matters is that we were able to believe in our illusions, that those illusions were part of our reality, they were interwoven with it, and clashed with it as well, of course they did, but they also helped to shape it. Our young people today have to get by without this fundamental experience: they have to project their dreams and ambitions on a world far from here, a world they only know from their parents' stories, from our stories, the stories of the older generation. In the world they see around them, in which they live day in day out, they are powerless and doomed to remain powerless. As I said, none of us can really know what it means to grow up like that.

'But Tommy knows.

'Tommy is subjected to it, every day of his young life. Who can blame him for trying to satisfy at least one of his longings, to do the one great, overwhelming, majestic thing that lay within his power? Because let us not forget that conquering a love can be a deed that makes us feel mightier than the mightiest king, more powerful than the most powerful warlord, richer than the richest man on earth. If one of you here present has not known that feeling, than he has never truly loved.'

Thra Kay Nay said, 'I don't need to mention the minor circumstances, the uncertainty about the fate of Ta Eh Shee's husband. The greater circumstance of living in a world in which you are of no importance, in which you are completely invisible, that is enough to make us be hesitant in our judgement. Let us look into our own hearts and ask ourselves the question as to whether or not we, under the same circum-stances, would have searched for a way to fulfil our own promise, to write our own history, if necessary in the deepest secrecy.'

Another long silence fell and again I didn't know exactly how to interpret it. I heard a nightjar fly overhead. I heard the clicking the bats use to measure echoes, a trick I would have been glad to learn.

'Pastor Marcus,' Saw k'Pru Thoo said at last, breaking the silence, 'the floor is yours.'

'Yes,' said the pastor, 'thank you. It will be nothing new to you if I say that adultery is an abomination in the eyes of the Lord, the God of Israel, who we believe to also be our God, the God our forefathers called Y'wah. I believe that we must instruct our children in the sanctity of marriage, not because marriage is holy in my eyes, but because it is holy in the eyes of God. In consequence I also believe that what Tommy and Naw Ta Eh Shee did was wrong – assuming that the things that other people have told us actually happened, because we mustn't forget that neither of them has been willing to speak. Is their silence a confession? Who is to say? Maybe it's pride, maybe it's shame. Maybe it's anger at something they experience as an intrusion on what people from the West call "privacy", a word that is almost impossible to translate into our language, because there was no need for such a word in the world in which we lived. But that need exists now, here, in this camp, where we are crammed in closer together than cattle.'

The pastor said, 'Of course I had to think of the story of Jesus, who was called the Christ, and the adulterous woman. She was brought before him by scribes who said, "Teacher, this woman has been caught in the act of adultery. The Law of Moses commands us to stone her. What do you say?" Jesus answered, "Let him who is without sin among you be the first to throw a stone at her." Jesus did not condemn, he only said, "Go and do not sin again."

The pastor said, 'I know that it is not easy to understand God's words correctly. I know that not everyone here believes in the God I pray to every day, who holds our people's future in His hand. But didn't the Buddha also say that we all commit our own evil and only we can avert it? Let us all seek the wisdom that suits us best, but let wisdom prevail over vengefulness. Once Tommy fought on the side of the Burmese army and took part in an attack that killed Saw Min Thein's wife, robbed him of his unborn child and deprived him of the light of his eyes. Saw Min Thein has forgiven him, we all forgave him and accepted him in our midst. Of course, he was still a child then, who didn't know what he was doing, but which of us can say that in love he has ever known exactly what he was doing. In love we are all blind.'

The nightjar stayed near us that night on the Mountain of Salvation and Prayer, and we kept hearing the bats as well. There was no wind. To me it seemed very possible that we might hear God whisper, that we would soon hear the swish of the wings of angels. It was a night that imposed silence.

Now and then someone said something in hushed tones. The brother of the betrayed husband related again what other people were saying about his family and how they were suffering from it. Thra Kay Nay told a story from his youth, about loneliness and rejection, about encountering a tiger at night, a moment that changed his life forever. The tiger let him go, the tiger gave his life back to him.

The pastor sang a song in a language we didn't know.

When the first birds announced the dawn of a new day, Saw k'Pru Htoo, the camp leader, spoke. He said, 'Let the sun rise and set again. Let us seek out the company of the people we love, the people who make us what we are. Let us seek wisdom and truth. When the sun rises again tomorrow, we will meet in my office. And from there, we will go to the place where Tommy is being held. In his presence I will pronounce my judgement.'

The world is a gigantic machine that takes people up and spits them out somewhere else, cutting one country into pieces and gluing another together, making war here and peace there. And my country is jammed somewhere inside that incomprehensible mechanism. Cogs turn without engaging, the machine squeaks and creaks and grinds, mechanics tighten nuts and remove pieces, they grease and oil, nothing seems to help. People get crushed, generations are lost, entire nations are cast adrift.

On a piece of paper above the entrance of a dingy house in a refugee camp in Thailand, not far from the place where the Moei River forms the border with Burma, it says in childish letters, 'All sins shall be forgiven the sons of men.'

Acknowledgements and sources

This book is the result of an unusual invitation. In the autumn of 2001, I was approached by Carla van Oss of the Netherlands Refugee Foundation. She explained a plan that basically came down to this: over a period of several years, the Refugee Foundation hoped to draw attention to forgotten groups of refugees by inviting Dutch authors to spend some time in a refugee camp and write a book about the experience – in whichever form they chose. Within a few months the plan had taken shape and I agreed to participate in it. We arranged that I would travel to Thailand in late 2002 and stay there for three months to immerse myself in the fate of the Burmese refugees housed in camps around the small town of Mae Sot.

In Thailand the Netherlands Refugee Foundation helps Burmese refugees by supporting clinics and schools. In other places around the world the foundation helps other refugees with emergency help in the form of tents, food, drinking water and medical supplies. The foundation also works toward the safe return of refugees and helps them to rebuild their countries and lives.

Although it is the rich countries of the North that complain the most about the influx of refugees, more than 95 per cent of all of the world's refugees remain within their own region. They are displaced within their own borders or get stranded in a refugee camp in a neighbouring country – like the Burmese in Thailand.

Of the many people who helped me with my work in Mae Sot, only a few can be named without endangering them. This book would have been impossible without Aung Naing, Aung Kyaw Oo and Nyein Wai. Also essential was the assistance of Minka Nijhuis, who shared her thorough knowledge of Burma and the region with me and established contacts between me and a great many people who proved highly valuable for my book. As always, Tiziana Alings took on the role of first reader and personal editor. Karin Kuiper and our daughters, Bobbie and Noa, endured not only the stay in Thailand and an arduous journey through Burma, but also the long months of my wrestling with *The Invisible Ones*. I am very grateful to them all.

While writing this book I drew on a great many written sources, including the following books:

The Dhammapada: The Sayings of Buddha. Translation and Commentary by Thomas Cleary. Thorsons/Harper Collins, London 1995

Europe and Burma. D. G. E. Hall. Oxford University Press, London/Madras 1945

Freedom from Fear and Other Writings. Aung San Suu Kyi. Penguin, London 1991

Inked Over, Ripped Out – Burmese Storytellers and the Censors. Anna J. Allot. PEN American Center, New York 1993

A Journalist, a General and an Army in Burma. U Thaung. White Lotus, Bangkok/Cheney 1995

The Karen People of Burma. Rev. Harry Ignatius Marshall. University at Columbus, Ohio 1922

The Legends and Theories of the Buddhists compared with History and Science. R. Spence Hardy. Asian Educational Services, New Delhi/ Madras 1993

Living Silence – Burma under Military Rule. Christina Fink. White Lotus, Bangkok 2001

On the Road to Mandalay. Mya Than Tint. White Orchid Press, Bangkok 1996

The World of Burmese Women. Mi Mi Khaing. Zed Books, London 1984

Karel Van Loon
Hilversum, August 2003

Also available from
WWW.MAIAPRESS.COM

Merete Morken Andersen OCEANS OF TIME
£8.99   ISBN 1 904559 11 5

A divorced couple confront a family tragedy in the white night of a Norwegian summer. International book of the year (*TLS*), longlisted for The Independent Foreign Fiction Prize 2005 and nominated for the IMPAC Award 2006.

Michael Arditti GOOD CLEAN FUN
£8.99   ISBN 1 904559 08 5

A dazzling collection of stories provides a witty yet compassionate and uncompromising look at love and loss, desire and defiance, in the 21st century.

Michael Arditti UNITY
£8.99   ISBN 1 904559 12 3

A film on the relationship between Unity Mitford and Hitler gets under way during the 1970s Red Army Faction terror campaign in Germany in this complex, groundbreaking novel. Shortlisted for the Wingate Prize 2006.

Booktrust London Short Story Competition
UNDERWORDS: THE HIDDEN CITY
£9.99   ISBN 1 904559 14 X

Prize-winning new writing on the theme of Hidden London, along with stories from Diran Adebayo, Nicola Barker, Romesh Gunesekera, Sarah Hall, Hanif Kureishi, Andrea Levy, Patrick Neate and Alex Wheatle.

Hélène du Coudray ANOTHER COUNTRY
£7.99   ISBN 1 904559 04 2

A prize-winning novel, first published in 1928, about a passionate affair between a British ship's officer and a Russian emigrée governess which promises to end in disaster.

Lewis DeSoto A BLADE OF GRASS
£8.99   ISBN 1 904559 07 7

A lyrical and profound novel set in South Africa during the era of apartheid, in which the recently widowed Märit struggles to run her farm with the help of her black maid, Tembi. Longlisted for the Man Booker Prize 2004 and shortlisted for the Ondaatje Prize 2005.

Also available from
WWW.MAIAPRESS.COM

Olivia Fane THE GLORIOUS FLIGHT OF PERDITA TREE
£8.99   ISBN 1 904559 13 1

Beautiful Perdita Tree is kidnapped in Albania. Freedom is coming to the
country where flared trousers landed you in prison, but are the Albanians
ready for it or, indeed, Perdita? 'Thoughtful, sorrowful, highly amusing' (*Times*)

Olivia Fane GOD'S APOLOGY
£8.99   ISBN 1 904559 20 7

Patrick German abandons his wife and child, and in his new role as a teacher
encounters a mesmerising 10-year-old. Is she really an angel sent to save him?

Maggie Hamand, ed. UNCUT DIAMONDS
£7.99   ISBN 1 904559 03 4

Unusual and challenging, these vibrant, original stories showcase the huge
diversity of new writing talent coming out of contemporary London.

Helen Humphreys WILD DOGS
£8.99   ISBN 1 904559 15 8

A pack of lost dogs runs wild, and each evening their bereft former owners
gather to call them home – a remarkable book about the power of human
strength, trust and love.

Linda Leatherbarrow ESSENTIAL KIT
£8.99   ISBN 1 904559 10 7

The first collection from a short-story prizewinner – lyrical, uplifting, funny
and moving, always pertinent – 'joyously surreal . . . gnomically funny, and
touching' (Shena Mackay).

Sara Maitland ON BECOMING A FAIRY GODMOTHER
£7.99   ISBN 1 904559 00 X

Fifteen new 'fairy stories' by an acclaimed master of the genre breathe new life
into old legends and bring the magic of myth back into modern women's lives.

Dreda Say Mitchell RUNNING HOT
£8.99   ISBN 1 904559 09 3

A pacy comic thriller about Schoolboy and his attempts to go straight in a world
of crime. An exciting debut, winner of the CWA John Creasey Award 2005.

Also available from
www.MAIAPRESS.COM

Anne Redmon IN DENIAL
£7.99   ISBN 1 904559 01 8

A chilling novel about the relationship between a prison visitor and a serial offender, which explores challenging themes with subtlety and intelligence.

Diane Schoemperlen FORMS OF DEVOTION
£9.99   ISBN 1 904559 19 0   Illustrated

Eleven stories with a brilliant interplay between words and images – a creative delight, perfectly formed and rich in wit and irony.

Henrietta Seredy LEAVING IMPRINTS
£7.99   ISBN 1 904559 02 6

Beautifully written and startlingly original, this unusual and memorable novel explores a destructive, passionate relationship between two damaged people.

Emma Tennant THE HARP LESSON
£8.99   ISBN 1 904559 16 6

With the French Revolution looming, little Pamela Sims is taken from England to live at the French court as the illegitimate daughter of Mme de Genlis. But who is she really? 'Riveting and very readable' (Antonia Fraser)

Emma Tennant PEMBERLEY REVISITED
£8.99   ISBN 1 904559 17 4

Elizabeth wins Darcy, and Jane wins Bingley – but do they 'live happily ever after'? Reissue of *Pemberley* and *An Unequal Marriage*, two bestselling sequels to Jane Austen's *Pride and Prejudice*.

Norman Thomas THE THOUSAND-PETALLED DAISY
£7.99   ISBN 1 904559 05 0

Love, jealousy and violence in this coming-of-age tale set in India, written with a distinctive, off-beat humour and a delicate but intensely felt spirituality.

Adam Zameenzad PEPSI AND MARIA
£8.99   ISBN 1 904559 06 9

A highly original novel about two street children in South America whose zest for life carries them through the brutal realities of their daily existence.

21